Whitley Stokes, Dominus Hadton

The Life of Saint Meriasek - Bishop and Confessor

a cornish drama

Whitley Stokes, Dominus Hadton

The Life of Saint Meriasek - Bishop and Confessor
a cornish drama

ISBN/EAN: 9783337383534

Printed in Europe, USA, Canada, Australia, Japan

Cover: Foto ©Andreas Hilbeck / pixelio.de

More available books at **www.hansebooks.com**

NS MERI

F SAINT

AND CON

ISH D

EDITED,

NSLATION A

BY

LEY STO

ONDON

CO., PAT

1872.

DUBLIN: PRINTED BY ALEXANDER THOM, 87 & 88, ABBEY-STREET.

PREFACE.

The following drama 'of the life of S. Meriasek, Bishop and Confessor,' was discovered about three years ago among the Hengwrt MSS. by Mr. Wynne of Peniarth. The first thirty-six lines were printed in the *Archaeologia Cambrensis* for 1869, p. 409, by the Rev. Robert Williams of Rhydycroesau, but the remainder is now for the first time published. I purpose in this preface, first, to describe the manuscript; secondly, to state the plot, and to print what I have found elsewhere concerning Meriasek; thirdly, to notice the names of the places mentioned in the play; and lastly, to make some remarks on the language and the metres in which it is composed.

1. *The Manuscript.*

The manuscript is a small paper quarto, measuring eight and a half inches by six, in an old brown leather binding now labelled on the back '310. Cornish Mystery,' and on the top side 'Legendary, &c. Lives of Saints, No. 2, 7 books, 310.' Inside the cover is a yellow label on which is printed 'R. WMES. VAUGHAN HENGWRT.' It contains 90 leaves paginated in pencil, and a leaf six and a quarter inches by six (marked 91^a, 91^b), inserted immediately before the forty-sixth leaf. The versos of leaves 49 and 90 are occupied with rude plans of the stage. Half of p. 97, and three-fourths of p. 179 are blank. The colophon states that the MS. was finished by 'Dominus Hadton,' in the year 1504. The whole book is, I think, in his handwriting, but the MS. has been corrected in several places by a subsequent possessor,* who also inserted the stage-directions to which I have prefixed a

---

* Here follows a list of these corrections: *vyth*, 97, corrected *veth. an* 293, inserted. *esco* 511, *p* added. before 526, *kernov* inserted. *piiadou*, 560, made *peyadov. oma* 783 inserted. *flogh* 846, inserted. *athulh* 856, corrected *athuth. tev*, 936, corrected *tav. vy*, 936, inserted. *ovs*, 1051, corrected *ov covs. se*, 1056, corrected *serys. vyth*, 1073, inserted. *purwar*, 1114, corrected *purwhar. C* 1147, corrected *M. glowas*, 1160, corrected *glowes. movle* 1166 corrected *mevle. afaff* 1177 corrected *keuyn. an* 1180, inserted. *alemen* 1389 corrected *alema. wytsa*, 1760, corrected *wetsa. wyn* 2202, inserted. *prey*, 2352, corrected *preysys. presner kyns* 2462, corrected *eseth kens. vetynens* 2809 corrected *venitens. vetenens* 2886 corrected *veneten[en]s. vetenens* 2951 corrected *venetenes. benyth*, 2999, corrected *benytha. sur*, 3027, inserted. *han clehy* 3057 corrected *pur defry. moys*, 3204, corrected *sur devethys*, 3240, corrected *drehevys. rer pesy* 3440 corrected *rer y pesy. gyyff* 3700 corrected *guyff. why*, 4252, inserted. *hag vohosogyen pur*, 4261, corrected *han v. pub. veth* 4448 corrected *vethe. gorth* 4535, corrected *gor.*

bracket, thus : [. The facsimile following this preface gives a
good idea of the handwriting and of the mode in which these corrections and additions are made. The MS. has suffered little
(ff. 11 and 13 have lost a small portion of the margin), and is care-
fully preserved at Peniarth, near Towyn, Merionethshire.

2. The Plot.

Mereadôcus, Meriadec (or, in Cornish mouths, Meriasek), son
of a Duke of Britanny, is sent to school with his parents' blessing
(lines 1–92). His studies and pious conduct are described (93–
166). He returns home already renowned for learning, goodness,
and courtesy (193–231). Conan, king of Armorica, wishing to
wed him to a wealthy princess (168–192) goes with his nobles
to the Duke's house (232–264), and after a feast (265–297) pro-
poses the marriage (298–307). The parents gladly accept
(308–319). But Meriasek refuses, declaring that he would be
'consecrated a knight of God' (320–355). After much vain
expostulation from the king and Meriasek's parents (356–473),
the king departs in anger (474–482); but the parents give their
son their blessing, and he goes to a bishop who ordains him
a priest (483–533). He thereupon performs his first miracles
(534–568). Then with the bishop's blessing, he sails for Cornwall, and after saving the crew from shipwreck lands near Camborne (569–648). There he builds an oratory, makes a well
spring up miraculously (649–677), and heals the sick, the maimed,
and the leper (678–758). A pagan lord, Teudar, hearing of this,
goes to Meriasek and, after discussing the doctrines of the Concep-
tion and the Redemption, requires him to deny Christ, and worship
false gods (569-915). Meriasek refusing, Teudar sends his torturers to slay him (916–982). Warned of his danger by a vision,
Meriasek hides under a rock, and escapes to Britanny (983–1096).
After miraculously taming a wolf (1097–1131), he becomes a
hermit, and builds a chapel on a bleak mountain near Pontivy
(1132–1152).

The scene of the drama then shifts to Rome. The Emperor
Constantine, still a pagan, sends forth his knights to persecute
the Christians (1153–1287). The souls of two of the martyrs are
received in heaven (1288–1305), and the persecutors scared by
lightning. Pope Silvester and his clergy bury the martyrs, and
flee to Mount Seraptyn (Soracte ?), while Constantine is stricken
with leprosy (1353–1369), and seeks a cure from a doctor and a
pagan bishop (1370–1439). The doctor cheats him (1440–1485),
and the bishop prescribes a bath of children's blood (1486–1521).
Constantine has three thousand children collected for slaughter
(1522–1626), but takes pity upon them and their mothers and
sets them free (1627–1682). The Apostles Peter and Paul
appear in a vision to Constantine, and desire him to send for Silvester and get baptized (1689–1724). This is done: the emperor

is healed by the baptismal waters, and establishes the Christian faith (1725–1865).

The scene shifts back to Britanny. Outlaws rob a merchant and a priest (1866–1935). The Earl of Rohan seeks Meriasek's hermitage (1936–1979), and after vainly trying to get him to return to the world (1980–2053), asks him to clear the land of robbers, and promises, thereupon, to establish three fairs (2054–2079). Meriasek agrees (2080–2084), and sends fire on the outlaws' forest (2085–2112). Then the outlaws calling on Meriasek are saved from death, and leave Britanny (2112–2204).

The Duke of Cornwall then for the first time hearing that Meriasek has been forced by Teudar to fly the country (2205–2277), marches with his men against that pagan (2278–2299). Teudar makes ready for battle (2300–2324), heartened by certain demons (2325–2356). After some parley Teudar is defeated (2357–2498), and the first part of the play concludes with a recommendation to the audience to drink and dance (2499–2512).

In the second part of the play the scene is laid first at Rome. Constantine announces the establishment of Christianity throughout his kingdom (2513–2521). The playwright then brings us to Brittany. A blind Earl Globus is led to Meriasek's hermitage, who rejects his offer of gold and land, but heals him for Christ's sake (2522–2627). Like miracles are also wrought on a demoniac and a deaf man (2628–2681). The Bishop of Vannes then dying, rich and poor desire Meriasek to succeed him, and the Earl of Vannes sends to Pope Silvester for the Bull authorizing Meriasek's consecration (2682–2762). Silvester gives the Bull (2763–2786); the messenger brings it to the Earl of Vannes, and the Earl, the Dean, and a Canon go to Meriasek and vainly endeavour to persuade him to accept the vacant bishopric (2787–2852). They return sorrowfully to Vannes, but at the instance of two Breton bishops, they and the Earl Globus make a second and successful attempt (2853–2909). Meriasek is led off to Dol and consecrated in St. Sampson's Church (2970–3030). He clothes the naked and heals lepers (3031–3155).

An episode from the *Miracula de Beato Mereadoco* is then introduced. The only son of a certain woman goes to the court of a King Massen, and joining in a hunting-party is taken prisoner by a heathen tyrant, who attacks and defeats the king (3156–3578). Tidings of her son's misfortune reach his mother, who entreats the Virgin on his behalf (3579–3600). The Virgin disregards the mother's prayer and the tyrant orders the son's execution (3601–3614). The mother, in revenge, carries off the child-Christ from the arms of the Virgin's image. Thereupon, the Virgin, with Christ's consent, descends from heaven, frees the prisoner, and restores him to his mother, who then takes back the stolen image of the bambino (3615–3802).

After this episode, the playwright returns to Meriasek, who miraculously restores a madman to his senses (3803–3853), performs severe penance, and is nourished by angels (3854–3895).

Again the scene is laid in Italy. Two heathen dukes go out to hunt, are attacked by a dragon, and flee to the Emperor Constantine. The heathen bishop before mentioned maintains that the existence of the monster must be due to Constantine's conversion. Pope Silvester is fetched and (heartened by S. Peter) he vanquishes the dragon and brings to life many whom it had slain, The heathen dukes are baptized and all go in procession to the Pope's palace (3896-4180).

Returning to Britanny and Meriasek, the playwright first sets forth a miraculous cure of a cripple (4181-4251), and then describes Meriasek's death, surrounded by his sorrowful clergy (4252-4330), and the reception of his soul in heaven (4331-4348). Bishops and earls, deans and canons bury the saint's body in a grave made and cleansed by those whom he had healed; and the second and last act concludes with a speech by the Earl of Vannes, in which, after invoking on the audience the blessing of Meriasek, of Mary of Camborne, and of the Apostles, he says—

> " Drink ye all with the play,
>   We will beseech you
>   Before going hence.
>   Pipers, pipe ye at once !
>   We will, every son of the breast,
>   Go to dance.
>   Go ye or stay,
>   Welcome shall ye be
>   Though ye be a week here."

The comic element necessary in all Cornish plays is here provided by Constantine's quack doctor (1408-1482), the *tortores* employed by Teudar (950-1040), Constantine and the tyrant (3245), the Breton outlaws and the bishops' crucifers.

It will be seen that the play is founded on three stories unskilfully pieced together, the legend of Meriasek, the legend of S. Silvester and Constantine, and the story of the Virgin's rescue of the *filius mulieris* (3156--3802). As to the origin of the last-mentioned episode I know nothing. Silvester's legend is widely spread and is well told by Mrs. Jameson in her Sacred and Legendary Art.* Meriasek's legend is thus given piecemeal by the Bollandists at June 7 :—

DE SANCTO MERIADOCO.

episcopo venetensi in Britannia armorica.

Ex variis recentioribus, Vita antiquiori usis.

SEC. VII.] *INter Gallicanas civitates Britanniæ Armoricæ est Episcopalis urbs* Venetensis, Venetum *&* Venetiæ *etiam dicta, vulgo* Vannes,

---

* *See* Irish versions (hitherto unpublished) in the notes to the Félire of Oengus, Jan. 18, and in a life of Silvester preserved in the *Lebar Brecc.*

olim Ducum Sedes, quæ ad hunc diem vii *Junii cultu sacro veneratur* S.
Meriadocum *vulgo* S. Mèriadec, *suum Episcopum.*
Memoria ejus ut Sancti apud varios.] *Hujus aliquam Vitā Gallice
edidit Albertus le Grand, inter Vitas Sanctorum* Britanniæ *Armoricæ, jam
altera vice recusas anno* MDCLIX : *& inter Auctores quibus se usum profitetur,
sunt Augustinus du Pas, Joannes Chenu, & Claudius Robertus in Catalogo
Episcoporum Venetensium. Sed hi nudum nomen exprimunt, tantum titulo*
Sancti *praefixo, & statuunt duodecimum aut decimum tertium hujus
Sedis Episcopum. Sammarthani decimum quintum :* de quo, inquiunt,
consule Proprium Sanctorum dioecesis Venetensis, ubi fertur, ipsum
obdormivisse in Domino vii Idus Junii.

cultus in Venetensi Proprio.] *Idem* Proprium *allegat etiam Albertus le
Grand, quod nos habemus Veneti excusum anno* MDCXXX ; *& inde subdimus
aliquod Vitæ Compendium, in tres Lectiones parvas, ad secundum Nocturnum in Matutinis recitandas, distinctum : quibus alibi additur hæc Oratio :*
Deus, qui de huius mundi inedia, per mediū paupertatis, Beatum Meriadocum, Confessorem tuum atque Pontificem, abstraxisti ad patriam
claritatis, tribue nobis quaesumus ; ut, ipso pro nobis intercedente, dirumpas nostrae vincula pravitatis.

Legenda ex MS. Vita gallica.] 2. *Praeterea idem Albertus allegat,* antiquum Legendarium manuscriptum detentum in ecclesia S. Joannis
Traoume Meriadec, Poigt dicta, in parochia Plongaznau [leg. *Plou-*]
dioecesis Trecorensis : *quam Vitam utinam sub finem edidisset : tunc
certior fides adhiberi posset iis quæ refert, & in Lectionibus non habentur.
Talia sunt, quod* S. Meriadocus anno 758 natus est : sed cifris transpositis opinamur legendum anno 578 aut 587, tunc autem valde senex fuisset
circa annum 659, quando in Lectionibus *dicitur consecratus Sacerdos.
Deinde, ait idem Albertus,* Meriadocum, post acquisitas inter studia
scientias, à parentibus ablegatum ad aulam regiam, in eaque quinquennio
vixisse à vitiis immaculatum, omni pietatis & sanctitatis exercitio deditum.
Postea oblatum ab eisdem matrimonium recusasse & præelegisse sacros
Ordines ; Sacerdotioque suscepto secessisse in locum solitarium in Vicecomitatu Rohanensi, haud procul ab oppido Pontivio, ubi hoc tempore extat
sacellum ejus nomini dicatum.

multa particularia continet.] Interim cum praedones vicina loca devastarent, eum instituisse apud Vicecomitem Rohanensem, ut dictos prædones
pelleret : eique se id nequaquam posse efficere respondenti, promisisse, se
id peracturum si tres celebres mercatus concederet in paroecia Noyal,
scilicet die sexto Julii, octavo Septembris, & primo Octobris.   Qua
conditione à Vicecomite accepta, dictos prædones solis S. Meriadoci
apud Deum precibus fugatos fuisse.   Denique, post administratum in
omni sanctitate Episcopatum, vita functum esse & in ecclesia Cathedrali
sepultum, ac tam in eo quam in loco solitudinis suæ claruisse miraculis :
multas etiam in Britannia hac dicatas S. Meriadoco ecclesias, interque
eas sacellum castri Pontivii, & aliud in paroecia Plou-gaznou, *supra
indicato. Haec inter alia Albertus le Grand.*

exhibetur elogium ex Saussaio.] 3. *Andreas Saussayus in Martyrologio
Gallicano, hoc cum exornat elogio :* Apud Venetum in Armorica, S. Meriadoci Episcopi & Confessoris, qui ex regia stirpe Conani, provinciæ
hujus Principis, editus, calcato temporalis gloriæ fuco, humilitatis Filii
Dei imitator, sese, ne natalium fulgor spectabilem mundo redderet,
indumentis vilibus tegens, in desertum locum, Deo soli ut serviret,

recepit : ubi diu in omni sanctitate vitam ducens eremiticam, delituit. At deinde clara virtutum lucerna, ne sub modio esset diutius, divino indicio propalata, super candelabrum evecta est. Patefactus enim cœlesti nutu Christi famulus, sublato è vivis Hinguthano Venetensi Episcopo, magna Cleri populi conspiratione, de solitudine dilectissima abstractus, electusque est Pontifex, atque Episcopus ordinatus : quamquam ipse subesse, non præesse, desideraret. Sic suscepto Pastorali munere, mores Episcopales ita induit, ut vix ullum, ante vel post ejus tempora, illa Ecclesia Praesulem viderit, qui majori solertia, doctrina, vigilantia, integritate, pietate, gregem rexerit commissum. Propter quarum virtutum excellentiam, & clara suæ sanctitatis ac gloriae, quæ cum vivus, tum defunctus prodidit, argumenta, à majoribus inter dioecesis hujus Tutelares praecipuos habitus, & in hunc usque diem à posteris sacris honoribus, qui beatis Opitulatoribus deferuntur, excultus, hoc ipso die, quo ad beatitudinem migravit, venerationis celebratur obsequiis.

& Lectiones novae] *Haec Saussaius. Vitae autem Epitome ex propriis Ecclesiae Venetensis, est quae sequitur :*
ubi narratur ejus ordinatio Presbyteralis, vita solitaria.] I. Meriadocus, illustri stirpe Conani minoris Britanniæ Regis editus, à teneris annis sese ad virtutum omnium studium comparavit : humilitatem vero maxime in deliciis habuit, Christi Domini vestigiis insistens. Legitimam adeptus ætatem, sacris ordinibus ordinatur ; et inania mundi nomina, quæ suspiciunt homines, & junioribus animos faciunt, aspernatus, bonis omnibus et honoribus cessit, recepitque se in locum quemdam, non procul à Pontiviensi castro, in quo solus degebat, perturbationum expers, vitæque compos securissimæ.

miracula : electio ad Episcopatum] II. Aegrotos ibi plurimos, qui ad eum sanitatis recuperandæ gratia confluebant, sospites restituit. Cumque insignis hujus virtutis & sanctitatis fama percrebuisset ; Venetenses cives concilium cogunt, Capitulumque & universum Clerum impensius obsecrant, ut Meriadocum in Episcopi nuper defuncti locum sufficiant. Quibus in id convenientibus, datum est negotium quibusdam Canonicis, ut Meriadoco, ipsummet populi precibus & Cleri concordibus animis cooptatum Episcopum, renuntiarent.

in eoque virtutes.] III. Et licet sibi delatum onus deprecaretur ; ita tamen ingeminatis omnium votis urgetur, ut iis tandem cesserit. Paucis post diebus in Ecclesia Cathedrali, celebri Episcoporum conventu, & magno populi concursu, fausta acclamatione plausuque consecratur circa annum sexcentesimum quinquagesimum nonum. Caritatem maxime & misericordiam erga pauperes et ægrotos exercuit, eorum inediam sublevando salutique consulendo. Cum verò pie & sancte vitam confecisset, miraculorum gloria celebris, septimo Idus Junii obdormivit in Domino.

Father Albert Le Grand, in his *Vies des Saints de Bretagne*, and D. Lobineau, in the second volume of his work bearing the same title, Paris, 1836, pp. 118–125, have translated or analysed in French the Bollandist legend.

D. Lobineau gives the name (Hingueten) of the bishop from whom Meriasek received priest's orders, and further states that there are many places in Brittany dedicated to him.

"Entre autres la chapelle du château de Pontivy, et une ancienne chapelle appelée *Traoun-Mériadec*, c'est-à-dire *le Val de Mériadec*, en la paroisse de l'lougasnou dans l'ancien diocèse de Tréguier, au lieu où est maintenant la chapelle de Saint-Jean-du-Doigt. Une autre chapelle du même saint se trouve dans la paroisse de Stival près de Pontivi. Cette chapelle est un lieu de pèlerinage assez fréquenté. On y conserve le chef du saint évêque, et l'on y montre une cloche de cuivre jaune, très-ancienne, de forme conique, et qu'on dit avoir appartenu à S. Mériadec ; on la sonne sur la tête de ceux qui sont affligés de surdité. Enfin il y a encore une troisième chapelle dédiée à son honneur, et presque aussi fréquentée que celle de Stival, dans la paroisse de l'lumergat.

' These' (writes Viscount de la Villemarqué), 'with the editors of the Propre du diocèse de Vannes, printed in 1660, and of the ancient breviary of Vannes (1589), are the only authors who, so far as I know, have concerned themselves, at least at any length, with St. Mériadec. Our contemporaries, such as abbé Tresvaux, in his new edition of D. Lobineau, M. de Kerdanet in his annotated reprint of Alb. Le Grand, M. de Garaby, *Vies de B. B.* or *Sts. de Bretagne*, and M. Levot, *Biographie bretonne*, have merely followed or corrected their predecessors.

' Ils les corrigent bien, je crois, en plaçant au vii⁰ siècle et non au xiii⁰, l'existence de St. Mériadec. Le *Catalogue* des évêques de Vannes, daté de l'an 1254, leur donne raison contre le légendaire du xv⁰ siècle qui fait mourir le saint en l'an 1302. On n'est pas moins dans le vrai en relèguant parmi les fictions inventées pour flatter les Rohan—qui n'existaient pas au vii⁰ siècle—tout ce qui est dit par ce dernier légendaire au sujet de la parenté et des rapports de St. Mériadec avec un Vicomte de Rohan et les foires franches obtenues de lui. Si le Saint y fut pour quelque chose, les Rohan n'y sont pour rien : leur illustre nom aura usurpé la place de je ne sais quel vieux nom obscur du pays de Porhoët.'

3. *The Names of Places mentioned in the Play.*

Except *Rome*, 1182, 2514, *Lumbardy*, 1534, *meneth Sereptyn* (Mount Soracte ?), 1342, 1534, 1735, and *Poly* (Pola ?), these relate either to Britanny (*breten* 2757, 2861, *bretyn* 4355, *breten byen* 517), or Cornwall (*Kernou*, 2294, 2860).

The Breton place-names are as follows :—

Kernou, 513, etc., now *Kernéô* or *Kerné*, ' la Cornouaille, un des quatres cantons de la Bretagne qui ont donné leur noms aux quatre dialectes principaux de la langue bretonne qu'on y parle.' (Legonidec).

an castel gelwys pontelyne (' the castle called Pontelyn') 1139, 1947. Of this Viscount de la Villemarqué writes as follows : 'There is no castle of Pontelyne,' au bord de la rivière, mais il y en avait un autrefois, nommé le *château du Thelem*. Je le trouve, après bien des recherches, et non sans un certain plaisir que vous comprendrez, cité dans une " Enquête" de l'an 1479, " touchant les droits et prérogatives de la Maison de Rohan." Voici le texte : " Le Sieur de Guémené mesme dépose que en la Vicomté de Rohan y avait anciennement plusieurs chasteaux et fortes places, scavoir est le *Chasteau du Thelem* . . . . esquelz on dit que anciennement y souloit avoir capitaine, guet et garde . . . . quelz par les Anglois furent ruinés et démolis."

'Ce vieux château du Thelem était situé à une lieue trois quarts de Josselin, au confluent de l'Oust et de la Lié (*aliàs* Eler) près du *Pont* du Camper (*aliàs* Kemper, confluentia). Il a donné son nom, sous la forme de *Pontelaine*, qui est à peu près celle de vôtre Mystère, à une famille dont je remarque un membre, en 1437, parmi les seigneurs châtelains de la Vicomté de Rohan."

an ryuer a Josselyne, 1142. Of this M. de la Villemarqué says —" Il n'y a pas de 'rivière de Josselin,' proprement dite, mais une rivière qui passe à Josselin; c'est l'Oust (*Ult* alias *Ulto* fluvius, *Ultum*, Cartul. de Redon, A. 834, 859—*Ost*,—D. Morice, 1205). Elle prend sa source dans le département des Côtes du Nord, et arrose un grand nombre de lieux de l'ancienne Vicomté de Rohan. Toutefois on ne peut douter que l'auteur de votre Mystère ait voulu l'indiquer."

Rohan 1936.

plu voala (leg. *plu noala*) 2078, 2202. "Le pays appelé *Plu-Voala*" (writes M. de la Villemarqué) "dans le mystère de St. Mériadec (lisez *N*oala, N au lieu de V) est le Plebs Nuial du Cartulaire de Redon, ad ann. 1082, le Noal de l'Abbaye de Bonrepos, ann. 1204; le Noyal d'un texte de 1219 cité par D. Morice, le Noual d'un autre texte de 1274, et pour ne pas reproduire toutes les formes de ce nom, la paroisse de Noyal d'aujourdhui, dite Noyal-Pontivy. Composée de 4 trèves et du Château de Pontivy, dans la Vicomté de Rohan, elle faisait partie du doyenné de Porhoët et est maintenant la plus grande commune du canton de Pontivy, département de Morbihan."

Venetens 2682, 2761, 2809 'Vannes.'

eglos sent Sampson (the first archbishop and metropolitan of Brittany): this church is in the town of Dôl.

The Cornish place-names are as follows :—

Cambron 644, 687, 730, 965, 982, 4293, now Camborne, a market town and parish in the hundred of Penwith, on the road from Redruth to Penzance. The late Dr. Oliver has shown that the patron saint of the church is Mereadocus. The Saint's Well is still known, and, according to Mr. Hunt, persons who washed in it were called *Merrasickers*.

Penwyth 783, *Penwith* 2217, now a hundred in Cornwall.

Carnebre 784, *Carnbre* 966, 'the cairn-hill,' near the sea, N.W. of Redruth, noticeable both from the English Channel and the Atlantic.

Castel an Dynas 2210, there is one place so named, 'an eminence' ('729 ft.) 'crowned with an embankment,' near S. Columb Major, and another north of Penzance.

Peddre 2211, now Pidar, one of the hundreds of Cornwall.

Tyndagyel 2214, now Tintagel, Arthur's birthplace, on the Bristol Channel, N.W. of Camelford.

Menek, 2267, 2288, now Meneage, a peninsular district in Kerrier hundred, south of the town of Helston, with the Lizard for its extreme southern point.

Les Teudar 2267, 2284, now Les-teader, in the parish of S. Keverne, Meneage.

Porder 2288, now Powder, one of the hundreds of Cornwall.

Goddren 2289, now Goodren, in the parish of Kea, hundred of Powder, on a branch of the Truro river.

Morvelys 3415, has not been identified.

Tamer 2208, is the river Tamar.*

4. *The Language and Metres of the Play.*

Except a few English, French, and Latin oaths, curses, and other phrases scattered through the play, its language is Middle-Cornish, but rather more modern than that of the *Passion*, and of the dramas published by Mr. Norris. Thus loanwords from the English are somewhat more numerous than they are in Mr. Norris's dramas. Again, the vowels *e* and *o* have often become *a* (exalt*ya* 15, wos*a* 22, my3tern*as* 154, than 1370, t*a*rthennou 1423, bohoso-gy*an* 472, soudory*an* 1354, calcory*an* 1375; m*a*ryasek 262: *y* sometimes occurs for *e* (beth*y*ns 818), and *e* for *i* (prence 924). In two or three instances a mute *th* is written for *gh* (bot*h*osek 779, my3ternas 154, berth*uth* 1376). In *pethy* (for *pethyth*) and *forna* 1104 (for *forthna*) *th* is dropt. In one word (*bedneth* 198, 224) *nn* has become *dn*. In *falge* 777, *calge* 2046, and *felge* 1273, *s* has become soft *g*, as in the Italian *Ambrogio* from *Ambrosius*; *v* for *f* occurs in goth*v*os 28, goth*v*as 104, o*v*e 248, ar*v*eth 3201. But these are mere phonetic corruptions. The grammar of the language is pure Middle-Cornish. The infixed and suffixed pronouns are regularly used. The verb is unimpaired. The syntax is that of the older dramas, save that the future of the verb substantive is sometimes used for the present. On the whole, the play may be regarded as filling the gap between the fourteenth century Oxford plays and the modern Cornish *Creation of the World*.

Most of the interesting Cornish words and grammatical forms are mentioned in the Notes: the following additional remarks may be useful to students of the text.

The long vowels are expressed in three ways—1st, by adding *y* or *i*, 2nd, by duplication, 3rd, by adding a mute *e*. Thus—

1st, t*ays* 295, r*ays* 319, m*ays* 534, b*eys* 340, br*eys* 342, p*eyth*

---

* For information regarding these places I am indebted to the kindness of the Rev. Dr. Bannister, vicar of St. Day, Scorrier.

445, we*yll* 466, vo*ys* 312, do*y* 457, 610, o*ys* 462, mo*ys* 689,=mo*is* 130, gro*yt* 3326, go*yt* 3325.   In glowa*es* 1160 an *e* is added.

2nd, gl*aa*n 1719, l*ees* 663, jugl*eer* 921, m*ee*n 1406, r*ee* 1509, f*eer* 2195, r*ee* 2308, r*ee* (faciet) 2836, p*ee* 3264, l*yy*nnyou 4446.

3rd, a*ye* 6, myt*er*ne 4, scol*e* 10, wor*e* 19, corf*e* 148, wyr*e* 205, ov*e* 248, ol*e* 366, mesk*e*, 434, hovl*e* 853, toul*e* 1168.

c is sometimes used for *s* : v*e*cyl 1519, gemer*c*ys 1837, *c*ydyr 1969, *c*ervyes 3595, *c*ervons 3651, gra*c* 215 : fe*c*y*c*yan 1484 : *s* for *c* : re*s*eves 452.

ʒ has two powers, *dh* (W. *dd*, English soft *th*) and *y* (ʒurl 1937, ʒesseys 2162, ʒethewon 2602, ʒches 4231).

g is either hard, or equivalent to English *j* (an *g*effa 20, marte*g*e 61).

sch in loanwords is sometimes for *sc* (oms*ch*umunys 1249), but generally for *sh.*

th has two powers : *dh* (cle*th*ethyou 1266, *th*efy 2475), or that of the sharp English *th.*

u is often = the consonant *v* (sc*u*ys 2).   It is sometimes= *i* (*y*) (cr*u*stunyon 539, m*u*ter 3010, t*u*ront 3206), or *e* (*u*goreff 3689, y*u*rlys 294, p*u*rfeth 1546, tr*u*spys 1116) : conversely *e* for *u* occurs in fort*e*n 1424, steth*y*a 1495.

v is either = the vowel *u* (*v*hell 4), or the consonant *v.*

w is generally a vowel (y*w* 1, g*w*lascur 3), or semi-vowel ; but it is sometimes = *v* (bar*w*ow 2309 dei*w*orijs 4178, *w*ur 668, *w*ryens 3963).

The stage-directions contain some curious words.   Thus, the mediaeval Latin verb *pompo, kalus,* p. 32, *exulatores,* p. 106 (which would perhaps have been better rendered ' exiles ' or ' fugitives '), *cardinale* p. 158, *crosser* (if this be intended for Latin) p. 164, *tentum* p. 192, *stallum* p. 200. *processonant* p. 242, *processconabiliter* p. 106.   Except in one or two instances, I have allowed the scribe's wonderful Latin to remain uncorrected.   The English *beryth* p. 76, *urnell* p. 80, *yledyt* p. 172, *bagyll* p. 174, *forling, suagynk* p. 220, *soudrys* p. 228 are also noteworthy.   Some of the strangest English loanwords are mentioned in the notes.

The Metres.

These are numerous and elaborate, and may be divided into ten classes—

I. The seven-syllabled rhyming couplet, e.g. 2536, 2537.

II. Quatrains.   Of these there are several kinds, in one the lines are seven-syllabled and the rhymes run thus : *abab* (e.g. 168—171). In another the first line has four syllables, the rest seven, and the rhymes are thus : *abba* (e.g. 126—129).   See also 391—394.

III. Five-lined stanzas : see 4324—4328, where the rhymes are thus : *aabab.*

IV. Six-lined stanzas. Examples are 25–30, 31–36, 258–262, 813–818, 819–824.

V. Seven-lined stanzas. Examples are 99–105, 264–271 (where the rhymes are thus: *aababab*) 519–525 (where the rhymes are thus: *aabaaab*). See also 4349–4355, 4386–4392, 4198–4204.

VI. Eight-lined stanzas. Examples: 9–16 (where the rhymes are thus: *abababab*), 118–125 (*ababcddc*), 278–285 (*aabccbcb*). There is a curious form in which the fifth line has four syllables, the others seven syllables, and the rhymes run thus: *ababcddc*. See 1–8, 17–24, 37–44, 45–52.

VII. Nine-lined stanzas: e.g. 90–98 (rhymes *aab ccb ddb*), 207–215 (rhymes *ab ab c ddd c*). And see 172–180, 363–371, 3179–3187.

VIII. Ten-lined stanzas: e.g. 154–163, 474–483.

IX. Eleven-lined stanzas: 632–642.

X. Twelve-lined stanzas: 142–153 (rhymes *ababab ab cddc*), and see 848–859.

In conclusion, a few words as to the mode in which I have edited the text and made the translation. The MS. abounds in contractions. These I have extended, but always printed the extensions in italics. The scribe uses capital letters capriciously. I have employed them only to denote the commencement of a stanza. He sometimes wrongly joins two words, and wrongly divides a single word, namely in the following instances :—

clapsens 936. *kewar* 1048. *mapguirhas* 1125. *speryssans* 1317. *empertek* 1411. *pendraleueryth* 1486. *whybath* 1512. *mylflogh* 1657. *gasabev* 1661. *lynebras* 1993. *warnalosal* 2413. *gulym* 2604. *roythym* 2847. *dothekynsu* 2934. *my nnoghoma* 3199. *hawarbarthom* 3244. *poby* 3311. *dywhylescyans* 3463. *fydis* 3509. *venentha* 3579. *polgeov* 3655. *dyalwethygov* 3690. *saban* 3711. *recovleferel* 3739. *nefrebetheheb* 3802. *gorthe* 3837. *thymokea* 4017. *braysogh* 4311. *halsebcwe* 4466. *moyden* 4492. *duavan* 4548.

Teu dar 759, 1048. *ar luth* 1430. *hel myv* 1522. *trem myl* 1776. *so yth* 2292. *at lyan* 2477. *hawa reegrueys* 2767. *otho mogyan* 3137. *guar nyany* 3272. *du a* 3976. *kyn sol* 4170.

I have corrected these errors. In other respects I have spared no pains to reproduce the text with exactitude. For ample opportunities to do this I am indebted to Mr. Wynne, who first at Peniarth gave me free access to the MS. for nearly a week, and afterwards, at my request, deposited it for three months in the library of Trinity College, Dublin.

The translation is merely intended to convey, line for line, to philologists the meaning of the original so far as I have been able to ascertain it. Hence, I have not only rendered the *chevilles* with which the Cornish text is intolerably overloaded, but I have often disregarded English idiom. I believe that my version is generally accurate, but there are some words and passages from which I have been unable to elicit any satisfactory meaning.* That these are not more numerous is due to the researches of Norris and Ebel and to the kindness of the Rev. Robert Williams, of Rhydycroesau, who read a proof of the work, and to whom I am indebted for many corrections and suggestions.

W. S.

5, Merrion-square, North, Dublin,
December 14, 1871.

---

* See lines 17, 103, 156, 293, 719, 908, 1035, 1044, 1307, 1475, 1476, 1901, 2328, 2385, 2419, 2681, 2738, 2883, 3303, 3927, 3083. Attention is requested to the Corrigenda at pp. 278, 279.

BEUNANS MERIASEK.

ORDINALE DE VITA SANCTI MEREADOCI.

p. 1.

HIC INCIPIT ORDINALE DE VITA SANCTI MEREADOCI EPISCOPI ET CONFESSORIS ∴

Pater mereadoci pompabit hic

[PATER MEREADOCI]

Me yw gylwys duk bryten
  ha seuys a goys ryel
ha war an gwlascur cheften
4   nessa ȝen myterne vhell
    kyng conany
aye lynneth purwyr y thof
gwarthevyas war gvyls ha dof
8   doutis yn mysk arlyȝy

Vn mab purwyr ȝyn y ma
  meriasek y hanow
ȝe scole lemmyn y worra
12   me a vyn heb falladow
dysky dader may halla
    mersyv gans du plygadow
y karsen y exaltya
16   may fo perhennek gwlasow

MATER

Arluth henna yv gwrys da
  y exaltye yredy
perfect ef a wore redya
20   grammer angeffa deffry
    y vyea tek
ha worshypp wosa helma
  yv ȝe voth mos a lemma
24   lauer ȝynny ov map wek

MERIADOCUS

A das ha mam ov megyans
  yv bos gorrys ȝe ȝyskans
    rag attendie an scryptur
28   gothvos ynweth decernya
omma ynter drok ha da
  yv ov ewnadow pup vr

HERE BEGINS THE PLAY OF THE LIFE OF SAINT MERIASEK, BISHOP AND CONFESSOR.

Meriasek's father shall here parade.

MERIASEK'S FATHER.

I am called Duke of Brittany,
   And raised from blood royal,
And over the country chieftain
4   Nearest to the high sovran,
      King Conany.
Of his lineage right truly am I,
Warden over wild and tame,
8   Feared among lords.

A son right truly we have,
   Meriasek his name.
To school now put him
12   I will without fail,
That he may learn goodness.
   If it be God's pleasure,
I should like to exalt him
16   That he may be owner of countries.

MERIASEK'S MOTHER.

Lord, that is done well
   To exalt him readily.
Perfectly he can read:
20   Grammar, that he shall have soon,
     It would be fair,
And worship after this.
Is thy will to go hence,
24   Tell to us, my sweet son?

MERIASEK.

O father and mother, my delight
Is to be put to learning,
   To attend the Scripture.
28 Knowledge likewise to discern
Here between evil and good
   Is my desire always.

p. 2.

PATER

Beneth du ᴣys meryasek
32 pup vr ty yv colonnek
   parys rag dysky dader
meseger scon alemma
kegy gans ov mab kerra
36   bys yn mester a grammer

PRIMUS NUNCIUS

Arlud ᴣe voth a vyth gvrys
   my a wor pur wyre yn ta
py ma an mester trygis
40   hag yᴣyv marthys densa
   sur worth flehys
meryasek pan vynnogh why
an forth dalleth yredy
44   ny a vyn ha pur vskys

MERIADOCUS

A das ha mam kekyfrys
   pesef agis bannothow
maym beua the well grays
48   benyᴣa yn ov dyᴣyow
   desky dader
rag agis benneth[ow] why
yv moy treasur ᴣymmo vy
52   es pyth an bysma neb vr

p. 3.

PATER

Ov mab wek ᴣys benneth du
   ham benneth vy benyᴣa
ny fylleth hedre ven bev
56   ath porpos gene neffra
   lemmen squyer
keᴣegy gans ov map dy
ha gveyth warnotho defry
60 ena ty a yl dysky
   martegen the vrys mur dader

MATER

Ov map benneth varya
   dys ham bennath vy neffra
64 thethe ganov mannafi amma
   ewne yv ᴣyn ᴣeth leuf kara
   meryasek wek

FATHER.

God's blessing to thee, Meriasek !
32 Always thou art hearty,
    Ready to learn goodness.
Messenger, forthwith hence
Go thou with my dearest son
36   Unto the master of grammar.

FIRST MESSENGER.

Lord, thy will shall be done.
    I know right truly well
40 Where the master is dwelling,
    And he is wondrous kind
    Surely to children.
Meriasek, when you wish
The way readily begin
44   We will, and right quickly.

MERIASEK.

O father and mother also
    I beseech your blessings
That I may live made the better
48   Ever in my days
    To learn goodness.
For your blessings
Are a greater treasure to me
52   Than the wealth of this world any time.

FATHER.

My sweet son, God's blessing to thee,
    And my blessing ever,
Thou shalt not fail whilst I may be alive
56   Of thy purpose by me always.
    Now squire,
Go thou with my son thither,
And take care of him truly.
60 There thou canst learn,
    If it be thy wish, much of goodness.

MOTHER.

My son, Mary's blessing
    To thee and my blessing for ever.
64 Thy mouth I would kiss it :
    Right is it for us to love thee dearly,
    Sweet Meriasek.

my a dryst yn du avan
68 pan ven ny sur coth ha gwan
gvreth agan revlys tek

ARMIGER DUCIS

Meryasek alemma duen
gervyth a scryve pluven
72 whath me ny won ʒe redya
nag aswen ov leʒerow
me a bys du karadow
roy ʒynny ynta spedya

p. 4.   *Hic magister pompabit*

MAGISTER

76 My yv mayster a gramer
gvrys yn bonilapper
vniversite vyen
my a wor mur yn dyvyn
80 pan ve luen ov ʒos a wyn
ny gara covs mes laten

PRIMUS NUNCIUS

Honour ʒyvgh master worthy
ha benytha mur reuerens
84 duk conan pur yredy
y vab rag cawas dyskans
sur danvenys
ateva ʒyugh doctor wek
88 dyskovgh ef yn maner dek
ha wy a vyth rewardeys

MAGISTER

Messeger na ʒovt an cas
my an dysk na vo yn gvlas
92 gramarion vᵗ ay parov
devgh seʒovg mereasck
yn myske an flehys pur dek
ha merovgh agis leffrov
96 pe dyth munys kewsovghwy
let veth orth agis dysky
ha mur nynsyv an gobrov

PRIMUS SCOLAR[IS]

Du gveras a b c
100 an pen can henna yv d
ny won na moy yn liuer

I trust in God above
68 When we shall be old and feeble
Thou wilt observe our rules fair.

THE DUKE'S SQUIRE.

Meriasek, let us go hence.
Never a word of pen-writing
72 Yet can I read.
I know not my letters.
I beseech loveable God,
May he grant to us well to speed.

Here shall the Master parade.

MASTER.

76 I am a master of grammar
Made in .... (?)
Of a small university.
I know much in citation :
80 When my tot may be full of wine
I love not to speak (aught) save Latin.

FIRST MESSENGER.

Honour to you, worthy Master
And ever much reverence.
84 Duke Conan right readily
His son to have learning
Surely hath sent.
Here he is for you, doctor sweet.
88 Teach him in a beautiful way,
And you shall be rewarded.

MASTER.

Messenger, fear not the case.
I will teach him so that there will not be in the country
92 Any grammarian of his peers.
Come, sit ye, Meriasek,
Amongst the children very fairly,
And look at your books.
96 If it be a little saying that ye speak,
There will be hindrance to teaching you,
And the rewards are not great.

FIRST SCHOLAR.

God keep A, B, C,
100 The end of the song, that is D.
I know no more in the book.

ny vef y*n* scole ru*m* levte
bys y*n*newer gor3ewar
104   3u*m* gothvas wosa lyfye
me a 3ysk moy ov mest*er*

SECUNDUS SCOLAR[IS]

E s t he*n*na yv est
pa*n*dryv nessa ny won fest
108   m*ur* na reugh ov cronkye
rag my ny ve3af the well
vnwyth a caffen hansell
me a russa ame*n*die

MAGISTER

112   Dyske moy gans 3e cowe3a
pan vy*n*nogh eugh 3e lyvya
meryasek wek eugh gansa
r*a*g wy yv tender yn oys
116   ha flehys yonk a gar boys
ha*m* bevnans vy yv henna

MERIADOCUS

Me a lever 3yvgh mest*er*
ha na vewy dysplesys
120   he3yv sur yv dugwener
da yv sevell worth vn p*ri*s
ha p*r*edery an ena
rag kere*n*sa a*n* passyon*n*
124   a porthes ihe*s*u ragon*
pynys hy3yv y fan*n*a

Ha pub gvene*r*
a vo sur drys an vly3an
128   gul peyadov my a vyn
ky*n*s eva na 3ybbry mevr

3e*n* chappell me a vyn mois
3e c*ri*st a scolyas y woys
132   3e v3yll ov peiadow
ha 3e varye y vam
ky*n*s eva na dybbry tam
helma yv ov vsadow

MAGISTER

136   Ov map gvra 3e vlonogeth
tevlys os 3*o* sansoleth
meriasek go*n* gvyr lemmyn

* MS. ragan.

I was not at school, by my loyalty,
 Until late (?) yesterday evening.
104 To my knowledge, after dining
 I will learn more, my master.

SECOND SCHOLAR.

E, s, t, that is *est*.
What thing is next I know not quite.
108 Do not beat me greatly,
For I shall not be better.
Once if I got a handsel
 I should amend.

MASTER.

112 Learn thou more with thy comrades.
When you will, go to dine,
 Sweet Meriasek, go with them,
For you are tender in age,
116 And young children love food,
 And my life is that.

MERIASEK.

I say to you, Master,
 And be not displeased,
120 To-day surely is Friday:
 Good it is to arise for a while
 And think of the soul.
For love of the Passion
124 Which Jesu bore for us.
 Penance to-day I desire.

And every Friday,
Which shall be surely throughout the year,
128 Make prayer I will,
 Rather than eat or drink much.

To the chapel I will go,
To Christ who shed his blood,
132 To make my prayer,
And to Mary his Mother,
Before drinking or eating a bit :
 This is my usage.

MASTER.

136 My son, do thy will.
Designed art thou for holiness,
 Meriasek, I know truly now.

ke ha due pan vy plesyes
140 myns may hyllen sur esyes
ty a vyth yn pup termyn

descendat solus ad capellam

MERIADOCUS *in capella*

Ihesu arlud nef han bys
ȝys y raf ov peyadow
144 iesu arlud my ad pys
orth temtacyon dewolow
iesu crist gvyth vy pupprys
lel ȝeth servye om dyȝyow
148 ihesu ov corfe ham spyrys
ol ov nerth ham cowgegyow
rof ȝeth gorthye
hag ath peys vvel ha clour
152 nefra na veua yn nor
trelyes ȝe lust an bysme

Marya myȝternas nef
a vagas crist gans ȝe leth
156 maria drefa ȝe luef
ȝen mab a skyentoleth
marya whek peys genef
byth nangeffa an iovl keth
160 warnaf power
nan beys ov escare arall
ham kyke yv escar teball
pur ysel me an temper

164 gans golyas ha gans pynys
me a garsa
crist ȝe plesya
a new⁺ hag a henys

et tunc ad magistrum

Hic pompabit rex conanus

REX CONANUS

168 Gelwys yȝof conany*
mytern yn bryton vyau
han gvlascor pur yredy
me a bev ol yn tyan
172 Der avys ov arlyȝy
mones y fannaf lemmyn
the duk pen an chevalry
nesse ȝymmo yn certan
176 par del yv ef

p. 7.

---

*MS. Conanus.

Go and come when thou mayest be pleased.
140 All we can, surely eased
    Thou shalt be at every time.

       Let him go down alone to the chapel.

    MERIASEK *in the chapel.*

Jesu, Lord of heaven and the world,
    To thee I make my prayer.
144 Jesu, Lord, I beseech thee
    Against devils' temptations.
Jesu Christ, keep me always
    Loyally to serve thee in my days.
148 Jesu, my body and my spirit,
    All my strength and my thoughts
      I give to worship thee,
And I pray thee, humble and pure,
152 That I never be on earth
    Turned to the lust of this world.

Mary, queen of heaven,
    Who fed Christ with thy milk,
156 Mary, upraise (?) thy hand
    To the child of knowledge !
Mary sweet, pray with me
    That never may the caitiff Devil have
160   Power over me,
Nor the world, my other enemy,
And my flesh is an evil enemy,
    Full low I will tame it

164 With watching and with penance.
    I would like
    To please Christ
In youth and in old age.

       And then to the Master.

   Here King Conan shall parade.
    KING CONAN.

168 I am called Conany,
    King in little Britain ;
And the country right readily
    I possess altogether.
172 By advice of my lords
    I would go now
To the Duke, head of chivalry,
    Next to me certainly
      As he is.

yma maryag galosek
cowsys ʒyn rag meryasek
mergh ʒe vyghtern gallosek
180 nynses brassa yndan nef

PRIMUS DOMINUS

Maryasek yv flogh fur
cortis hag vvel yn sur
drys oll flehys an powma
184 my a lever arlud flour
y terfensa myrgh emperour
ʒy par kefis mara peya

SECUNDUS DOMINUS REGIS

Meriasek yv kerys
188 anotha y ma notyes
mur a ʒadder yn povma
p. 8. me a leuer ʒyvgh heb flows
ay cowᵗ ny clowys cows
192 moy gracyus flogh yn bysma   [finit

MERIADOCUS

Me agis pesse mester
mar a pewy sur plesijs
mones ʒe dre heb awer
196 ʒe vyras ov ʒas vskys
hav mam kefrys
bedneth ʒyvgh am vestrigy
me a yl lour y bysy
200 genovgh tek yʒof dyskys

MAGISTER

Banneth crist ʒys meriasek
ham benneth pur colonnek
luen os a venegycter
204 yn ov scole ny ve bythqueth
ʒyso gy purwyre cowyth
yn discans nag yn dader

descendit cum armigero et redit ad patrem

MERIADOCUS

Lowena ʒum tas worthy
208 ha reuerens bys bynyʒa
lowena ʒum mam defry
enour ha dader neffra
pesef agys leun vanneth

There is a mighty marriage
Spoken of to us for Meriasek.
A daughter to a mighty sovran.
180   There is not a greater under heaven.

FIRST LORD.

Meriasek is a wise child :
Courteous and humble surely
    Beyond all the children of this country.
184 I say, flower of lords,
He would deserve an emperor's daughter
    For his mate, if she were found.

SECOND KING'S LORD.

Meriasek is loved,
188 Of him is noted
    Much of goodness in this country.
I say to you, without a flout,
Of his comrade I never heard tell.
192   The most gracious child in this world !

MERIASEK.

I would beseech you, Master,
    If you would be surely pleased,
To [let me] go home without sorrow
196   To see my father forthwith
      And my mother likewise.
A blessing to you for my schooling !
I can enough beseech it.
200   By you well am I taught.

MASTER.

Christ's blessing to thee, Meriasek.
And my blessing right hearty.
    Full art thou of blessedness.
204 In my school never was there
To thee truly a comrade
    In learning nor in goodness.
        He goes down with the squire and
          returns to his father.

MERIASEK.

Joy to my worthy father,
208   And reverence for ever !
Joy to my mother truly,
    Honour and goodness !
    I beseech your full blessing.

212 lemmyn grace an spyrys sans
re woloways ov skyans
yma zym perfect dyskans
    grac the crist pen an eleth

p. 9.

PATER

216 Meryasek welcum yn tre
    ham luen vanneth y rof zys
mar kyssys ynta spedie
    me yv sur ze well plesijs
220   an keth trana
marrogyon parusugh wy
haneth omma yredy
    mytern connan sur a thua

MATER

224 Meriasek bedneth crist zys
    ha bedneth ze vam neffra
gvyf os the vos welcummys
    hag enoris gans henna
228   rag ze zadder
ahanas vs zyn cowsys
du asota mur presijs
    dres ol breton : heb awer

CONANUS REX ad ducem

232 Reuerens zyvg ser duk worthy
    par del ovgh corf a galloys
me redeth omma defry
    drefen agen bos vnwoys
236   ze kestalkye
lowena zyvgh arlothes
ha zen map ker vs genes
    meryasek ov goys nesse

p. 10.

PATER MEREADOCI

240 Wolcum ogh ov lyche worzy
wolcum ogh omma deffry
    wy hag ol agis pobell
ze lowenna rag blythan
244 me a vyth yn pur certan
    agis gvelas om castell

MATER MEREADOCI

Welcum ogh agan soueran
yn keth plassma pur certan
248   plesijs one agis gwelas*

* MS. gwlelas.

212 Now the grace of the Holy Ghost
Hath enlightened my knowledge,
I have perfect learning,
   Thanks to Christ the head of the angels.

FATHER.

216 Meriasek, welcome home,
   And my full blessing I give to thee.
If thou leftest to speed well
   I am surely the better pleased
220   Of that same thing.
Knights, prepare you.
To-night here readily
   King Conan will come.

MOTHER.

224 Meriasek, Christ's blessing to thee,
   And thy mother's blessing ever.
Worthy art thou to be welcomed,
   And honoured therewithal
228   For thy goodness.
Of thee it is told to us,
Pardie, that thou art much praised
   Throughout all Brittany, without grief.

KING CONAN *to the Duke.*

232 Reverence to you, worthy Sir Duke.
   As you are a body of might.
I have come here indeed,
   Because of our being one blood,
236   To talk together.
Joy to you, lady,
And to the dear son that is with thee,
   Meriasek, my nearest blood !

MERIASEK'S FATHER.

240 Welcome are you, my worthy liege !
Welcome are you here indeed,
   You and all your people.
The gladder for a year
244 I shall be very certainly
   To see you in my castle.

MERIASEK'S MOTHER.

Welcome are you, our sovran,
In this same place very certainly
248   Pleased are we to see you.

welcumma* den benary
nefre ny ʒue yn ov chy
kynteffov ʒas am denes

MEREADOCUS

252 Welcum omma lych ryall
del ogh pen ha princypall
dreson ny ol yn tyan
worthy rag cawas reuerens
256 drefen agis governens
rewlys on brays ha byan

REX CONANUS

Gramercy ʒywy warbarth
my a vyn kyns es dyburth
260 muvye omma certan tra
rag dader hag honester
ʒe varyasek heb awer
ow goys nessa

PATER MEREADOCI DUX

264 Ny a vyn purwyr kensa
mones warbarth ʒe ʒybry
dun yn palys ʒe setha
bras ha byan pub huny
268 spencer yv parys pub tra
lauer ʒym del om kerry
ma yllyn mos ʒe lyfya
ov lych gans y arlyʒy

descendunt omnes in placeam

p. 11.

PINCERNA DUCIS BRITANIE

272 Pup tra oma yv parys
an arlythy desethys
bethens genogh meriasek
ny a kergh vytel in chy
276 trompys cleryons wethugh wy
lemen then fest lowenek

MERIADOCUS

Ov arluth lich a esa
omma purguir an kynsa
280 hav thays theragtho inweth
ham mam ger in pen an voys
orlyans duk a galloys
esethugh oma purfeth
284 han arlythy yonk ha loys
ran arak ran aberveth

---

* MS. welcumma ma.

More welcome man never
Will come into my house,
 Though may come my father that reared me.

MERIASEK.

252 Welcome here, royal liege,
As you are head and principal
 Over us altogether
Worthy to receive reverence
256 Because of your governance
 Ruled are we, great and small.

KING CONAN.

Gramercy to you altogether!
I will before separating
260 Move here a certain thing,
For goodness and decency,
To Meriasek, without grief,
 My nearest blood.

MERIASEK'S FATHER THE DUKE.

264 We will, truly, first
 Go together to eat.
Let us come into the palace to sit,
 Great and small, every one,
268 Spencer, is everything ready?
 Tell me as thou lovest me,
That we may go to dine,
 My liege with his lords.

All go down into the open space.

THE SPENCER of the Duke of Brittany.

272 Everything here is ready.
Let the lords seated
 Be by you, Meriasek.
We will seek victual within.
276 Trumpets, clarions, blow ye
 Now to the joyous feast!

MERIASEK.

My liege lord shall sit
Here right truly the first.
280 And my father before him also.
And my mother dear at the head of the table.
Orleans, Duke of power,
 Sit ye here perfectly,
284 And the lords, young and gray,
 Part before, part in the middle.

C

DUX ORLYANS

Gromercy meryasek wek
agis norter yv mar dek
288 maythogh keris gans lues
hagis manerov a plek
kefrys the letrys ha lek
  parov thyugh in bys nynsues
    Hic mimi ludent melodiam

MERIADOCUS

292 Ov lich kyng bethugh mery
inweth oll an kyff nywy
  dukis ʒurlys marogyon
p. 12. ov thays hav mam am denys
296 omgersyogh me agis peys
  a luen golon

CONANUS REX

Gromercy meryasek wek
  mar luen oys a corteysy
300 me ath ra den galosek
  trest am bus pur eredy
me a wor py kefyth gruek
neb yv mergh mytern worthy
304 ha gensy y feth tra dek
  maners trefov castylly
theth tus ha dyso mar plek
  me a leuer pyv ew hy

PATER MERIADOCI DUX

308 Gromercy agen lych da
mur gras y wothen nefra
  thywy agis bolnogeth
the greffe y fyen ny
312 y voys maryys eredy
  ha moghheys agen roweth

MATER

Ny yv plesijs hag a vyn
boys revlijs drethogh certeyn
316 ha meriasek kekefrys
ken the vlamya y fyen
why yv pen agen chen
  gouerner lich a fur rays

DUKE OF ORLEANS.

Gramercy, sweet Meriasek,
Your nurture is so sweet,
288   That you are loved by many,
And your manners are pleasing
Likewise to lettered and to layman.
      Peers to you in the world are not.

Here the mimes shall play a melody.

MERIASEK.

292 My liege lord, be you merry :
Likewise all shall have gaiety (?),
      Dukes, Earls, Knights.
My father, and my mother who suckled me,
296 Comfort yourselves, I beseech you,
      From a full heart.

KING CONAN.

Gramercy, sweet Meriasek,
    So full art thou of courtesy,
300 I will make thee a mighty man,
    Trust have I right readily,
I know where thou wilt find a wife,
    Who is a worthy king's daughter,
304 And with her will be a fair thing—
    Manors, houses, castles.
To thy people and thee, if it pleases,
    I will say who she is.

MERIASEK'S FATHER THE DUKE.

308 Gramercy, our good liege !
Much thanks I give ever
      To you for your wish.
We should be the stronger
312 Were he married readily,
      And our sway greatened.

THE MOTHER.

We are pleased and we will
Be ruled by you certainly,
316   We and Meriasek likewise :
Otherwise to blame we should be.
You are head of our tribe,
      Governor, liege of great grace.

MERIADOCUS

320 Ov arluth lich thyugh mur grays
   thym agis bolnogeth da
ha na vewy dysplesijs
   peseff aragogh omma
324   ov ascusia
wy ham tays hav mam kefrys
ny vanna omry then beys
   na domethy benytha

PATER

328 Tav dymmovy meryasek
   ty a thommeth ov map wek
   the neb arlothes worthy
ha ny a veth the creffa
332 der an maryach benitha
   hag ol the lynnyeth defry

MATER

Domethy mar ny reva
tus ara agen scornya
336   meriasek na govs folneth
wath bythqueth in bysma sur
acontis y fus flogh fur
   gvyth the hanov da rag meth

MERIADOCUS

340 Na govsogh ger war an beys
   benytha ov domethy
the ken forthov sur ov breys
yma syttis credy

PATER

344 Pan forthov yv an rena
   meryasek thym lauer
lemen mar mynnyth dotya
trueth vya ov map ker

MERIADOCUS

348 Na vanna dre grath ihesu
   me a leuer ov thays wek
ov bolnogeth purguir yv
   rag gorthia crist galosek
352 bones sacris marrek du
   an order mar thym a plek
benitha hedre ven byv
   me a garse lowenek

MERIASEK.

320 My liege lord, to you much thanks
For your good will to me.
And be not you displeased.
I beseech before you all,
324 To excuse me,
You and my father and my mother likewise.
I will not give myself to the world,
Nor marry me ever.

THE FATHER.

328 Be silent for me, Meriasek!
Thou wilt marry thee, my sweet son,
To some worthy lady,
And we shall be the stronger
332 Through the marriage ever,
And all thy lineage surely.

THE MOTHER.

If he do not marry him
Folk will scorn us.
336 Meriasek, speak not folly.
Still ever in this world surely
Thou hast been accounted a wise child,
Keep thy good name for shame!

MERIASEK.

340 Speak ye not a word in the world
Ever to marry me.
To other ways surely my mind
Is set already.

THE FATHER.

344 What ways are those?
Meriasek, say to me.
Now if thou wilt dote
It would be a pity, my dear son.

MERIASEK.

348 I will not through Jesu's sake,
I say, my sweet father.
My will right truly is
To worship mighty Christ.
352 To be consecrated a knight of God,
Of the order that pleases me,
Ever as long as I may be alive
I should like gladly.

CONANUS REX

356 Pan othem vs thysogy
a naha roweth an beys
ha ty genys eredy
abarth tays ha mam kefrys
360 nynsyv worschyp theth ehen
the conseyt in pur certen
ov map preder forthov guel

PATER

Ellas ov map meryasek
364 bythqueth 3° gora 3° scole
ty rum gruk vy morethek
a skyans prest nynsus ole
ty the desky
368 ny a veth scorne ol an pov
pytha an tyr han trevov
us thynny heb feladov
mar ny vynnyth domethy

MERIADOCUS

372 A das gruegh crist agis er
bo ens y then goys nessa
pythellens nefre numduer
ganse ny vanna melya

p. 15.   CONANUS REX

376 Me a greys sur meryasek
nagote re skyansek
gul erbyn the days hath vam
ny won pendrussis in scoll
380 a thader byth nynsus oll
ov map ty the dysky tam

MERIADOCUS

Crist indelma a leuer
ov sywa neb a vynna
384 forsakyans byen ha muer
teryov trefov an bysma
y days hay vam
y nessevyn hay cothmans
388 hag eff a gvayn roov cans
bys benitha an bevnans
in neff awartha heb nam

warlergh sen luk
392 me an kyff lell
thyugh in awell
screfis yv kepar del yn gruk

KING CONAN.

356 What need is there to thee
Of refusing the sway of the world ?
And thou (well-) born surely
On side of father and of mother likewise.
360 It is not respect to thy tribe
Thy conceit very certainly.
My son, think of better ways.

THE FATHER.

Alas, my son Meriasek,
364 That thou ever wert put to school !
Thou hast made me sorrowful.
Of knowledge there is now nought at all
To teach thee.
368 We shall be the scorn of all the country.
Where will go the land and the villages
That are ours without fail,
If thou wilt not marry thee ?

MERIASEK.

372 O father, make Christ your heir,
Or let them go to the nearest blood,
Whither they may go concerns me not :
With them I will not meddle.

KING CONAN.

376 I believe surely, Meriasek,
Thou art not overwise
To act against thy father and thy mother.
I know not what thing thou didst in school :
380 Of any goodness there is not,
My son, that thou learnest aught.

MERIASEK.

Christ thus saith :
Whoso would follow me
384 Let him forsake small and great,
Lands, houses of this world,
His father and his mother,
His kinsmen and his friends,
388 And he shall gain a hundred gifts
For ever of life
In heaven above without fault.

According to Saint Luke
392 I will find it loyally
For you in the gospel :
It is written as he made it.

CONANUS REX

Pyraga na ylta gy
396   domethy oma in beys
del fue lius den worthy
  ha gans y du purgerys
  ran sens in neff
400 genes ythoff dysplesijs
gul theth *tus* bones gesijs
  kemeres duen ha greff

MERIADOCUS

Rag kerense *crist* an neff
404   me a vyn ag*is* pesy
na gem*er*re denv^t greff
  na duwen am govys vy

CONANUS

p. 16.   Coyl ortheff vy meryasek
408   me ath desyr dre tekter
bonyl ty a feth edrek
  open dys me a leue*r*
  *pr*eder inta
412 the days ha me ny a yl
statya an tyr dyogeyl
mar mynen the den areyl
  na thefo d*is* benytha

416 In vrna avel begyer
ty a veth sur heb awer
  sensys in pov
hag ol the kerens blamys
420 ella's mar pethen schamys
  wath *pr*eder a guel forthov

MERIADOCUS

Mar peth stat the den arel
grueys annotho dyogel
424   ov liche wek me yv plesijs
henna thymo ny ra greff
mar calla cafus tyr neff
  fy the plos lust*is* an beys

CONANUS REX

428 Mur a varth yv genevy
  pan fyghythrychyth an beys
bewe pel ny elte gy
  heb peth na denvyth genys

KING CONAN.

Why canst thou not
396   Marry thee here in the world,
As were many worthy men,
    And by them God was purely loved ?
    By the saints in heaven,
400 With thee I am displeased,
To cause thy folk to be jeered,
    To take dole and grief !

MERIASEK.

For love of the Christ of the heaven
404   I will beseech you
That no one take grief
    Or dole because of me.

CONAN.

Listen to me, Meriasek,
408   I desire thee through fairness,
Or else thou wilt have repentance,
    Openly I say to thee.
      Consider well.
412 Thy father and I, we can
Limit the land, certainly,
If we will, to another man,
    That it come not to thee ever.

416 Then as a beggar
Thou wilt be surely without grief
    Held in the country,
And all thy kinsmen blamed.
420 Alas, if we be shamed !
    Yet think of better ways.

MERIASEK.

If an estate to another man be
Made thereof certainly,
424   My sweet liege, I am well pleased.
That to me will not cause grief.
If I can find heaven's land
    Fye on the foul lusts of the world !

KING CONAN.

428 Much marvel have I
    When thou *fyest* the riches of the world.
Live long thou couldst not
    Without wealth, nor (could) any one born.

432   drc rychyth ha chevalry
    den a veth degemorys
    inban in meske arlythy
    ha ganse prest enorys

p. 17.   436 Der y peth grueys den ryel
    ha gorys then stat vhel
      pendra dal an bohosek
    kyn fo brays y devethyans
440 ef a dryk pennoth in hans
      nynguel an rych galosek

MERIADOCUS

    Na govsugh a chevalry
      byth moy rychys numdur man
444 tollys yv lues huny
      der peyth an beys yn certan

    A dyves del redyn ny
      rych lour o in pup termen
448 py theth y ena defry
      the yfern then pcyn belen

    Lasser o den bohosek
    a thuk lavyr pur anwek
452   abraham an reseves
    pan o marov dotho eff
    hag in y hascra heb greff
      in golovder an gvythes

CONANUS REX

        [*surrexit circa placeam*

456 Serys kemerugh in ban
    drog yv gena doys oma
    a meryasek guas belan
    dar soposia a reta
460   den rych nefra
    mones then neff da ny yl
    me a greys dotyys oys vyl
      ha muscugys rum cna

p. 18.   ### MERIADOCUS

464 An scriptor* lcferel grua
    den rych then neff dyogcl
    mage fur weyll yv dotha
    moys avel capel gorhel
468   der trov nasweth

---

* MS. scripctor.

432 Through riches and chivalry
    A man will be accepted
Above amongst lords,
    And by them quickly honoured,

436 Through his wealth made a royal man,
And put to the high station.
        What thing is the poor man worth ?
Though great be his lineage,
440 He will remain bareheaded down below :
        Him the rich powerful (man) will not see.

MERIASEK.

Talk you not of chivalry :
    Never more do riches concern me :
444 Deceived is many a one
    By the wealth of the world certainly.

Of Dives as we read
    Rich enough was he at every time.
448 Whither went his soul really ?
    To hell, to the villanous pain.

Lazarus was a poor man
Who bore labour right unsweet :
452   Abraham received him,
When he was dead, unto him,
And in his bosom, without grief,
    Kept him in light.

KING CONAN.

[he rose (and walked) round the open space.

456 Sirs, get you up.
    I am sorry that I came here.
O Meriasek, villanous fellow,
    Dost thou suppose
460   That a rich man never
Can go to the good heaven ?
I believe thou art doting vilely
    And distracted, by my soul !

MERIASEK.

464 The scripture doth say
    A rich man to the heaven certainly,
As great a labour is it for him
    To go as (for) a ship's cable
468   To go through a needle's eye.

henna gans y destrowhy
a yl boys spedijs defry
indellan den rych besy
472 the vohosogyan guet ry
in cheryte part ath peth

CONANUS REX

Farwel ser duk
re crist am gruk
476 the vap yv fol
ganso omgrua
ov herth oma
galles the col
480 ham lafuryans
the lee nefra
war ov ena
me an car in ov bevnans   [*finit*
                                  [*tranceat conanus*

PATER

484 Ov arluth dywy mur grays
ov profia dotho dadder
ellas ragos ov map rays
na vennyth dre onester
488 bones revlys
yma pensevyk an gluas
dysplesijs purguir genas
the days hath vam kekefrys

MERIADOCUS

492 Kynthogh geneff dysplesijs
ythyv ol am anvoth vy
trest ambus boys acordys
orth ihesu crist a vercy
496 agys bannothov kefrys
tays ha mam thymmo gruegh ry
me a vyn mones uskys
wath de thesky dadder moy
500 rag kerense an drensis
na temptyogh vy the foly

p. 19.   PATER

Inter dula du avan
ov map gruaff the kemynna
504 kemer the rovle the honan
gul nahen me ny alla
ov banneth dis   [*finit*

That by destroying it
May be sped certainly.
So the rich busy man,
472 Take care to give to the poor
In charity part of thy wealth.

KING CONAN.

Farewell, Sir Duke,
By Christ who made me
476 Thy son is mad.
By him is caused
My journey here
To go to loss,
480 And my labouring.
To lessen thee ever,
On my soul,
I shall like it in my life.

[Let Conan pass off.

THE FATHER.

484 My lord, much thanks to you
Showing goodness to him.
Alas for thee, my son of grace!
Thou wilt not through decency
488 Be ruled.
The prince of the country is
Displeased right truly with thee,
Thy father and thy mother likewise.

MERIASEK.

492 Though you are displeased with me,
It is all against my will.
Trust have I that I am in accord
With Jesus Christ of mercy.
496 Your blessings likewise,
Father and mother, give ye to me.
I will go straightway
Yet to learn more goodness.
500 For love of the Trinity
Tempt me not to folly.

THE FATHER.

Between the hands of God above,
My son, I do commend thee.
504 Take thine own rule:
Do ought else I cannot:
My blessing to thee!

MATER

Amen p*r*est ham banneth vy
508 ov map dore thym the vay
morethek assoff defry
ov tyberth sur the orthys   [*finit*
[*her meriasek weryth a p*r*est ys govn*

Hic episcopus kernov hic pompabit

Me yv escop in breten
512 in conteth gelwys kernov
mur yv ov rays pup t*er*men
cowethe thym yv tanov
pa*r*let mar stovt
516 p*r*ence war an vebyen lyen
nynsus in brete*n* vyen
ov pa*r*ov purguir heb dovt

MERIADOCUS

Ser epscop thyugh lowena
520 ag*is* pesy y fanna
a ry dy*m*mo vy ordys
p*r*onte*r* boys me a ga*r*sa
corff ihe*s*u thy venystra
524 mar myn ov descans se*r*vya
genogh pan ve*n* apposijs
[*descendit episcopus kernov in placeam*

EPISCOPUS KERNOV

Wolcu*m* oma meryasek
m*c* re glowes ov map wek
528 ahanes covs mur thadde*r*
p. 20.   ry dys ordys me a vyn
in hanov ihe*s*u lemyn*
sacrys gena betheth suer

[*genuflectit*

532 cryst roy d*is* in pup termyn
omguythe p*r*est in glander

CECUS

Banneth du genogh tus vays
me yv dal na yl guelays
536 regh dym ag*is* alusyon
ha ragogh y raff pesy
the.c*r*ist ihe*s*u a ve*r*cy
selwadour an crustunyon

* MS. lemys.

THE MOTHER.

Amen ever, and my blessing.
508 My son, give me thy kiss!
Sad am I indeed
 At parting surely from thee.
  [Here Meriasek wears a priest's gown.

Here the Bishop of Kernou shall parade.

I am bishop in Brittany
512 In a county called Kernou.
Great is my grace always:
 Comrades are few to me
  A prelate so proud,
516 A prince over the sons of reading.
There are not in little Britain
 My peers right truly without doubt.

MERIASEK.

Sir Bishop, joy to you!
520 You I will beseech
 To give me orders.
A priest I should like to be,
Jesu's body to administer it
524 If my learning will serve
 By you when I may be appointed.
[The Bishop of Kernou goes down into the open space.

THE BISHOP OF KERNOU.

Welcome here, Meriasek,
I have heard, my sweet son,
528 Of thee much good spoken.
Give thee orders I will.
In Jesu's name now
 Consecrated by me thou wilt be surely.
    [He kneels.
532 May Christ grant to thee alway
 To keep thyself ever in purity!

A BLIND MAN.

God's blessing (be) with you, good folk!
I am a blind man who cannot see.
536 Give me your alms!
And for you I will pray
To Christ Jesu of mercy,
 The Saviour of the Christians.

KALUS*

540 Me yv inweth efrethek
am esely podrethek
gyllys in gron
schanlour y halla kerthes
544 me a pysse kynweres
the orthugh a luen golon

MERIADOCUS

[genuflectit

Ihesu arluth me ath peys
gueres an den ma yv dal
548 ihesu crist mytern glorijs
roy y syght dotho heb fal
ihesu arluth luen a rays
inweth sav an den arall
552 ihesu arluth map guirhays
dyswe the gallus ryall
lemen oma
in nomine patris et filij
556 virtu crist rebo yly
a dus gvan dyugh in torma

CECUS

Cryst ihesu dys ren tala
me a weyl lemen inta
560 benyges the peyadov†
me a wor bones oma
ha glorijs prest the geryov

p. 21. ### KALUS

Ha me yv sawys purdek
564 neb a fue sur efrethek
lues blethen in bysma
galer numbus
grays the ihesus
568 ha then denma

[finit
[tranceat in placeam

EPISCOPUS KERNOV

Meryasek dyso reuerans
keris gans du a seluans
gon guir lemen the vota
572 me ath peys trych genevy
ha sur nefre thysogy
me ny falla

---

* Leg. χωλός or claudus ?
† The original scribe wrote *piiadov*, but this is crossed out and *peyadov* written over it.

A CRIPPLE.

540 I am also maimed,
My limbs rotten
    Become in a heap.
Scarce enough can I walk.
544 I would beseech a common cure*
    From you with a full heart.

MERIASEK.

[He kneels.

Lord Jesu, I beseech thee,
    Cure this man who is blind !
548 Jesu Christ, glorious King,
    Give his sight to him without fail!
Lord Jesu, full of grace,
    Heal the other man likewise.
552 Lord Jesu, son of a virgin,
    Display thy royal power
    Now here.
In nomine Patris et Filii.
556 May Christ's virtue be a salve,
    O weak folk, to you this turn !

THE BLIND MAN.

Christ Jesu repay it to thee !
I see now well.
560   That thy prayer blessed
Is here, I know,
And glorious ever thy words !

THE CRIPPLE.

And I am healed right well,
564 (I) who was surely maimed.
    Many years in this world
Sickness I had.
Thanks to Jesus
568   And to this man !

BISHOP OF KERNOU.

Meriasek, reverence to thee !
Loved by God of salvation
    I know truly now that thou art.
572 I pray thee dwell with me,
And thee surely never
    Will I fail.

---

* A cure in common with the blind man.

MERIADOCUS

Ser epscop dywy mur grays
576 lafurya sur the ken gluas
avesijs off alemma
banneth genogh oll an sens
han sansesov myns del ens
580 hagis compny ben(itha)

CROCIFER EPISCOPI KERNOV

Banneth du thys meryasek
ny a vya lowenek
a mynnes oma tre(ga)
584 erbyn the voth
thynny ny goth
sur the lettya

[*ascendit episcopus kernov*

MERIADOCUS

Marners dorsona dywy
588 the kernov mar segh defry
mones genogh y carsen
the ry nammur me numbus
sav me a beys crist ihesus
592 thagys socra pup termen

p. 22.

NAVTA

Wolcum oys genen dremas
ny ath wor the pen an gluas
dre voth du kyn pen sythen

[*ascendit in navim*

596 dus aberveth oma scon
hav marners tennogh dyson
an goyl thym in ban lemen

SERVUS NAVTE

At eve fast bys in top
600 nov mata make fast the rop
yma an gvyns ov wetha
han mor ov terevel fol
me a greys kellys on ol
604 ha buthys pur guir oma

(NAV)TA

A gony pan vuen genys
warbarth ny a veth kellys
ens pup the ʒeys thy gela
608 nynsus oma forth nahen
ahanan ny vev vn den
tru gony doys then pletma

MERIASEK.

Sir Bishop, to you much thanks
576 To go onward surely to another country
　　　I am advised hence.
The blessing of all the saints
And the saintesses as many as there are
580 　　With you and your company ever!

THE BISHOP OF KERNOU'S CROZIER-BEARER.

God's blessing to thee, Meriasek!
We should be glad
　　If thou wouldst stay here.
584 Against thy will
It behoves us not,
　　　Surely, to hinder thee.
　　　　　　[The Bishop of Kernou goes up.

MERIASEK.

Mariners, a blessing to you!
588 To Cornwall if you are going now
　　　I should like to go with you.
To give I have not much,
But I will beseech Christ Jesus
592 　　To succour you always.

THE SAILOR.

Welcome art thou with us, honest man.
We will put thee to the end of the country,
　　Through God's will, before a week's end.
　　　　　[He goes up into the ship.
596 Come thou in here at once;
And, my mariners, quickly haul
　　The sail up for me now!

THE SAILOR'S SERVANT.

Lo it is quite up to the top.
600 Now mate, make the rope fast.
　　　The wind is blowing,
And the sea rising madly.
I believe we are all lost
604 　　And drowned right truly here.

THE SAILOR.

Ah woe is us that we were born!
Together we shall be lost!
　　Let every one go to confess to his fellow.
608 Here there is no other way.
Of us not one man will live.
　　Sad, woe is us, to come to this plight!

MEREADOCUS

A bethugh a confort da
612 crist agen gueres a ra
  ha me a vyn y pesy
mar pe y voth indella
na rella den peryllya
616 in tyr na mor in bysma
  mar creya war crist ha my

p. 23.   NAVTA

Meryasek gorthys reby
drethos ol sawys on ny
620 a peryl sur in torma
kegy in tyr a dremas
in kernov the ihesu gras
  theth desyr ty re dufa
       [descendit in cornubia

MEREADOCUS

624 The ihesu rebo grasseys
the pov astrange devethys
  me yv oma
kerthes in tyr me a vyn
628 ihesu arluth cuff colyn
  the teller da rum gedya
gorthya crist ker may hallen
han werhes flour maria

632 Devethys off in tereth
  ha squeth me yv ov kerthes
maria mam ha maghteth
  mara sus dis chy na plaes
636 oges oma
grua ov gedya vy bys dy
rag mur y carsen defry
guthel thymmo oratry
640 in herw^t chy maria
densa lowena dywhy
  pan a chapel yv henna

p. 24.   DOMESTICUS

Me a leuer dys dyson
644 chapel maria cambron
  gelwys yv an keth chyna
a py le in govynnyth
lauer henna dymo weyth
648 a cow^t da

MERIASEK.

O be ye of good comfort !
612   Christ will save us,
      And I will beseech him,
  If his will be thus
  That no one shall be in danger
616   On land nor sea in this world
      If he cry on Christ and me.

THE SAILOR.

Meriasek, worshipped be thou !
Through thee we all are saved
620   From peril surely this turn.
Go thou on land, O honest man !
In Cornwall, thanks to Jesu,
     According to thy desire thou hast come.
              [He lands in Cornwall.

MERIASEK.

624   To Jesu be thanks !
  To a strange country come
     Am I here.
  Walk on land I will,
628   May Lord Jesu, dear heart,
     To a good place guide me,
  That I may worship dear Christ,
     And Mary, the flower of maidens !

632   I am come on land,
     And weary am I walking.
  Mary, mother and maiden,
     If thou hast a house or place
636   Near this,
  Do guide me even unto it,
  For much I should like really
  To make me an oratory
640   Near Mary's house.
  Kind (sir), joy to you !
     What chapel is that ?

A HOUSEHOLD SLAVE.

I will tell thee at once.
644   Mary of Camborne's chapel,
     That same house is called.
  From what place dost thou ask it ?
  Say that to me yet,
648   O good fellow !

MEREADOCUS

A vreten sur then povma
dresen mor me re dufa
 del vynnas du ov desky
652 hag omma gul me a vyn
ryb chapel maria wyn
 thym oratry
us dour omma in oges
656 rag nefre nahen dewes
 nynsa om ganov defry

DOMESTICUS

Dour yv mur ascant oma
reys yv polge da alema
660 mones certen thy gerhes
corff bo gvyn a cafen vy
dour ny effsen eredy
 na ny vye rag ov lees

MERIADOCUS

664 North yst then chapel omma
me a vyn mos the guandra
 dour thymmo sur rag weles

   Tranceat ad pratum
     [*genuflectit*

p. 25. Ihesu arluth me ath peys
668 ihesu gront dovyr a wur speys
 ihesu dymmo der the graes
del russys kyns the moyseys
 an men cales
   [*her y⁰ wyll sprynggyth vp water*

DOMESTICUS

672 Densa benyges reby
dovr oma ov try thynny
 mar dek thagen confortya
kerys oys purguir gans du
676 prevys open oma yv
 the ragon in teller ma

HOMO FEBRICOSUS

A thu ellas pendrama
lader cleves thym yma
680 a veth gelwys an seson

MERIASEK.

From Brittany surely to this country
Over the sea I have come,
    As God teaching me willed.
652 And here I will make,
By blessed Mary's chapel,
    For me an oratory.
Is there water here at hand ?
656 For never other drink
    Shall go into my mouth surely.

THE HOUSEHOLD SLAVE.

Water is very scanty here.
Needful is it a good bit hence
660   To go certainly to fetch it.
Ale or wine if I could get,
Water I would not drink readily,
    Nor would it be for my good.

MERIASEK.

664 North-east of the chapel here
I will go to wander,
    Water for me surely to seek.

Let him go across to the meadow.
        [He kneels.
Jesu, Lord, I beseech thee,
668 Jesu, grant water in great abundance,
    Jesu, to me through thy grace
As thou didst before for Moses
    From the hard rock.
      [Here the well springeth up water.

THE HOUSEHOLD SLAVE.

672 Kind (sir), blessed be thou,
Bringing here to us water
    So fair to comfort us !
Loved art thou right truly by God,
676 It is clearly proven here
    Before us in this place.

A FEVER-PATIENT.

O God, alas, what thing is it ?
A thief of a disease I have,
680   Which is called the season.

ganso me ambeth schorys
pup deth nansyv lues mys
    rag peyn feynt yv ov colon

CONTRACTUS

684 Me yv efrethek heb fal
du thym a sevya mal
    appeua marov an beys
yma tregys in cambron
688 den ov cul merclys dyson
    guel yv dyn moys dy us(kys)
hay besy a lue*n* colon
    thynny ny guthel guereys

trancit ad meriadocum

p. 26.
HOMO FEBRICOSUS

692 Lowene dys meriasek
ny yv dev then bohosek
    me grefijs gans an febyr
han keth de*n* ma sur yv mans
696 na nyl susten na pegans
    ny yllen dendyl the guir
grua gueres dynny dyblans
    rag kere*n*se ihesu ker

MERIADOCUS *[genuflectit*

700 Ihe*s*u arluth neff han beys
    yehes dywy re grontya
ihe*s*u arluth me ath peys
    lem*m*en sav an keth tusma
704 maria mam lue*n* a rays
    peys theth vap arluth rag*t*ha
maria mam ha guerhays
    gueres ov pesy gena
708 sevugh inban a tu*s* vays
    fetel omglowugh o*m*ma

CONTRACTUS

Gorthyans the cr*i*st me yv sav
yagh yv ov corff ham garrov
712   kerthes heb greff me a yll   [*finit*

HOMO FEBRICOSUS

ha me yv yagh the cr*i*st grays
meryasek wek lue*n* a rays
    fortyn du dotho ny fyl
716 thy worthya ny yv senses
    hag a vyn awos p*e*ryl   [*finit*

With me I have marks
Every day, now it is many months.
 For pain faint is my heart.

A CRIPPLE.

684 I am maimed without fail—
God for me has raised a desire
 If (only) I were dead from the world !
There is dwelling in Camborne
688 A man working miracles at once.
 Better is for us to go to him quickly
And to beseech him with a full heart
 To help us.

He goes across to Meriasek.

THE FEVER-PATIENT.

692 Joy to thee, Meriasek !
We are two poor men,
 I grieved with the fever,
And this same man surely is maimed.
696 Neither sustenance nor goods
 Can we earn of a truth.
Help us clearly
 For love of dear Jesu.

MERIASEK [*kneels.*

700 May Jesu, Lord of heaven and of the earth,
 Grant healing to you !
Lord Jesu, I beseech thee
 Now save this same folk !
704 Mary Mother full of grace,
 Beseech thy Son (the) Lord for them.
Mary Mother and Virgin,
 Help, beseeching with me !
708 Rise ye up, O good folk,
 How do you feel yourselves here ?

THE CRIPPLE.

Worship to Christ ! I am whole.
Healed are my body and my legs.
712 I can walk without grief.

THE FEVER-PATIENT.

And I am cured, thanks to Christ !
Meriasek, sweet, full of grace,
 God's fortune to him will not fail.
716 To honour him we are bound,
 And will, notwithstanding peril.

MERIADOCUS

Grassegh the crist a tus vays
adar trav^t dymmo vy
720 omma lemen fondya plays
dre voth ihesu a vercy
sur me a vyn
awose helme eglos
724 the worthya crist deth ha nos
y feth omma thum porpos
ryb chapel maria wyn

MORB[OS]US

Ellas ellas pendrama
728 in ov fays cothys yma
cleves vthyk num car den
in ca[m]bron me re gloways
yma prest vn methek brays
732 ov sawya tus in certen
me a vyn moys the verays
gul gueres dymo mar men

[ad meriadocum

Lowene dis meryasek
736 thymo vy den bohosek
awoys crist lemen gueres
in ov fays cleves yma
mana car tus an beysma
740 neb lues sur ov gueles

MERIADOCUS [genuflectit

Arluth neff reth weresa
naamam kyns es helma
a sawyas an cleves mur
744 gans dour y raff the golhy
ihesu crist du a vercy
theth gueres mar tuth an nur

DOMESTICUS

Ty then gylleth boys lowen
748 sawys tek oys in certen
grasse the meryasek wek
rag eff yv lenwys a grays
ha kerys gans du a rays
752 del welyn letrys ha lek

[finit

MORB[OS]US

Meryasek dywhy mur grays
me a beys crist luen a rays

MERIASEK.

Give thanks to Christ, O good folk,
 Say nothing to me.
720 Here now found a place,
  Through the will of Christ of mercy,
   Surely I will.
 After this, a church,
724 For worshipping Christ day and night,
 Shall be here, to my purpose,
  By holy Mary's chapel.

A SICK MAN.

Alas, alas, what thing is this ?
728 On my face is fallen
  A frightful disease, no one loves me.
 In Camborne I have heard
 There is now a great leech
732 Healing folk certainly.
 I will go to see
  If he will cure me.

         [To Meriasek.

Joy to thee, Meriasek,
736 To me, a poor man,
  For Christ's sake now help.
 In my face is a disease,
 So that the folk of this world love not,
740 Not many surely, to see me.

MERIASEK *[kneels.*

May Heaven's Lord help thee !
Naaman before this
 He healed of the great disease.
744 With water I do wash thee :
 Jesu Christ, God of mercy,
  To help thee if he has come on the earth.

THE HOUSEHOLD SLAVE.

Thou, O man, mayst be joyful.
748 Well healed art thou certainly,
  Thank sweet Meriasek.
 For he is filled with grace,
 And loved by God of worth,
752 As we see, lettered and lay.

THE SICK MAN.

Meriasek, to you much thanks !
I beseech Christ full of grace

in neff thywhy re*n* tala
756 han wyrhes maria splan
du assus lues de*n* gvan
  sawys genogh in bysma   [*tranceat*
  [*hic meriadocus expectat apud cambron*

  hic tevdarus pompabit

Tevdar me a veth gelwys
760   arluth regnijs in kernov
may fo malhu*m* enorys
  ov charg yv heb feladov
  oges ha pel
764 penag a worthya ken du
y astev* peynys glu
  hag inweth mernans cruel

NUNCIUS

Heyl dyugh se*r* a[r]luth tevdar
768   yma gena nowothov
sav ny vethe sur heb mar
  y covsel thyugh gans ganov
  na vethe nes
772 del won inta
war ov ena
  ny veth ov les

p. 29.   TEVDARUS

Pyv an iovle us warfethys
776   laue*r* thy*m*mo ty lorde*n*
ay covs ty falge negethys
  dar ny glov an plos iovde*n*
covs vnw* ty bothosek
780   covs myscheff yth vryonse*n*
ay covs ty map molothek
  an iovl rebo the worfen

NUNCIUS

Yma oma in penw*
784   nebes a weyst the carnebre
vn pronte*r* ov cuthel guyth
  sawya tu*s* dal in bysme
  bother ha mans
788 ha pup cleves ol in beys
a thu ny vyn boys covsis
  mas a c*r*ist a thuk me*r*nans
pan o marov dase*r*rys
792   y methe bue the vevnans

In heaven to you may he pay it,
756 And the Virgin Mary bright.
Pardie, there are many weak men
Healed by you in this world. [*Let him go off.*
[*Here Meriasek waits at Camborne.*

Here Teudar shall parade.

Teudar I am called,
760 Lord reigning in Cornwall.
That Mahound be honoured
Is my charge without fail,
Near and far.
764 Whosoever worship another god,
They shall have keen pains,
And likewise a cruel death.

A MESSENGER.

Hail to you, Sir Lord Teudar!
768 With me are news,
But it would not be safe without doubt
To say them to you with a mouth
That should be nearer.
772 As I know well,
Upon my soul,
It will not be my advantage.

TEUDAR.

What the devil is it that has happened?
776 Tell to me, thou lurdane.
Ah, speak, thou false rascal!
Ruin! the dirty scoundrel will not hear.
Speak (at) once, thou beggar!
780 Speak! mischief in thy throat!
Ah, speak, thou son accursed!
May the devil be thy end!

THE MESSENGER.

There is here in Penwyth,
784 Somewhat west of Carnbrea,
A priest doing a work,
Healing blind folk in this world,
Deaf and maimed,
788 And every disease in the world.
Of [thy] god he will not that there be a thought,
But of Christ who died.
When he was dead, raised,
792 He says that he was, to life.

TEVDARUS

Out govy rag galarov
 py dol an iovle ythama
out govy na vuff marov
796 kyns doys a dor ov dama
 govi rag schame
sovdoryan duen alemma
may hallen ganso rekna
800 the develys name

PRIMUS MILES

Ov arluth genogh ny a
me re glowes an denna
 nansyv mysyov tremenys
p. 30. 804 tus dal eff a ra sawya
ha tus vother mageta
 inweth gul dethe cloweys [finit

SECUNDUS MILES

Tevdar dyugh me a leuer
808 an keth denna grueys yv muer
 purguir yn pov
mar ny vethe chastijs
a vahum ny veth sensys
812 moy es ky heb feladov

TEVDARUS [descendit

Duen ny in kerth
gans mur a nerth
 ov marogyon
816 py ma tregys
thym leferys
 bethyns dyson

NUNCIUS

Sur me an guel
820 arluth ryel
 enos in plen
mes an chapel
pur thyogel
824 doys a ra len

TEVDARUS

Ty bagcheler treyl war tuma
the hanov thym lafara
 quik hath cregyans

TEUDAR.

Out, woe is me, for sorrows !
  What devil's hole am I in ?
Out, woe is me that I was not dead
796   Before coming from my mother's womb !
  Woe is me ! for shame !
Soldiers, let us come hence
That we may reckon with him.
800   The devil's name !

FIRST SOLDIER.

My lord, we will go with you.
I have heard of this man,
  Now there are months past.
804 Blind folk he doth heal,
And deaf folk as well,
  Also he maketh them to hear.

SECOND SOLDIER.

Teudar, to you I say
808 That same man is made great,
  Right truly in the country.
If he be not chastised
Of Mahound there will not be thought
812   More than a hound without fail.

TEUDAR [*descends.*

Let us come away
With much of strength,
  My knights.
816 Where is he dwelling ?
Said to me
  Let it be forthwith.

THE MESSENGER.

Surely I see him,
820 Lord royal,
  There in the plain.
Out of the chapel
Right certainly
824   He doth come loyally.

TEUDAR.

Thou bachelor, turn on this side !
Thy name to me tell
  Quick, and thy belief

828 gothfes henna
sur a vanna
hath devethyans

p. 31.

MERIADOCUS

Meryasek yv ov hanov
832 sevys a lyne conany
in crist ihesu caradov
ytheseff prest ov cresy
y vos lel du
836 genys ay vam maria
ha hy maght¹ aywosa
helma ov cregyans ythyv

TEVDARUS

Sevys oys a woys worthy
840 meryasek beth avysyys
rag dovt cafus velyny
na govs tra na fue guelys
me a leuer
844 crbyn reson yv in beys
heb hays gorryth thymo creys
bones flogh vyth concevijs
in breys benen heb awer

MERIADOCUS

848 Nynsesos ov attendya
an laha del vya reys
omma an genegygva
a ihesu crist war an beys
852 hay pascyon ker
avel hovle der weder a
heb y terry del wylsta
indella crist awartha
856 a thuth in breys maria
heb mostye iunt v¹ in suyr
der an sperys sans kerra
concevijs y fue the guir

p. 32.

TEVDARUS

860 Na wyle gene flatra
kynfes nefre ov clattra
the ihesu ythese tays
mage lel avel y vam
864 nynsus ger guir malbe dam
wath in ol the daryvays

828 Know that
Surely I would,
And thy race.

MERIASEK.

Meriasek is my name,
832   Raised from Conan's line.
In Christ Jesu the loveable
Am I ever believing.
That he is true God
836 Born of his Mother Mary,
And she a maiden notwithstanding ;
This is my belief.

TEUDAR.

Raised art thou of worthy blood.
840   Meriasek, be advised,
For fear of getting disgrace,
Speak not aught that has not been seen,
I say.
844 Against reason it is in the world,
Without a man's seed, believe me,
That a child should ever be conceived
In a woman's womb, without grief.

MERIASEK.

848 Thou art not considering
The law as need should be,
Of the birth here
Of Jesus Christ on the world,
852   And his dear Passion.
As (the) sun goes through glass
Without breaking it as thou seest,
So Christ above
856 Went into Mary's womb
Without defiling any joint surely.
Through the Holy, dearest Spirit
He was conceived, of a truth.

TEUDAR.

860 Seek not to talk with me.
Though thou wert for ever clattering
To Jesus there was a father
Just as well as his mother.
864 There is not a true word, malbe dam,
Yet in all thy declaration.

MERIADOCUS

Du avan prest o y days
a cothfes y attendya
868 rag prenna adam hay hays
doys y fynnas then bysma
mernans tyn eff a porthas
eneff map den gruk sawya
872 ese in colmen satnas
eff as dros the lowena

TEVDARUS

Marso du avan y days
me a leuer meryasek
876 eff a alse der y rays
selwel rych ha bohosek
heb boys marov
ath daryvas schame ythyv
880 pan othem o the vap du
boys lethys avel carov

MERIADOCUS

Der pegh adam agen tays
eff hay lynnyeth o dampnys
884 sav an devgys a vynnays
arta y vones prennys
the saluascon
an map a fue concevijs
888 ha densis a kemereys
rag na ylly an devsys
gothe pasconn

p. 33.   ## TEVDARUS

Ny thue les agen argya
892 kyn feny oma vyketh
meryasek crist denaha
ha the cothmen me a veth
may fo guelys
896 epscop worthy me ath ra
chyff peb les oll an povma
na moy me ny deserya
mas gorthya mahum pup preys

MERIADOCUS

900 Ima guel forth es honna
grua thegy crist ker gorthya
ken maner kyllys os suir
.

MERIASEK.

God above was his father.
Thou oughtest to consider it.
868 To redeem Adam and his seed
He would come to this world.
Sharp death he bore :
Man's soul he saved
872 Which was in Satan's bond.
He brought it to joy.

TEUDAR.

If God above was his father
I say, Meriasek,
876 He could through his grace
Have saved rich and poor,
Without being dead.
Of thy assertion shame is !
880 What need was there for God's son
To be slain like a hart ?

MERIASEK.

Through the sin of Adam our father
He and his lineage were damned,
884 But the Godhead wished
Again that he should be redeemed
To salvation.
The Son was conceived
888 And took manhood,
For that the Godhead could not
Suffer passion.

TEUDAR.

Profit will not come of our arguing,
892 Though we be here for ever.
Meriasek, deny Christ
And I will be thy friend
So that it may be seen.
896 A worthy bishop I will make thee,
Chief of the whole breadth of this country.
I desire nothing more
But to worship Mahound always.

MERIASEK.

900 There is a better way than that :
Do thou worship dear Christ,
Otherwise thou art lost surely.

TEVDARUS

Vu ger na campol a gryst
904 ha mar qureth me ath wra trest
wath coyl orthef ha beth fuir
rag pan deffen ha moys fol
an iovle a thue mes ay dol
908 kyns es ov ruthy purguir

Drok yv gena
war ov ena
meryasek wek
912 gul dis mas da
ha gorthyans grua
thum dewov tek

p. 34.
MERIADOCUS

Theth dewov try mylw᪲ fy
916 rag sur dewolov ens y
nys gorthya vy benytha
ortheff na wyla pythays
nahy mar mynnyth boys vays
920 foyl oys mar trestyth inna

TEVDARUS

Out warnes ty fals jugleer
defya ov dewov flour
ty a crek in cloghprennyer
924 rag perel prence hag emperour
omma the foyl
the voy nefre me ath cays
outlayer fyys ath wlays
928 covs vn geer erbyn ov rays
ha ty an noyll

Me yv empour
ha governour
932 conquerrour tyr
arluth worthy
mur ov mestry
gothfeth ha myr

MERIADOCUS

936 Tav thymo vy the clap sens
speyna a reth mur a gvyns
oma sur in sevureth
p. 35.
guel yv dis bones cristyan
940 gorthya crist a luen golan
ha my lemmen ath vygeth

TEUDAR.

One word do not talk of Christ,
904 And if thou dost I will make thee sad.
Yet listen to me and be wise.
For when I should come and go mad
The Devil will come out of his hole
908 Rather than make me easy (?) right truly.

Sorry am I,
On my soul,
Sweet Meriasek,
912 To do thee aught save good.
Ah do worship
To my beautiful gods!

MERIASEK.

On thy gods three thousand times fie!
916 For surely devils are they.
I will never worship them.
Of me seek not affection,
If thou wilt refuse to be good.
920 Mad art thou if thou trustest in them.

TEUDAR.

Out on thee, thou false juggler,
To defy my flower of gods!
Thou shalt hang in prison,
924 For peril of prince and emperor,
Here, thou fool.
The more ever will I hate thee.
An outlaw thou hast fled from thy country.
928 Speak a word against my grace
And thou shalt catch it.

I am emperor,
And governor,
932 Conqueror of land,
A worthy lord,
Great is my mastery.
Know and see!

MERIASEK.

936 Silence for me! hold thy prate!
You do spend much of wind
Here surely in seriousness (?)
Better is it for thee to be a Christian,
940 To worship Christ with a full heart,
And I now will baptize thee.

TEVDARUS

Out govy gesugh thym spath
alema quik rag feya
944 deve an iovle the rag ov fath
ʒᵉ vynnes ov begithia
marov off in kres an plath
na pel mar trege omma
948 mahum darber hardygrath
ʒᵉ neb a 'ruk ov throbla

[*ascendit*

Tormentoris dugh in plen
tormentoris marsogh len
952 tormentoris dugh dym scon
ay ay ay dar ny regh vry

[*descendit*

reys yv age herhes y
pan yv mogh ol ov duwon

[*her yerdis aredy for tevdar and hys men*

956 Hov hov pythesogh matis
y besche reb your patis
pendra reny dar napya
ay num clewugh ov kelwel
960 tannegh honthsel kyns sevel
go to dalethugh frappia

[*et verberabunt eos*

p. 36.   ### PRIMUS TORMENTOR

Ser arluth na cronk na moy
ha lauer the voth thynny
964 ny an grua purthyogel

TEVDARUS

Eugh thymo bys yn cambron
awest the carnbre dyson
ena wy a gyff in lel
968 guas ov theria heb questron*
esel yv then tebel el

Meryasek ythyv gelwys
in crist yma ov cresy
972 genogh why bethens sesijs
gruegh y tormontya besy
crist mar ny veth denehys
pegh then horsen trewesy
976 genogh kynfove lethys
me agis menten defry

* leg. question.

TEUDAR.

Out, woe is me, leave me a space !
Hence quick to flee (?)
944 The devil has come before my face
To wish to baptize me!
Dead am I in the midst of the place
Any longer if thou stayest here.
948 Mahound, provide hard grace
For him who hath troubled me !

[*He ascends.*

Torturers, come into the field.
Torturers, if ye are loyal,
952 Torturers come to us at once !
Ay, ay, ay, ruin, you don't regard

[*He descends.*

Need is it to fetch them
Since all my grief is a mockery.

[*Here staves ready for Teudar and his men.*

956 How, how, where are ye, mates ?
I will baste ye (?) by your pates.
What thing shall we do . . . . . . (?)
Ah, you hear me calling ?
960 Take handsel before rising.
Go to, begin striking !

[*And they shall beat them.*

FIRST TORTURER.

Sir lord, beat no more,
And tell thy will to us :
964 We will do it full certainly.

TEUDAR.

Go ye for me as far as Camborne
Westward of Cambrea, quickly.
There will ye find loyally
968 A lad tarrying : without question,
A limb is he of the evil angel.

Meriasek is he called :
In Christ is he believing.
972 By you let him be seized
Do ye torment him.
If Christ be not denied,
A thrust to the doleful whoreson !
976 Though he be slain by you,
I will maintain you certainly.

SECUNDUS TORTOR

Arluth henna ny a ra
desempys duen alema
980 aspyans pup ay quartron
me agis gyd rum ena
  pur uskis bys in cambron

        [trancit tevder domum

MERIADOCUS

Then arluth rebo grasseys
984 dre besyon ythoff guarnys
  may thellen mes an povma
arta the breten uskys
  han falge tevdar avodya
988 an porpos yv erverys
  wath eff a fyl annotha

p. 37. Omma me re fundyas plas
  ryb maria a cambron
992 ihesu crist darber 3 grays
  in keth chyma pup seson
may fo prest an drensys tays
  inno enoris dyson
996 ha maria
han sacrements vij
kefris gol ha guyth
  menystrys wose helma

1000 Grefons ha cleves seson
mar angeveth lel crystyan
  hav remembra in plasma
ihesu arluth cuff colan
1004 y grefons gura sewagya

Inweth an dour ov fenten
rag den varijs in certen
  peseff may fo eff ely
1008 thy threy arta thy skyans
ihesu arluth a selwans
  gront helma der 3° vercy

Ov banneth genes a plas
1012 reys yv vodya a vur spas
  oges yma ov envy
me a vyn guythe then won
hag omma powes dyson
1016 indan an garrek defry

[her meryasek schall hydde hym sylfe vnder ye rokke

SECOND TORTURER.

Lord, that will we do.
Straightway let us go hence.
980   Let every one spy from his quarter.
I will guide you, by my soul,
    Very quickly, as far as Camborne.

              [Teudar goes away home.

MERIASEK.

To the Lord be thanks!
984   By a vision I am warned
    That I should go out of this country
Again to Brittany forthwith,
And avoid the false Teudar.
988   The purpose is designed
    Yet he will fail thereof.

Here have I founded a place
    By Mary of Camborne.
992   Jesu Christ, provide thy grace
    In this same house, every season,
So that the Father's Trinity be always
    Therein honoured forthwith,
996   And Mary,
And the seven sacraments
Likewise on feast and work (day)
    Administered after this.

1000 Grievance and disease of the season,
If a loyal Christian have it,
    And remembers me in this place,
Jesu, Lord, dear heart,
1004   His grievance will assuage.

Likewise the water of the fountain
For a man insane certainly
    I pray that it be a salve
1008 To bring him again to his sense.
Jesu, lord of salvation,
    Grant this, through thy mercy.

My blessing with thee, O place!
1012 Need is it to quit (thee) in a short time,
    Near is my enemy.
I will keep to the field
And here stay quiet
1016   Under the rock certainly.

    [Here Meriasek shall hide himself under the rock.

p. 38.

SECUNDUS TORTOR

A wylste gy meryasek
in cambron an lagasek
nynsusy eff malbe dam

TERTIUS TORTOR

1020 bener regyffy the con
galles eff in mes then won
rengeffo moleth y vam

CALO

Aspyen orthen buschys
1024 hag orth an karrek kefrys
mar asethe the cutha
gase ny vyn boys kefys
duen ny the dre alema

PRIMUS TORTOR

1028 Py dol an iovle ythetha
tevder mes y skyans a
pan glowe y vos scappys

SECUNDUS TORTOR

avesyans eff ahena
1032 praga na ruk y sesya
orth y ganov pan govsis

TERTIUS TORTOR

[ad teuder

Heyl tevder in agis tour
meryasek an povma dor
1036 galles ny ny wothen ken
in trefov hag in gonyov
ny ren welas sur heb wov
annotho covs ny wor den

p. 39

TEVDARUS

1040 Out govy harov harov
an pov mar sewe fyys
ny vensen heb feladov
awoys dyv ran peth an beys
1044 na vensen* mes
a pennov methov
o¹ in ov dythyov
creyaff warnogh ladron drues

* leg. vese?

SECOND TORTURER.

Sawest thou Meriasek?
In Camborne, the quick-of sight
   He is not . . . .

THIRD TORTURER.

1020 Never mayest thou have thy supper!
He has gone out to the field.
   May he have his mother's curse!

A DRUDGE.

Let us spy at the bushes
1024 And at the rock also.
   If he is sitting to hide.
He will not allow (himself) to be found.
   Let us go home hence.

FIRST TORTURER.

1028 What hole of the devil has he gone to?
Teudar will go out of his wits
   When he hears that he has escaped.

SECOND TORTURER.

Let him consider thereof
1032 Why he did not seize him (Meriasek)
   By his mouth when he spoke.

THIRD TORTURER.

                 [*To Teudar.*

Hail, Teudar in thy tower!
Meriasek from this country quite
1036   Has gone : we know not otherwise.
In villages and on downs
We have not seen him surely, without a lie.
   Of him no one can speak.

TEUDAR.

1040 Out! woe's me! *haro, haro!*
If he be fled the country.
I would not, without fail,
   For sake of two parts of the world's wealth
1044   That he should be away.
Ah, drunken heads,
Out ! in my days
   I cry on you bold thieves !

CALO

1 48 Ay tevdar ke war the gam
molleth du the vapp the vam
pyraga nan guythte gy
pan eses ganso ov covs

1052 ny vyn y thu eff heb flovs
orto cafus belyny

[*descendit tevder*

TEVDARUS

Yv helma ol an confort
ambethe deworthugh wy

1056 ay serys yma thyugh sport
pan vs dewen dymmo vy
wel wel na for(s)
re appolyn ov du splan

1060 kyns dyberth ny warth mas ran
me a pe ȝen hebyhors
hay cowetha
have that iiij^{ar} lorel

1064 hag arta perthugh coff guel
pendrellen the comondya

[*verberat eos*

p. 40.   MERIADOCUS

The ihesu rebo grasseys
omma me re poweseys

1068   pur guir indan an menina
ov envy in kerth galsons
ov metya byth ny alsons
du a vynnas indella

1072   carek veryasek holma
gelwys vyth wose helma

Me a vyn sensy then mor
the weles thymmo tru mach

1076 dorsona dyugh mester flor
du re wythe orth damach
agis lester
mar mynnogh moys the vreten

1080 me a bysse pur certen
mones genogh heb awer

NAVTA

Ty a hevelsa dremas
dus in hanov du an tas

1084   lemen aberveth genen

A DRUDGE.

1048 Ah Teudar, go on thy way.
God's curse on thy mother's son!
 Why didst thou not keep him
 When thou wast with him talking?
1052 His God will not, without flout,
 Have villainy upon him.

     [Teudar goes down.

TEUDAR.

Is this all the comfort
 That I should have from you?
1056 O sirs, it is a sport to you
 When it is grief to me.
  Well, well, no matter!
By Apollo, my bright god,
1060 Before separating not a laugh but a cry.
 I will pay to the hobby-horse,
  And her comrades.
Have that, (ye) four lorels,
1064 And again remember better
  What I may command.

     [He beats them.

MERIASEK.

To Jesu be thanks!
Here I have rested
1068 Right truly under this stone.
My enemies have gone away.
Meet me they could never.
  God willed so.
1072 Meriasek's rock this
 Shall be called hereafter.

I will hold to the sea
 To seek for me true mates.
1076 A blessing to you, flower of masters,
 May God keep from damage
  Your ship!
If ye will go to Brittany,
1080 I would pray right certainly
 To go with you without grief.

THE SAILOR.

Thou wouldst seem an honest man.
Come in God the Father's name,
1084 Now on board with us.

ten an gol inban mata
an guyns thagen corse dufa
cowel ny a wey'l breten   [*finit*

SERVUS

1088 Tremenys yv dyogel
lemen genen an chanel
  may fe holmyv spede dek
devethys on bys in tyr
1092 lemen quik thag*is* desyr
  grueghwy londia me*r*yasek   [*descendit*
an men re ruk inclynyn
in ty*r* rag the receva
1096   gras the ih*e*su galosek

p. 41.   ### MERIADOCUS

Du re*n* tala thyugh t*us* vays
arluth ih*e*su lue*n* a rays
  ru*m* gedya in forth wella
1100 thu*m* nessevyn mar a saff
gans*e* te*m*ptijs ysethaff
  trolie ha lust an bysma

BRITTONNUS

Dremas beth war pythylly
1104 blyth brays in forna defry
  purguir yma
mar a tue in the ogoys
eff a ra scollya the goys
1108 ellas at eve ena

MERIADOCUS

Best thys me a worhe*m*my*n*
thy*m*mo na rylly dregy*n*
  na the crystya*n* benytha
1112 na gy*m*me*r* ovn vyth dremays
thy handla sur eff am gays
  myr purwhar in ketelma
ov sywa eff a levays
1116 truspys vyth ny ra p*r*ofia.

BRITTONNUS

Sur ty yv de*n* benygays
lues de*n* eff re lathays
  ha flehys p*r*est in povma

Hoist up the sail, mate.
The wind has come to our course,
   Fully we shall see Brittany.

THE SAILOR'S SERVANT.

1088 Passed is safely
Now by us the Channel
   So that this was fair speed.
Come are we to shore
1092 Now quick to your desire
   Do you land, Meriasek.   [*He lands*.
The stone has bent down
On the shore to receive thee.
1096   Thanks to mighty Jesu!

MERIASEK.

May God pay it to you, good folk,
May Lord Jesu, full of grace,
   Guide me in the best way.
1100 To my kinsmen if I go,
By them I shall be tempted
   Towards them and the lust of this world.

A BRETON.

Honest man, be wary where thou mayst go.
1104 A great wolf in that way indeed,
   Right truly is.
If he come anear thee
He will spill thy blood.
1108   Alas, behold him there!

MERIASEK.

Beast, to thee I command
That to me thou do no mischief
   Nor to a Christian ever.
1112 Have no fear at all, honest man.
He will surely let me handle him.
   See, quite gently thus
He has ventured to follow me:
1116   Any violence he will not offer.

THE BRETON.

Sure thou art a blessed man!
Many men hath he slain
   And children ready in this country.

1120 thyso gy sensys asson
at eva kepar hag on
a vo doff orth 5ᵉ sywa   *[finit*

p. 42.   MERIADOCUS

Gul truspys thym ny profias
1124   nag eff nyngeveth dregyn
in hanov crist map guirhas
thys best me a worhemyn
moys then guelfos
1128 gans map den na ra mellya
nefra a wose helma
aberth ihesu awartha
yth forth grua mos

1132 Me a vyn moys then guylfoys
ena crmet purguir boys
may hallen gorthya ov du
na ven temptis
1136 gans tus an beys
hedre ven byv

Omma sur ryb an castel
gelwys pontelyne defry
1140 war an meneth dyogel
hag orth an ryuer surly
a josselyne
chapel guthel me a vyn
1144 rag gorthya maria wyn*
kynthyv teller guyls ha yne

                [ascendit ad montem

Gorthyans the crist map maghteth
M pas sur yv an meneth
1148 the worth an grond byteweth
du am gueres
ov chy fundia
sur ha grondya
1152   manneff uskyes

    [chappell aredy. Her a weryth a rosset
        mantell and a berde.

p. 43.   HIC INCIPIT VITA SANCTI SILUESTRY

    Constantinus hic pompabit dicens

Drefen ov boys corff hep par
ha dovtijs gans an bobil
ov hanov in guir† heb mar
1156   yv costyntyn the nobil

___
* MS. *why.*   † MS. *guire*, but the *e* is in a later hand.

1120 To thee we are bound.
Lo he is like to a lamb
That may be tame following thee.

MERIASEK.

He did not offer to do violence to me,
1124 Nor shall he have hurt.
In the name of Christ, the Virgin's Son,
To thee, Beast, I command
To go to the wilderness.
1128 With a son of man meddle not
Ever hereafter.
By will of Jesu above
On thy way do go.
1132 I will go to the wilderness
There a hermit right truly to be,
That I may be able to worship my God.
(And) that I may not be tempted
1136 By the folk of the world
Whilst I may be alive.

Here surely by the castle
Called Pontelyne really
1140 On the mountain certainly,
And by the river surely
Of Josselyn,
A chapel I will make
1144 To worship blessed Mary,
Though it is a place wild and cold.

[He goes up to the mountain.

Worship to Christ the Maiden's Son !
A thousand paces surely is the mountain
1148 From the ground ever.
God help me !
Found my house
Surely, and ground (it)
1152 I will forthwith.

*[A chapel ready. Here he wears a russet
mantle and a beard.*

HERE BEGINS THE LIFE OF SAINT SILVESTER.

Constantine shall here parade, saying,

Because of my being a body without peer,
And dreaded by the people,
My name truly without doubt,
1156 Is Constantine the noble,

F

emperour worthy
map then vyternes helen
neb yv pen ol y ehen
1160   del glowas lues huny

Yma in pov falge cregyans
   ov cul dym angyr an iovle
mar tur na pel ov bevnans
1164   me as temper by my sovle
hag as gor ol then mernans
   der eselder peyn ha mevle
me re lathes lues cans
1168   hag indella yv ov thovle
   wath dyswul moy
tormentoris guesyen fol
tormentoris dugh thym ol
1172   aberth mahum ha soly

Hic pompabunt tortores [w swerdys

1172ª Heyl costenten the nobil
del onny* the lel bobil
   devethys ython warbarth
rag enour dis ha gorthyans
1176 benitha the eskerans
   mar as keuyn sur ny warth

CONSTANTINUS

Wolcum kynghtis euerych on
   reys yv dywy lafurya
1180 rag chastya an crustunyon
   drest ol an gluas rome alemma

p. 44.   Myns a greys in map maryon
   der peyn gruegh age latha
1184 byth na thovtyogh dampnasconn
   me agis menten nefra

SECUNDUS TORTOR

Ny thovtyn peryl na pegh   ·
yma debron thum ij vregh
1188   mar bel ov boys ov powes
heb moldra an crustunyon
ornogh thynny sovdoryon
   na garra sevel in cres

CONSTANTINUS IMPERATOR

1192 Tus arvov genogh ytha
ij cans purguir alemma
   guetyogh omprevy manly

* MS. *onneny*, but the *e* is in a later hand.
† The corrector has struck out the *s*.

A worthy Emperor,
Son to the queen Helena,
Who is head of all his tribe,
1160   As many a one has heard.

There is in the country a false belief
    Causing me the devil's anger.
If my life no longer endures
1164   I will tame it, by my soul,
And will put it all to the death
    Through baseness of pain and disgrace.
I have slain many hundreds,
1168   And thus is my will
        Yet to undo more.
Torturers, mad lads,
Torturers, come ye all to me
1172   In behalf of Mahound and Sol.

Here the torturers shall parade [with swords.

1172ᵃ Hail, Constantine the noble!
As we are thy loyal people
    Come are we together.
For honour to thee and worship.
1176 Thy enemies ever,
    If we take them, surely will not laugh.

CONSTANTINE.

Welcome, knights, everyone!
    Need is it for you to go on
1180 To chastise the Christians
    Over all the kingdom of Rome hence.

All that believe in Mary's Son
    By torment slay them.
1184 Never fear damnation.
    I will support you ever.

SECOND TORTURER.

We fear not peril nor sin.
There is an itching in my two arms
1188   That I should be resting so long
Without murdering the Christians.
Order for us soldiers
    That love not to stand quiet!

EMPEROR CONSTANTINE.

1192 Armed men shall go with you
Two hundred right truly hence.
    Take care to prove yourselves manly,

then cristunyan scollya goys
1196 na sparyogh yowynk na loys
eskerans ov du soly

TERTIUS TORTOR

Na ren purguir costyntyn
y asteveth torment tyn
1200 myns a worth crist an brebour
duen in kerth scon cowetha
pup ay du gruens aspya
ov quandra mar sus treytour

CALO

1204 Me a weyl enos ij guas
sur orth fysmens age fays
crustunyon yth havalsens
p. 45. serys leferugh thynny
1208 pana cregyans us dywy
oma scon war beyn mernans

COMES

In crist ihesu ny a greys
awos ovn a then in beys
1212 ny forsakyn y hanow
neb na cresse in della
the peyn yfern sur ytha
the torment pan vo marov

PRIMUS TORTOR

1216 Out warnes ty plos brathky
na hanw crist theragon ny
ha mar qureth y feth mernans
rag dyswul an crustunyen
1220 danvenys gans costenten
ny yv then povma dyblans

DOCTOR IN FIDE*

Awoys ovn a costenten
nag a peynys neb termen
1224 ihesu ny ren dynaha
thynny mar quregh velyny
cryst yv pen an arlythy
a ra agys aquytya

* *in fide* added by the corrector here and before l. 1245.

To spill blood for the Christians,
1196 Spare not young nor grey,
  Enemies of my god Sol.

THIRD TORTURER.

We would not do [so], right truly, Constantine.
They shall have sharp torment,
1200   All who worship Christ the beggar.
Let us come away forthwith, comrades!
Let each on his side spy
  If there be a traitor wandering.

A DRUDGE.

1204 I see there two lads.
Surely by the semblance of their faces
  Christians they would seem.
Sirs, say to us
1208 What belief you have
  Here forthwith on pain of death.

THE EARL.

In Christ Jesu we believe.
For fear of man on earth
1212   We will not forsake his name.
Whoso may not believe thus
To hell's pain surely shall go,
  To torment when he shall be dead.

FIRST TORTURER.

1216 Out on thee, thou foul hound!
Name not Christ before us,
  And if thou dost thou shalt have death.
To undo the Christians
1220 Sent by Constantine
  Are we to this country clearly.

A DOCTOR IN THE FAITH.

For dread of Constantine
Or of tortures at any time
1224   We will not deny Jesu.
If ye do outrage to us
Christ, who is the head of lords,
  Will he acquit you?

SECUNDUS TORTOR

1228 Ty horsen agen* brag ny
thys mylw^t ha ȝ⁰ crist fy
dynagh uskis y hanov

[y' gulovs aredy

p. 46.

gorth quik iovyn ha soly
1232 bo ty a vyrwe eredy
oma dre peynys garov

COMES

Guel yv genen ny merwel
es gorthya devle dyogel
1236 in bysma yv grueys apol
tru a thu asogh goky
na worthyogh crist a vercy
a thuk mernans ragon oll

TERTIUS TORTOR

1240 Rag covs geryov mar velen
in cloghprennyer purcerten
oma y fetheth cregys
inweth an treytour arall
1244 ryb the scoth kepar ha gal
genevy a veth hangys

DOCTOR IN FIDE

Maria myternes neff
maria agen eneff
1248 peys mengeffo saluasconn
a pobyl omschumunys
remembrogh agis sperys
rag dovt cafus dampnasconn

[finit

CALO

1252 Tav gays thym the ombrene
pur a wylsta war an kee
gesys yn bysma enaff
p. 47.
kynfo porthov neff degeys
1256 wath yferne a veth aleys
pencyl ellen fors ny raff

COMES

lhesu arluth cuff colon
ihesu grond thyn saluasconn
1260 rag oma reys yv merwell

* leg. nagen ?

SECOND TORTURER.

1228   Thou whoreson, insult us not.
On thee and on Christ a thousand times fie !
    Deny his name forthwith.
                    [The gallows ready.
Worship quickly Jove and Sol,
1232   Or thou shalt die at once
    Here through rough pains.

THE EARL.

Better is it with us to die
Than to worship a devil certainly.
1236   In this world Apollo is made.
Pity, O God, you are (so) foolish
That you do not worship Christ of mercy,
    Who bore death for us all !

THIRD TORTURER.

1240   For saying words so villainous
In a prison right certainly
    Here thou shalt be gibbeted.
Likewise the other traitor
1244   By thy shoulder like a villain
    By me shall be hung.

A DOCTOR IN THE FAITH.

Mary, queen of heaven,
Mary, pray that our soul
1248   May have salvation.
O accursed people
Remember your spirit
    For fear of getting damnation !

A DRUDGE.

1252   Be silent, leave me to redeem myself.
Hast thou really seen on the way
    A soul left in this world ?
Though heaven's gates be shut
1256   Yet hell will be wide open.
    Unto which of the two I may go I care not.

THE EARL.

Jesu, Lord, dear heart,
Jesu, grant us salvation,
1260   For here need is to die.

benyges rebo an *preys*
ihesu dyso ov *sperys*
me a gemen dyogel [*finit*

PRIMUS TORTOR

1264 Lemen pan vsons in crok
vskys moghheen age drok
duen drethe gans clethethyov
an tenewen thy gela
1268 mar guir an iovle res pela
helme at eve marov

SECUNDUS TORTOR

Der y gela me a reys
ny gara sevel in creys
1272 atta hy der y *pottis*
me an felge a drus then pen
may teffo y ompynnen
ha skynnya avel *mottis*

p. 48.

TERTIUS TORTOR

1276 *Parys* on ny the gul drok
neb na vo rengeffo crok
cothys then doyr attonsy
age corff warbarth yv trogh
1280 dyghtys ens kepar ha brogh
a vo squerdis gans mylgy

CALO

Nefre cosker ongrassyas
menogh a ra bostov bras
1284 neb tebel dorne pan vo grueys
mas hap drok orthugh askyn
gase farwel me a vyn
molleth du in cowetheys
[*trancit calo et tortores expectant in placea*

IHESUS *in celo dicens**

1288 Ov eleth gvyn avel grueys
an enevov mertherijs
drewhy scon the lowena
rag age lauer in beys
1292 grontis yv dage sperys
an ioy a thur bys nefra

* In the corrector's hand: the original scribe wrote *Deus.*

Blessed be the time !
Jesu, to thee my spirit
I commend certainly.

FIRST TORTURER.

1264 Now since they are on the gallows
Quickly let us greaten their evil.
Let us come through them with swords
From one side to the other.
1268 So truly may the devil peel them !
This one, look, is dead.

SECOND TORTURER.

Through the other I will run.
I like not standing quiet.
1272 Look at it through him put !
I will slit him across to the head
So that his brains may come
And ascend like motes.

THIRD TORTURER.

1276 Ready are we to do evil :
May he who is not have the gallows !
Look at them fallen to the ground !
Their bodies together are broken :
1280 Dighted are they like a badger
That may be torn by a greyhound.

THE DRUDGE.

Ever an ungracious set
Often will make great boasts
1284 When any evil turn may be done.
But an ill hap will fall on you.
I will leave a farewell.
God's curse on the company.
[*The drudge goes off and the torturers wait in the open.*

JESUS *in heaven saying.*

1288 My angels white like crystal !
The martyred souls
Bring ye soon to joy.
For their labour in the world
1292 Granted is to their spirits
The joy that dureth for ever.

MICAEL

Ihesu the voth a veth grueys
neb yv in beys mertherijs
1296   y a due de lowena
del yv dynny comondys
lel pup vr ol y feth grueys
    hag y tegoth in della

p. 49.   GABRIEL

1300 A enevov mertherijs
ioy neff yma dyugh grontys
    gans crist ihesu awartha
drefen an torment in beys
1304 thagis corfov rebue grueys
    why agys beth lowena

               [her ye sovlys aredy

PRIMUS TORTOR

Out duen in kerth cowetha
the neb hensy rag cutha
1308   ken warbarth ython leskys
in neys rum caradevder
yma cothys golovder
    dretho maythoff amuwys

Hic Sanctus Siluester Incipit dicens

1312 Gefugh* creys vfel ha clovr
    in hanov du dy lawe
neb a formyas neff ha novr
    in bysma gans y dule
1316   map den a pry
tays ha map ha sperys sans
iij ferson hag vn substans
henna yv an lel cregyans
1320   del deske sans eglos dynny

Lemen warbarth ov flehys
    ny a vyn moys alemma
the anclethias an dus vays
1324   us mertherijs del glowa
    gans drok pobyll
p. 50.   tus an empour costenten
gasa crystyen byv ny ven
1328   in povma purthyogel

             [descendit
             [ye tumbe aredy

* Perhaps *Gesugh.*

MICHAEL.

Jesu, thy will shall be done.
Whoso are martyred on earth
1296   They shall come to joy.
As is commanded unto us
Loyally always it shall be done,
    And thus it behoveth.

GABRIEL.

1300 O martyred souls,
Heaven's joy is granted to you
    By Christ Jesu above.
Because of the torment on earth
1304 Which was done to your bodies
    You shall have joy.

        [Here the souls ready.

FIRST TORTURER.

Out! let us come away, comrades!
To some ways (?) to hide,
1308   Else together we are burnt.
Anear, by my loveableness,
Is fallen lightning
    So that I am startled thereby.

   Here Saint Silvester begins, saying,

1312 Ye shall have peace, lowly and clear.
    In God's name, praise to Him
Who made heaven and earth,
    In this world with his two hands,
1316   The son of man of clay.
Father and Son and Holy Ghost,
Three Persons and one Substance,
    That is the true faith,
1320   As holy Church teaches us.

Now together, my children,
    We will go home
To bury the good folk
1324   Who as I hear are martyred
    By evil people.
The folk of the Emperor Constantine
Will not leave a Christian alive
1328   In this country right certainly.

        [He descends.
        [The tomb ready.

CARDINALE

Seluester agen tays wek
ihesu arluth galosek
  pup vr regen gueresa
1332 at oma an dus varov
goren y scon in bethov
  ha fyyn quik alemma

        [her they beryth them

SILUESTER

Lemmen pan vsons in beth
1336 ihesu crist pen an eleth
  gorw^t age enevow
ny a vyn polge avodya
mar a kyllyn omguytha
1340 orth costentyn in torma
  ken ganso bethen marov

Then meneth a seraptyn
mones purguir ny a vyn
1344 in rome dyn ny dal trege
gena ov mebyen lyen
dugh lemen bras ha byen
  mar kyllyn polge omguythe

     [ascendit ad montem seraptyn

    [a vysour aredy apon Constantyn ys face

p. 51. SECUNDUS TORTOR *[ad constantinum*

1348 Heyl ser arluth costynten
crustunyon marov genen
  yma sur neb try vgans
ran cregys ran debynnys
1352 ran orth lostov mergh draylys
  ran leskis in tan dyblans

        [tranceat

CONSTANTINUS

Eugh the dre ov sovdoryan
an iovle thagis covya
1356 yma ortheff lovrygyan
  cothys ha ny won fetla
  ellas ellas
ythoma gyllys leper
1360 del leuer pup ol hager
  ny gar den gueles ov fas

A CARDINAL.

Silvester, our sweet Father,
May Jesu, (the) mighty Lord,
   Always help us !
1332 Lo here are the dead folk :
Let us put them forthwith in tombs,
   And let us flee quickly hence.
                    [Here they bury them.

SILVESTER.

Now, since they are in the tomb,
1336 Jesu Christ, the head of the angels,
   Preserve their souls !
We will for a little while go away,
If we can keep ourselves
1340 From Constantine this turn,
   Else by him we shall be dead.

To the mountain of Soracte
Right truly we will go :
1344   In Rome it behoves us not to stay.
With me, my disciples,
Come now, great and small,
   If we can for a little while keep ourselves.
          [He goes up to Mount Soracte.

      [A mask ready upon Constantine's face.

SECOND TORTURER *to Constantine.*

1348 Hail, Sir Lord Constantine !
Christians dead with us
   There are surely some three score.
Some hung, some beheaded,
1352 Some dragged at horses' tails,
   Some burnt in fire clearly.
                  [Let him pass off.

CONSTANTINE.

Go home, my soldiers,
   The Devil to remember you !
1356 There is leprosy on me
   Fallen, and I know not how.
     Alas, alas !
I am become a leper,
1360 As every one says, ugly.
   No one loves to see my face.

A govy pendra yv guel
ortheff lemmen the voys grueys
1364 a me revue ree cruel
orth crustunyan me a greys
a tekter rychys farwell
nebes ioy ambus an beys
1368 mensen stak omma merwell
in meske tus na ven guelys

JUSTUS

Danvenogh than epscobov
han doctours bras doys oma
1372 y a lefer der lyfryov
marsus savment in bysma
orth an cleves
rag y yv calcoryan vrays
1376 ha na berthuth ovn in cays
then deseys y a gueres

p. 52. ### CONSTANTINUS

Maseger a thesempys
kergh thym an epscop omma
1380 han doctour brays kekefrys
yv gelwys flour an bysma
sur in clergy
mar cothens dym leferel
1384 boys neb gueres dyogel
orth an cleves ambus vy

SECUNDUS NUNCIUS

Heyl ser emperour costentyn
oma ythese parys
1388 rag lafuria pur ylyn
alema in the nygys
ny raff strechya
an epscop han doctour flour
1392 me as kergh uskis theth tour
moys a raff in vn trettya

Hic pompabit Episcopus Poly* vel Doctor

SECUNDUS NUNCIUS

Heyl ser epscop in the dour
heyl inweth dywhy doctour
1396 metijs da ogh in vn chy

* *poly* here and elsewhere is added by the corrector.

Ah woe is me, what thing is best
To me now to be done ?
1364 Ah, I have been overcruel
To Christians, I believe.
Ah beauty of riches, farewell !
Little joy have I of the world.
1368 I would wish for a tether here to die :
Amongst folk I would not be seen.

A JUSTICE.

Send ye to the bishops
And the great doctors to come here.
1372 They will say by books
If there be salve in this world
For the sickness.
For they are great caulkers ;
1376 And have you no fear in the case :
They will cure the disease.

CONSTANTINE.

Messenger, straightway
Fetch to me the Bishop here,
1380 And the great Doctor, likewise,
That is called flower of this world
Surely in learning.
If they can tell me
1384 That there is any aid certainly
Against the sickness that I have.

SECOND MESSENGER.

Hail, Sir Emperor Constantine !
Here I was ready
1388 To go on right clean
Hence in thy business.
I will not walk slowly.
The Bishop and the flower of doctors
1392 I will fetch them quickly to thy tower.
I will go in a turn.

Here the Bishop of Pola or the Doctor shall parade.

SECOND MESSENGER.

Hail, Sir Bishop in thy tower !
Hail, also to you, Doctor !
1396 Ye are well met in one house.

the costenten reys yv doys
prederugh inta kyn moys
gorthebov fur reys yv ry

EPISCOPUS POLY

1400 Wolcum maseger ylyn
oys oma war ov ena
pendra wer the costyntyn
dar nynsusy in poynt da
1404 lauer thynny
mar a sywe dyscrasiis
meen drethon a veth kefys
may fo purlowen defry

p. 53. ### DOCTOR

1408 Mayl at eua bargyn da
maseger tek
lauer thymo in preytha
then emper tek
1412 pendrus werys

SECUNDUS NUNCIUS

claff deberthys eff yv sur
ny welys in beys na mur
denvith del ywa dyghtijs

DOCTOR

1416 A haha me a wothya
bakcheler ienkyn in preytha
heth ov lefer a fysek
dokhy indan the gasel
1420 ha grua thegy ov gormel
ov boys fecycyen connek

[erthyn pott. y' bovke aredy And
the vrnell enspektad

CLERICUS IANKYN*

Rag esya an pedrennov
ha rag stopya tarthennov
1424 yma thywy forten tek
a caffogh sur benewen
polge ryb agis tenewen
why a protfse den connek
[descendit ad constantinum

* jankyn is added by the corrector.

To Constantine need is to come.
Consider well before going.
   Answers wise need is to give.

BISHOP OF POLA.

1400 Welcome, fair messenger,
   Thou art here on my soul.
What has happened to Constantine?
   Is he not in good point
1404   Say thou to us.
If he be disgraced
Means through us will be found
   So that he may be very glad really.

DOCTOR.

1408 *Mal*, lo here is a good bargain,
   Sweet messenger,
Say to me, in good time,
   To the fair emperor
1412   What thing has happened ?

THE MESSENGER.

A separated leper he is surely.
I have not seen on earth or sea
   Any one as he is dighted.

DOCTOR.

1416 Ah, haha, I knew.
Bachelor Jenkyn, in good time
   Fetch my book of physic,
Carry it under thy armpit,
1420 And do thou praise me
   That I am a cunning physician.

        [An earthen pot : the book ready;
        and the urinal [to be] inspected.

CLERIC JANKIN.

For easing the buttocks,
And for stopping tertians,
   You have good luck.
1424 If you got a woman
For a while by your side
   You would prove a cunning man.
        [He goes down to Constantine.

EPISCOPUS POLY

1428 Gorthyans in se
ha lowene
    thyugh arluth gluas
omma wharee
1432 ny redufe
    gans an gannas

p. 54.

CONSTANTINUS

A wolcum ser epscop flour
wolcum inweth ser doctour
1436   dugh inban me agis peys
ov cleves prest wy a weyl
nynsyv grefons me an geyl
    a wothogh gul dym guereys

DOCTOR

1440 Mannaff gueles agys dour
hag in vrna an empour
    angeveth gorthyb in cays

JUSTUS

me a prederys henna
1444 y vryn atta oma
    tovle in the wedyr glays

DOCTOR

Hoc vrum malorum
et nimis rubrorum
1448   aha me a wor inta
dus oma bacheler ienkyn
myr warvan drefe the vyn
    ay lok up byscherev tha

1452 Annotho na gymmer gloys
kynthus ganso sawer poys
    gor dotho nes the frygov
helma yv mater tykly
1456 lemen me a wor defry
    pendra yv an clevegov

p. 55.

Pendra vynnogh dym the ry
ha sawys pur eredy
1460   costentyn bethugh gena
dre weres ov du soly
me a vyn gul drynk dywhy
    mar cafa stoff the perna

BISHOP OF POLA.

1428 Worship on (thy) seat
And joy,
　　To you, lord of the kingdom!
Here anon,
1432 We have come
　　With the messenger.

CONSTANTINE.

O welcome, sir flower of bishops!
Welcome, also sir doctor!
1436 　　Come ye up, I pray you.
My disease at once you shall see:
It is not a grievance I conceal:
　　Can ye do me a cure?

DOCTOR.

1440 I will look at your water
And then the emperor
　　Shall have an answer in the case.

JUSTICE.

I thought of that.
1444 His urine lo is here:
　　Throw it into thy blue glass.

DOCTOR.

Hoc urum malorum
Et nimis rubrorum,
1448 　　Aha, I know well.
Come here, bachelor Jenkyn
Look up, raise up thy lip!
　　O look up, beshrew thee!

1452 Thereof do not take pain
Though there be with it a heavy savour.
　　Put thy nostrils nearer to it.
This is a ticklish matter.
1456 Now I know certainly
　　What are the diseases.

What thing will you give to me,
And cured full readily,
1460 　　Constantine, you will be by me?
Through aid of my god, Sol,
I will make a drink for you,
　　If I get the stuff to buy (it).

CONSTANTINUS

1464 Tan at omma thys x puns
in dalleth an rema syns
grua vy sav hag y feth guel
benithe in the vevneyns
1468 me ath ra parlet vhel

DOCTOR

Mayl an rema a ra les
me a vyn pesy cumyes
rag mones dre
1472 arta me a thue deth yov
oma dyugh gans dewosov
a relle agis sawye
descendit cum clerico. [*Expectat episcopus
poly ibidem*

Rum fay ny alla peragh besse
1476 teka pemont nansyv wesse
re du soly numdarfa
sav malbe dam a won vy
gueres the cleves defry
1480 byteweth reys yv bewa
mar ny weres falsury
fecessyon ny thereff nefra [*finit*
[*tranceat domum*

p. 56. ### CLERICUS

Me ny won guel losowen
1484 in bysma rag fecycyen
by my troyth es del yv gov [*finit.*
[*trancit domum*

CONSTANTINUS

Epscop pendra leueryth
ny won us methegyeth
1488 am gruelle sav der lyfryov

EPISCOPUS POLY

Nag us arluth rum lovta
me rebue sur ov stuthya
in lyfryov nansyv tremmys
1492 why ny vethugh sav nefra
marnes golhys in bysma
a vewhy purguir in goys

CONSTANTINE.

1464 Take, lo here ten pounds for thee !
In the beginning, hold these.
  Heal me and thou shalt have better
Ever in thy life.
1468   I will make thee a high prelate.

DOCTOR.

Mâl, these will do good !
I will beg leave
  To go home.
1472 Again I will come on Thursday
Here to you with potions
  Which will heal you.

*He goes down with the clergyman. [The Bishop
of Pola waits in the same place.*

By my faith I cannot . . . .
1476 Fairer payment, now is a . . .
  By god Sol, has not happened (?) to me.
But, *malbe dam*, if I know how
To heal thy disease certainly.
1480   Ever need is to live.
If falsehood helps not
  A physician will never rise.

CLERIC.

I know not a better herb
1484 In this world for a physician,
  By my troth, than falsehood is.

    [He goes off home.

CONSTANTINE.

Bishop, what sayest thou ?
I do not know through books
1488   That there is medicine that would heal me.

BISHOP OF POLA.

There is not, lord, by my loyalty.
I have been surely studying
  In books, it is now three months.
1492 You will never be whole
Unless washed in this world
  You be right truly in blood.

PRELATUS

Ny revue ov stethya sur
1496 a pegh golhys dre goys pur
wy a fya tek sawys
ha benitha ken maner
del govs thynny an lefer
1500 ny yllogh bones yaghheys

CONSTANTINUS

Pana goys a veth henna
na sparyogh best in bysma
mar a kylla boys kefys
1504 othommek me a vya
del welogh the voys sawys

p. 57.   **EPISCOPUS POLY**

Ny dal dotho boys goys best
flehys purreys yv dyugh fest
1508 the kuntel dres ol an pov
ha specyly ree ov tena
goys glan yma then rena
a dremen pup elyov
1512 gruegh why bath in lycorna
hag y fethugh pur salov

PRELATUS

Danvenogh sovdrys in pov
the kuntel an flehyggyov
1516 ea numbyr a tremmyl
han rena bethens lethys
hage goys pur ysawys
tek a glan yn vn vecyl
1520 pan vegh in henna golhys
ythegh gvyn avel crystel   *[finit*

CONSTANTINUS

Helmyv tra a yl boys grueys
tormentoris desempys
1524 tormentoris scon thym dugh
tormentoris gans mur greys
tormentoris dufunugh

PRIMUS TORTOR
               [ad constantinum

Heyl ov arluth costentyn
1528 kekefrys gal ha brentyn
oma ython devethys

PRELATE.

We have been studying surely.
1496 If you were washed in pure blood
        You would be healed fair,
And never otherwise,
As saith the book to us,
1500   Can you be cured.

CONSTANTINE.

What blood will that be?
Spare ye not a beast in this world
        If it can be found
1504 Wanting I would be,
        As you see, to be healed.

THE BISHOP OF POLA.

It ought not for him to be a beast's blood,
Children very needful is it for you
1508   To gather over all the country,
And specially some a-suckling.
Pure blood, those have,
        Which excels every salve.
1512 Bathe in that liquor
        And you will be quite whole.

PRELATE.

Send soldiers into the country
To gather the children,
1516   Yea, a number of three thousand,
And let them be slain,
And their pure blood be saved
        Fair and clean in a vessel.
1520 When you shall be washed therein
        You shall go white as chrystal.

CONSTANTINE.

This is a thing that may be done.
Torturers, straightway,
1524   Torturers, come quick to me!
Torturers, with much strength.
        Torturers, awake!

FIRST TORTURER.

                                [*To Constantine.*

Hail, my lord Constantine!
1528 As well rascal as noble,
        Here we are come.

del grese awoys gul da
ny russugh agen creya
1532   na thywhy nynso vsijs
        [yͨ *wymmen aredy w' ther chyldryn*

p. 58.   CONSTANTINUS

Eugh thymo dres ol an pov
   kefrys rome ha lumbardy
kuntullugh an flehyggyov
1536   a vo pur certen achy
    the try blythy
dens omma hage mammov
tremmyl orth nyver heb wov
1540   nynsus forse kyn fens cans moy

Ens pup oll in y quartren
parcel tus arvov certen
    intrethogh rennys a veth
1544 neb a kuntel an moghya
angeveth an grays brassa
    ea ha reward purfeth
                  [*armatores aredy*

SECUNDUS TORTOR

Arluth the voth a veth grueys
1548 quart[r]on meyny desempys
    dugh genavy alemma
benen gans the flogh byen
hath kentrevoges certen
1552 trussogh quik the costentyn
    bo my agis lath omma

TERTIUS TORTOR

Namsus thym vj vgons flogh
dywans then empour trussogh
1556   may hallons boys dewogys
kepar ha porhel bo lugh
lemen sovdoryen waryogh
    na schappya benen in beys

CALO

1560 Kuntullys gena yma
viij vgons flogh rum ena
    lour yv henna thum parte vy
serrys yv age mammov
1564 pan vo an rema marov
    wegennov ny a ra moy

As I should believe, for sake of doing good
You would not have cried to us:
1532   Not for you is this usual.

[The women ready with their children.

CONSTANTINE.

Go ye for me all over the country,
    Likewise Rome and Lombardy,
Gather the children,
1536   That may be right certainly at home
        Up to three years.
Let them and their mothers come here,
Three thousand by number without a lie—
1540   It is no matter though they be a hundred more.

Let every one go into his quarter
A parcel of armed folk certainly
        Among you shall be divided.
1544 He that gathers the most
Shall have the greatest thanks,
        Yea, and a perfect reward.

[Armed men ready.

SECOND TORTURER.

Lord, thy will shall be done.
1548 A quarter of the household straightway
        Come with me hence.
Woman, with thy little child
And thy neighbouress certainly
1552 Pack ye quick to Constantine,
        Or I will slay you here.

THIRD TORTURER.

Now I have six score children !
Quickly pack to the emperor
1556   That they may be bled
Like a porker or a calf.
Now, soldiers, take care
        That not a woman in the world escape.

A DRUDGE.

1560 Gathered by me are
Eight score children, by my soul !
        Enough is this for my part.
Troubled are their mothers.
1564 When these shall be dead
        We will make more sweetlings.

PRIMUS TORTOR

[ad constantinum cum mulieribus
et [pueris] plurimis

Heyll costentyn in the dour
lafuryys rag the pleysour
1568   a dro in pov me revue
at oma xix cans flogh
y feth sur colonov trogh
     pan weller age lathe

SECUNDUS TORTOR

1572 Costentyn devethys dre
me yv hag yma gene
     vi *cans* flogh inweth y tek
parys thage dewosa
1576 me a veth ov arluth da
     merugh an babyov wek

p. 60.   TERTIUS TORTOR

Heyl costentyn the nobyl
molothov mur a bobyl
1580   rag the plesya me ru*m*bue
malbev an flogh a scappyas
colonov ran a crakkyas
viij *cans* sur me re gavas
1584   gruegh scon age dewose

CALO

Heyl costentyn in the dour
xj *cans* flogh theth enour
     ha moy me re ruk kuntel
1588 aban ethe mes a dre
me re ruk flehys ievvje
     ragas tevery ancoel

PRIMA MATER

Ellas emperour debyta
1592 mar mynnyth oma latha
     flehys bythqueth na pehes
yma dywhy guan cusel
a du an neff tayl dyel
1596   warnogh a tus ongrassyes   *[finit*

p. 61.   JUSTUS

Na vragyogh brays lafarov
y a veth purguir marov
     rag cafus sur age goys

FIRST TORTURER.

[To Constantine with the women
and very many children.

Hail, Constantine in thy tower.
Laboured for thy pleasure
1568   About in the country have I.
Lo, here are nineteen hundred children !
There will be surely broken hearts
    When their slaughter is seen.

SECOND TORTURER.

1572 Constantine, come home
Am I, and here with me
    Six hundred children likewise I have brought.
Ready to bleed them
1576 I am, my good lord.
    See ye the sweet babes !

THIRD TORTURER.

Hail, Constantine the noble !
Curses great from the people
1580   For pleasing thee I have had.
. . . . the child has escaped
Hearts of some have broken :
Eight hundred surely I have found
1584   Have them bled at once.

THE DRUDGE.

Hail, Constantine, in thy tower !
Eleven hundred children to thy honour
    And more have I gathered.
1588 Since I went out from home
I have made for thee, *je vous dis,*
    Children really dying.

FIRST MOTHER.

Alas, Emperor pitiless !
1592 If thou wilt here slay
    Children that never sinned,
This is to you a weak counsel.
O God of heaven wreak vengeance
1596   On you, O graceless folk !

JUSTICE.

Do not brag big words !
They shall right truly be dead
    To get their blood, surely,

1600 an empour flour they golhy
may fo tekkeys eredy
kefys yv der an clergy
 sav in delma y hyl boys

CONSTANTINUS

1604 Py sul yv sum an flehys
 us kuntullys thym omma
ythyv sur mur a ponfeys
 mar peth reys age latha
1608 trueth ambus ov queleys
 age mammov ov thola
ha lowen certen зeheys
 thum corff me a gemersa

PRIMUS TORTOR

1612 Ima oma iij myl flogh
 thum gothfes ha vij vgans
bethens marov na sparyogh
 ha wy a veth purthyblans
1616 in agis lee me as lath
heb ovn oma na truath
 moy es carov gvyls a coys

SECUNDUS TORTOR

Me a vyn dewose myl
1620 trehy age bryonsen
an corfov ny a ra pyl
 hag as gor in dor certen
 the develys name
1624 ny sense moy latha flogh
es dyswul gauer py bogh
 rag in mater ny coth schame

p. 62.   CONSTANTINUS

Dynyte an goys ryel
1628 yv in rome pur thyogel
 del recorde agen latha
neb a lath flogh in batel
sensys y feth den cruel
1632 ov geryov gruegh attendya
poys yv gena dyswuthel
 heb ken an keth flehys ma
ny won awose merwel
1636 a vetha peyn thum ena

1600 (And for) the flower of emperors, to wash him,
That he may be beautified readily.
Found is it through our learning
That he may be whole.

CONSTANTINE.

1604 How many is the sum of the children
That are gathered for me here?
It is surely much of trouble
If needs be to slay them.
1608 Pity have I seeing
Their mothers wailing,
And gladly certainly health
For my body I should get.

FIRST TORTURER.

1612 Here are three thousand children,
To my knowledge, and seven score.
Let them be killed! spare ye not!
And you shall be very clear.
1616 In your place I will kill them
Without fear here nor pity
More than (for) a wild hart of the wood.

SECOND TORTURER.

I will bleed a thousand
1620 (And) cut their throats.
The bodies we will strip,
And put them in earth certainly.
The devil's name!
1624 I would not hold killing a child more
Than destroying a goat or a buck,
For in the matter shame is not becoming.

CONSTANTINE.

Dignity of the blood royal
1628 Is in Rome right clearly.
As our law records:
Whoso shall slay a child in battle
Will be held a cruel man.
1632 Consider ye my words.
Heavy am I to destroy
Without pity these same children.
I know not, after dying,
1636 Whether there will be pain to my soul.

TERTIUS TORTOR

Ser empe*r*our bethens lethys
rag savment dywhy leme*n*
mar ny vyn du the coweys
1640   an iovle a vyn pur lowen
wose helma
omgolhough in age goys
sav nefre mar mynnogh boys
1644   ha ny as lath knak oma

CALO

Pan gol us awoys latha
an chett*is* mowes ha mav
in vn noys mar lefara
1648   me a russe dywhy ix
an keth sort ma
mar mynnogh arluth brentyn
me a dregh y vreonsen
1652   hag an dewoys knak oma

[*tranceunt tortores et mulieres
expectant in placea*

p. 63.   CONSTANTINUS

A wek wegov agys mam
thywhywy y fye cam
boys lethys am govys vy
1656   trueth vye del wothogh
latha o*m*ma iij myl flogh
awoys sawya vn body

Guel yv genavy me*r*wel
1660   in cleves bras indelma
ha gasa bev dyogel
an iij myl flogh us o*m*ma
es del yv gena purlel
1664   gul mernans mar thebyta
me a vya de*n* cruel
mar lathe*n* oll an re ma

Regh an flehys thage mam
1668   war beyn tenna ha cregy
me a charge na ve heb nam
flogh vyth lethys eredy
ha me a vyn
1672   the*n* benenes ry mona
boys ha dewes the pe*r*na
ha the*n* flehys delles da
the dre mammethov tota
1676   why hag*is* flehys vyan

THIRD TORTURER.

Sir Emperor, let them be slain
   For healing to you now:
If God will not aid thee
1640   The devil will right gladly.
   After this
Wash yourself in their blood
If you will ever be healed,
1644   And we will slay them here, snap!

A DRUDGE.

What loss is it for slaying
   The chits, girl and boy!
In one night, so I say,
1648   I would make for you nine
   Of this same sort.
If you will, Lord sovran,
I will cut their throats
1652   And bleed them here, snap!

        [The torturers go off and the women
            wait in the open.

CONSTANTINE.

O sweet sweets of your mothers!
To you it were a wrong
   To be slain because of me.
1656 Pity were it, as you know,
To slay here three thousand children
   For sake of healing one body.

I had liefer die
1660   In great disease thus,
And leave alive certainly
   The three thousand children that are here,
Than by me right truly
1664   Do a death so pitiless.
I should be a cruel man
   If I slew all these.

Give ye the children to their mothers.
1668   On pain of drawing or hanging
I charge that there be not, without exception,
   Any child slain verily;
   And I will
1672 To the women give money
To buy food and drink,
And to the children good raiment.
Home, nurses, quickly,
1676   You and your little children!

p. 64.

SECUNDA MATER

Ser emperour dywhy mur grays
agys boys mar pytethays
   orth benenes bohosek*
1680 rag sawya agen flehas
du re tharbara ʒehas
   thywhy arluth galosek   *finit*

CONSTANTINUS

Me a vyn moys thum guely
1684 nansyv noys pur eredy
   squyth off omma am bevnans
thum corff am beua ʒehas
y rosen hanter ov gluas
1688   hag ol ov mebyl dyblans

           [claudat hostium

IHC.

Pedyr ha povle eugh lemen
then norveys the costenten
   dren pyte a gemeras
1692 orth flehys gruegh ha byen
seluester in pur certen
   dotho ef a ree ʒehas

PETRUS

Arluth the voth ny a ra
1696 broder povle duen alema
   the confortya costenten
rag na scollyas
goys an flehas
1700   gueresys y feth certen

      [descendunt petrus et paulus ascendit
         in turrim constantinus

p. 65.

PAULUS

Constentyn mar qureth cosca
golsov orthen ny oma
   danvenys dys rag ʒehas
1704 drefen kemeres pyta
an flehys gruerght† del rusta
   ihesu a vyn the weras

---

  * perhaps *vohosek*.   † leg. *gruegh ?*

SECOND MOTHER.

Sir Emperor, much thanks to you
That you are so pitiful
   Towards poor women.
1680 For saving our children
May God provide health
   For you, mighty Lord!

CONSTANTINE.

I will go to my bed,
1684 Now it is night, right readily:
   Weary am I here of my life.
For my body that I might have health
I would give half my kingdom,
1688   And all my chattels clearly.
          [*Let him close the door.*

JESUS.

Peter and Paul, go now
To the earth unto Constantine :
   Through the pity he has had
1692 Towards children tiny and little
Silvester very certainly
   Shall give him health.

PETER.

Lord, thy will we shall do.
1696 Brother Paul, let us come hence
   To comfort Constantine,
For he spilt not
The blood of the children.
1700   He shall be healed certainly.
       [*Peter and Paul descend. Constantine*
          goes up to the tower.

PAUL.

Constantine, if thou dost sleep
Hearken to us, here
   Sent to thee for healing,
1704 Because of taking pity
On the tiny children, as thou hast done,
   Jesu will cure thee.

H

PETRUS

Drefen na russys scollia
1708 goys then ynocens oma
    crist dys agen danvonas
    pur salov grueys may festa
    the syluester donfon grua
1712   may teffo eff theth gueras

PAULUS

An pap syluester defry
in meneth sur neb vsy
    seraptim hennyv gelwys
1716 eff a ra prest the golhy
    may festa sav eredy
    heb moldra floghv^t in beys   [*finit*

PETRUS

Ha pan vesta sav ha glaan
1720 gueyt dustruya in tyan
    ol templys an falge dewov
    grua socour ha menteyna
    myns may hylly in bysma
1724   the ihesu crist eglosyov

        [*tranceat ad celum*

p. 66.   CONSTANTINUS

Benedicite pana syght
    ambuevy haneth in noys
thymo y tuth ij den vryght
1728   degeys an darasov cloys
      hag a covsis
donfon wa[r]lergh seluester
hag y fethen heb awer
1732   a oll ov cleves sawys

Maseger gans mur a greys
kergh seluester thym uskys
    in mont sareptim yma
1736 ov cuthe gans y clergy
lauer dethe eredy
    may teffons dymmo omma

SECUNDUS NUNCIUS *ad constantinum*

Arluth costentyn pup preys
1740 the volnogeth a veth grueys
    genevy a fur termyn

PETER.

	Because thou didst not spill
1708	The blood of the innocents here,
	Christ has sent us to thee,
	Right sound that thou mayst be made.
	To Silvester send
1712	That he may come to cure thee.

PAUL.

The pope Silvester, certainly,
Who is surely on a mountain,
Soracte that is called,
1716 He will readily wash thee,
So that thou wilt be whole at once
Without murdering any child in the world.

PETER.

And when thou shalt be whole and clean,
1720 Take care to destroy completely
All the temples of the false gods.
Succour and maintain,
As many as thou canst in this world,
1724 Churches for Jesu Christ.

[*Let him pass to heaven.*

CONSTANTINE.

Benedicite, what a sight
I had this very night!
To me came two bright men,
1728 The doors shut close,
And said
To send after Silvester
And I should be without grief
1732 Healed of all my disease.

Messenger, with much strength,
Seek Silvester for me quickly.
On Mount Soracte he is,
1736 Hiding with his clergy.
Tell them at once
That they come to me here.

SECOND MESSENGER [*to Constantine.*

Lord Constantine, always
1740 Thy will shall be done
By me in a short time.

H 2

marogyen duen alema
me ny won in fays pyma
1744   an keth meneth na certyn
        [*ad siluestrem in monte seraptim*

Heyl seluester hath clergy
na fella cuthe defry
    wy ny regh in keth plasma
        [*The ymagis aredy w^t syluester*
           of pyter and povle

p. 67.   1748 the costyntyn an emperour
reys yv dyugh lafurya dour
    eff a erhys indella

SELUESTER

Arluth neff' rebo gorthys
1752   me a wor lemen inta
gothe mernans dyn a reys
    byth ny yller y sconya
    ov bredereth
1756 duen alema kescolon*
ihesu map a saluasconn
    regen guerese pup deth

                [*ad constantinum*
Heyll costentyn in the dour
1760   me a wor ty a wetsa
bones grueys dyso enour
    ha the cregyans a pe da
    ny an grussa
1764 rag the voys in dysgregyans
awos ovn gothe mernans
    inclenya dys ny vanna

                     [*ascendit*

CONSTANTINUS

Seluester wolcum owhy
1768   nynsyv awos drokcoleth
ythogh kerhys dymovy
    repreff na cam nygis beth
desesijs bras off defry
1772   kekefrys ha nos ha deth
cusullys der ov clergy
    o tus a fur skentoleth
    sur me a fua
1776 tremmyl flogh gruergh the latha
bath may rellen in v[r]na
    in goys tum an flehys na

       * MS. kescolen.

Knights, let us come hence.
I know not well where is
1744 That same mountain certainly.

     [To Silvester on Mount Soracte.

Hail, Silvester, and thy clergy !
Hide any longer
  You shall not in this same place.

    [The images of Peter and Paul ready
      with Silvester.

1748 To Constantine the emperor
Need is it for you to go on vehemently:
  He has ordered so.

     SILVESTER.

Heaven's Lord be worshipped !
1752 I know now well
To suffer death he has given to us.
  Never can it be refused.
    My brethren,
1756 Let us come hence with one heart.
May Jesu, Son of salvation,
  Protect us every day !

       [To Constantine.

Hail, Constantine, in thy tower !
1760 I know thou deservest
That honour be done to thee,
  And that thy belief should be good
    We would cause it.
1764 Because of thy being in unbelief,
For fear of suffering death
  Incline to thee I will not.

      [He goes up.

    CONSTANTINE.

Silvester, you are welcome :
1768 It is not on account of an ill deed
That you are fetched to me.
  Reproof nor wrong ye shall not have.
Greatly diseased am I,
1772 Likewise day and night
Counselled by my clergy,
  Who were folk of much knowledge,
    Surely was I
1776 Three thousand tiny children to slay,
Bathe that I should then
  In the warm blood of those children.

p. 68.

1780   Tremmyl a fue kuntulys
      thymo oma rag an cays
   mur trueth y kemerys
     latha prest kemys flehas
      awoys vn den
1784 me as ornes in fyv dre
   sav noswyth a thyuvne
      syght coynt y welys certen

   Dev then a thuth dym in nos
1788   gans nerth bras a wo[lo]vde[r]
   hau darasov degeys clos
    ny won rum caradovder
     pyv ens y suer
1792 dymo y a covsis cler
   donfon warlergh seluester
   may renlen quik heb awer
   eff ath wolgh purlan kyn moys
1796   may fo sav the cleves mur
   pyv ylly an rema boys
   a wothogh wy seluester
    ov guarnya vy
1800 del grese dev thu ens y

SELUESTER

   Nynso an rena dewov.
    me a leuer costentyn
   ij abostel caradov
1804   y o 3e crist cuff colyn

p. 69. Myr age ymach heb wov
    mar syns y havel certyn
   ha thyso age hanov
1808   me a leuer pur ylyn

CONSTANTINUS

   Ren ena us om body
   poren an rena ens y
     henna gans an alwethov
1812 hay cowt a thek cletha
   in nos y a fue gena
   teka syght war ov ena
    ny welys in ov dethyov
1816 mercy war crist y creya
    boys crystyan menna heb wov

SELUESTER

   Me ath wra* cathecumynys
   ha lemen ty a penys
1820   vn sythen heb feladov

         * Seems *rora*.

Three thousand were gathered
1780 To me here for the case.
Much pity I took
 To slay so many children
 On account of one person.
1784 I ordered them alive home:
But at night-time I awoke:
 A strange sight I saw certainly.

Two men came to me at night
1788 With a great strength of radiance,
And the doors shut close.
 I know not, by my loveableness,
 Who they were surely.
1792 To me they said clearly
Send after Silvester
That I should quickly without grief—
"He will wash thee full clean before going,
1796 So that thy great disease shall be healed."
Who could these be,
 Know ye, Silvester,
 Warning me?
1800 As I believed, two gods were they.

SILVESTER.

Those were not gods,
 I say, Constantine.
Two loveable apostles
1804 They were to Christ the dear heart.
Behold their images without a lie
 If they are like them certainly,
And to thee their names
1808 I will tell very fairly.

CONSTANTINE.

By the soul that is in my body
Exactly those they were!
 That one with the keys,
1812 And his comrade bore a sword.
At night they were with me.
Fairer sight, on my soul,
 I have not seen in my days.
1816 Mercy I cry on Christ.
 Be a Christian I will without a lie.

SILVESTER.

I will make thee a catechumen,
And now thou shalt do penance
1820 A week without fail.

war lergh henna begythys
ty a veth sur ha golhys
may fy salov

CONSTANTINUS

1824 Penys purguir yv ov luyst
ha creya pup vr war crist
mercy rag ov fehosov
p. 70. then guan ha tus omthevas
1828 in dewelyans am pehas
manneff ry alesonov

SELUESTER

[descendit.   holy water aredy

Lemmen gruaff the vegethya
in hanov map maria
1832 omma atte ty golhys
neb a vyrwys in grovs p[r]en
re gronntya dyso lemen
del in peseff luen yehey(s)
[ye vysour away

Cum   in   aquam   descendisset   baptismatis
mirabilis enituit splendor lucis Sic inde
mundus exiuit et christum se vidisse asseruit

IHC.

1836 Costentyn rag the pyte
a gemercys an flehys
han tregereth warnethe
age lathe na vynsys
[ye processyon aredy

1840 me a vyn sur the sawye
a pegh pan ota golhys
mercy neb a gemerre
mercy an gueres pup preys

CONSTANTINUS

1844 Benedycite pan wolov
revue oma sollebreys
ihesu crist pen elyov
pur thefry me re weleys
1848 aleys ol y wolyov
the ragoff sur disquetheys
ys guelys cleth a dyov
ha tek eff am confortycys

After that baptized
Thou shalt be surely, and washen,
   That thou mayst be healed.

CONSTANTINE.

1824 To do penance right truly is my desire,
And to cry always on Christ
   Mercy for my sins.
To the weak and orphan folk
1828 In atonement of my sin
   I will give alms.

SILVESTER.

[He descends.   Holy water ready.

Now I do baptize thee
In the name of Mary's Son.
1832   Lo, here thou art washen.
May he who died on the cross-tree
Grant to thee now,
   As I beseech him, a full healing!
              [The mask away.

*When he went down into the water of baptism
there shone forth a marvellous splendour of
light. So thence he came forth clean, and
declared that he had seen Christ.*

JESUS.

1836 Constantine, for thy pity
   Which thou tookest on the children,
And the mercy upon them
   That thou wouldst not slay them
              [The procession ready.
1840 I will surely heal thee
   When thou art washen from sin.
Whoso may have mercy
   Mercy shall heal him always.

CONSTANTINE.

1844 Benedicite, what a light
   Was here some time ago!
Jesus Christ, head of healing,
   Right certainly I have seen.
1848 Widely all his wounds
   Before me surely uncovered,
I saw them left and right,
   And fairly he comforted me.

SILUESTER

1852   Ty a yl boys lowenek
kyntheste claff anhethek
    grasse the crist ythoys sav
nyn fus teka
1856   den na weka
    thum gothfes in the dethyov

CONSTANTINUS

The crist ihesu ingrassaff
    ha thys seluester nefra
1860   theth palys lemen manaff
    gans procescyon the gora
dres an gluas y comondyaff
    du mas crist gorthys na ve
1864   ha me a ra mar pewaff
    the lays ihesu cresyae

ad palacium pape procesc[i]onabiliter
[et postea tranceat domum

[And John ergudyn aredy a horse bakke y^t was y^e
Justis w^t constantyn ffor to play ye marchont*

p. 72.   *Exulatores hic pompabunt vel vnus pro omnibus*

PRIMUS EXULATOR

Me yv outlayer in coys
moy reovte in ov oys
1868   bythqueth purguir numdarfa
pan vo due ov stoff achy
ware me a provy moy
    nynsyv marnes sportt raffna

SECUNDUS EXULATOR

1872   Nansyv preys aspya pray
due yv an mona rum fay
    mester in agen mesk ny
aspyen gvas gans pors poys
1876   mar kyllyn den sans eglos
    whare y a kuntel moy

PRIMUS EXULATOR

In sol matis duen in kerth
aspyogh gans mur an nerth
1880   py fo marchont ov quandra

* Here, in a third hand, follow the words: *Pax vos omnes nos sumus melyores vyrgilius.*

SILVESTER.

1852 Thou mayst be joyous.
Though thou wert a loathsome leper,
  Thanks to Christ, thou art whole.
There has not been a fairer
1856 Man, nor a sweeter,
  To my knowledge, in thy days.

CONSTANTINE.

To Christ Jesu I give thanks,
  And to thee, Silvester, ever.
1860 To thy palace now will I
  With a procession put thee.
Throughout the kingdom I will command
  That no god but Christ be worshipped,
1864 And I will cause, if I live,
  Belief in Jesu's laws.

*To the pope's palace in procession-wise,
  [and thereafter let him go home.*

*[And John Ergudyn, who was the Justice with Con-
  stantine, on horseback ready to play the merchant.*

Outlaws shall here parade, or one for all.

FIRST OUTLAW.

I am an outlaw in the forest.
More sway in my age
1868   Never right truly has fallen to me.
When my stuff at home shall be ended
Soon I will try more.
  Naught save sport is it to rob.

SECOND OUTLAW.

1872 Now's (the) time to look out for prey.
Ended is the money, by my faith,
  Master, amongst us.
Let us look out for a lad with a heavy purse,
1876 If we can, a man of holy Church.
  Anon they will gather more.

FIRST OUTLAW.

Up, mates, let us come away.
Look out with much of strength
1880   Where a merchant may be wandering.

y dalhenna na sparyogh
me a omgem*er* ragogh
    hag*is* men*ten* benytha

descendit

TERTIUS EXULATOR

1884   Me a weyl guas war geyn margh
na fella ny vanna p*ar*gh*
    gene at eve sesijs
p. 73.   deyskyn then dor mata
1888   ha the borse mes ath ascra
    me ambeth hath margh usk*is*

MERCATOR

A serys clowugh ov leff
dovtyogh drok thag*is* eneff
1892   pan dremen*n*ogh an bysme
agys sper*ys* sur an pre*n*
in anken ha m*ur* a peyn
    a thu go ef an ene

[*y° prest aredy*

PRIMUS EXULATOR

1896   Pur a wylste war an kee
eneff map de*n* in bysmae
    ov repe*n*tya rag y throk
mar nu*m*kem*er* du certen
1900   an iovle a ra purlowen
    inagefery† avel hok

QUARTUS EXULATOR

Me a weyl guas in gon hyr
pront*er* ef a hevel suyr
1904   yma mona gans henna
ser p*ar*son bona dyes
me a vyn changya porses
    be my fay kyns mos lema

PRESBITER

p. 74   1908   A te then pr*eder* ath du
y volnogeth byth nynsyv
    bones grueys in ketelma
terry y wormenadov
1912   a regh why heb feladov
    gothvethugh y attendya

---

* MS. *paragh.*   † MS. perhaps *inagescry.*

To lay hold of him spare not.
I will betake myself before you,
And support you ever.

[*He goes down.*

THIRD OUTLAW.

1884   I see a lad on horseback.
No further will I forbear.
By me behold him seized.
Get down to the ground, mate,
1888   And thy purse out of thy bosom
I will have, and thy horse quickly.

MERCHANT.

O sirs, hear my voice!
Fear evil to your soul,
1892   When ye pass from this world
Your spirit surely shall pay for it
In grief and much of pain
O God, woe is it the soul!

[*The priest ready.*

1896   ### FIRST OUTLAW.

. . . hast thou seen on the way
The soul of a son of man in this world
Repenting for her sin.
If God will not take me certainly
1900   The devil will very gladly
Into his number (?) like a . . . .

FOURTH OUTLAW.

I see a lad in a long gown.
A priest he seems surely :
1904   There is money with that one.
Sir parson, *bona dies,*
I will change purses
By my faith before going hence.

THE PRIEST.

1908   Ah thou man, think of thy God!
His will is not at all
To be done thus.
Break his commandments
1912   You do without fail,
Ye know (how) to attend to him.

PRIMUS EXULATOR

Neb a gemer ovn y thu
ny sewen henna neb tu
1916   mata orthen ny na set
sav dascor ol the vona
bo annyl the quartrona
oma me a ra heb let

PRESBITER

1920   Galles genogh mens ambus
termen a thue crist ihesus
interthon a ran an gvyr
prederugh helma deth brus
1924   pemont thymmo gruegh in suyr

PRIMUS EXULATOR

A vethe preys* bys deth brus
ny thue henna in trogel
ty a gel moy an pyth us
1928   adro dyso dyogel
streppyogh y queth
p. 73.   eff re ros thyn deth hyr lour
pan vo an vrus wy a wour
1932   an pement na hyns ny veth

SECUNDUS EXULATOR

At eve strepys in noth
in delma guthel y coth
then guesyon astefe peth

[expectant in placeu

HIC COMES ROHANI

1936   Me yv chyff arluth rohan
zurl worthy nangeves par
meryasek in certan
o thymo pur oges car
1940   in kerth galles
forsakis y das hay vam
ha ny won py theth heb nam
ragtho may thoma serres

PRIMUS NUNCIUS

1944   Ser zurle arluth galosek
yma purguir meryasek
devethys oma then pov

* Perhaps peys.

FIRST OUTLAW.

Whoso has fear of his God
He will not succeed on any side.
1916   Mate, do not set (thyself) against us,
But deliver all thy money,
Or else quarter thee
      Here I will without hindrance.

PRIEST.

1920 Gone with you is all I have.
The time of Christ Jesus will come
      Between us the True will divide.
Think of this, on doomsday
1924   You will surely make payment to me.

FIRST OUTLAW.

Should there be time until doomsday,
    That will not come in the body.
Thou shalt lose more, the wealth that is
1928   Around thee surely.
      Strip off his garment !
He has given to us a day long enough.
When the Judgment may be you know.
1932   The payment will not be before.

SECOND OUTLAW.

Lo, he is stript naked.
Thus ought to be done
      To the lads who have wealth.

          [They wait in the open space.

HERE THE EARL OF ROHAN.

1936 I am a chief, lord of Rohan,
    A worthy earl, who has not a peer.
Meriasek certainly,
    Who was to me a very near relation,
1940   Went away,
Forsook his father and his mother,
And I know not where he went, without mistake,
      So that for him I am vexed.

FIRST MESSENGER.

1944 Sir Earl, mighty Lord,
Meriasek right truly is
      Come here to our country :

ryb pontelyne eredy
1948 avel hermyt purthevry
speyna a ra y dethyov

p. 76. COMES ROHANI

Me a vyn mones dotha
hay cothmens purguir gena
1952 y temptya mar a kyllyn
rag treyla thy eretons
y nessevyn sur ymons
serris dretho in certyn

COGNATUS COMITIS ROHANI

1956 Yma eff in meneth bras
del glowevy sur myl pas
theworth an grond a woles
hag ena prest nos ha deth
1960 y honen ol eff a veth
y vos hay susten nebes

[*descendit* [leg. *ascendit*] *comes ad montem*
et cognatus et agnatus]

MERIADOCUS

The ihesu rebo grasseys
omma ythese tregys
1964 avel hermyt in guelfos
in le ov delles ourlyn
purpur pannov fyn certyn
lemen me a wesk queth los

1968 In ov nesse hevys ruen
ny eve cydyr na gwyn
na dewes marnes dour pur
hag erbys an goverov
1972 a veth ov bos thum preggyov
na vo ree fors ov nattur

p. 77. AGNATUS

Oma yma meryasek
ov corthya du galosek
1976 poren in top an meneth
myl pas in ban alemme
then chapel purguir ymae
acontis gans tus purgoeth

By Pontelyne indeed
1948   As a hermit full really
    He doth spend his days.

THE EARL OF ROHAN.

I will go to him,
And his friends truly with me,
1952   If we can tempt him
To return to his inheritance.
His kinsmen surely are
    Vexed through him certainly.

A RELATION OF THE EARL OF ROHAN.

1956   He is on a great mountain,
As I hear, surely a thousand paces
    From the ground at the bottom.
And there always, night and day,
1760   He himself is,
    His food and his little sustenance.
    [*The Earl goes up to the mountain, with the
    relation, and the agnate.*

MERIASEK.

To Jesu be thanks !
Here I have been dwelling
1964   As a hermit in the wilderness.
In lieu of my raiment of silk,
Purple cloths fine certainly,
    Now I wear a grey garment,

1968   Nearest me (is) a shirt of horsehair.
    I quaff not cider nor wine
    Nor any drink, unless pure water,
And herbs of the brooks
1972   Are my food for my meals,
    So that my nature be not overstrong.

THE AGNATE.

Here is Meriasek,
Worshipping mighty God,
1976   Right on the top of the mountain.
A thousand paces up from hence
To the chapel right truly is it
    Accounted by folk full old.

114

COMES ROHANI

1980 Meryasek lowene dys
omma duthen theth vereys
    hag inweth theth confortia
ha gul dyso aswonfos
1984 the nessevyn in ponfos
    y mons ragos in bysma

MERIADOCUS

Prag ymons y in ponfos
ny ruk truspus thum gothfos
1988   dethe na the den in beys
myns may hallen omguythe
na ny garsen benythe
    gans weres du benegeys

COMES ROHANI

1992 Trueth mur yv ahanas
den yv sevys a lyne bras
    ty the vynnes mar sempel
p. 78.   bones omma in ponvos
1996 the car the honen nynsos
    me a veth y leferel

MERIADOCUS

Da dym ythyv
nesse the du
2000   hay gorthya eff
guthel y voth
kepar del goth
    may hallen dendyl gluas neff

COGNATUS COMITIS ROHANI

2004 Ty a also gorthya du
del us lues den hythyv
    ov pewe tek hag onest
dus alema genen ny
2008 ellas trueth ambus vy
    the vos oma avel best   [*finit*

MERIADOCUS

Bohogogneth abreth du
remoconn then cur ythyv
2012   wose helma

THE EARL OF ROHAN.

1980 Meriasek, joy to thee!
Here we have come to see thee,
  And likewise to comfort thee,
And to cause thee to know
1984 Thy kinsmen in trouble
  Are for thee in this world.

MERIASEK.

Why are they in trouble?
I have not done violence, to my knowledge,
1988   To them, nor to anyone on earth.
To go that I may worsen myself
I should never like
  With help of blessed God.

THE EARL OF ROHAN.

1992 Great pity is of thee,
A man that is raised of a great line.
  That thou wishest so simply
To be here in trouble.
1996 Thine own friend thou art not,
  I shall be to say it.

MERIASEK.

Good to me it is
To draw near to God,
2000   And to worship Him,
To do His will,
As behoveth,
  So that I may earn heaven's kingdom.

THE RELATION OF THE EARL OF ROHAN.

2004 Thou mightest worship God
As there are many men to-day
  Living fair and decently.
Come thou hence with us
2008 Alas, pity have I
  That thou art here like a wild beast.

MERIASEK.

Poverty on behalf of God
Is removal to the Court (of heaven)
2012   After this,

I 2

hag inweth mam a yehes
ny wothogh why ov flehes
    pendryv ol boys an ena

p. 79.

COMES ROHANI

2016 Meryasek nynsos fur
gorthya du ty alse sur
    kyn fy reoute an beys
meth yv gans ol the cufyon
2020 the vones omma dyson
    avel begyer desethys

MERIADOCUS

A war agys cam why pobyl
helma yv bevnans nobyl
2024   termen a thue
ha then ena sur megyans
ythyv rag cafus selwans
    ol then ene

2028 Lust an kyk y ra vodya
han beys eff a ra gasa
    the trettya indan y dreys
byth ny ra cam the neb den
2032 gallus an iovle pup termen
    dretho a veth confundijs
megyans then ena certen
    ha ioy neff dretho guanys

p. 80.

COMES ROHANI

2036 Ima lues den heb greff
a theseff mones then neff
    ha wath a gar peth an bys
indelle te a alse
2040 gul worschyp* mur theth nesse
    ha boys selwys

MERIADOCUS

Pyth an beys ha reovte
ha rychyth bras rum lovte
2044   benithe me nys care
nynsyns the trestye mas falge
annethe kyn feste calge
    war na ra fethye inne

* MS, worsthyp.

And also a mother of healing.
Ye know not, my children,
    What is all the food of the soul.

THE EARL OF ROHAN.

2016 Meriasek, thou art not wise
Worship God, thou mightest surely
    Though thou shouldst have sway of the world.
Shame is with all thy dear ones
2020 That thou art here at once
    Like a beggar seated.

MERIASEK.

Go on your way, you people.
This is a noble life.
2024   An end will come,
And to the soul a sure delight,
It is to have salvation
    All to the soul,

2028 The lust of the flesh it will expel,
And the world it will leave
    To be trodden under its feet.
Never do wrong to any one.
2032 The devil's power always
    Thereby will be confounded.
Delight to the soul certainly
    And joy of heaven gained thereby.

THE EARL OF ROHAN.

2036 There are many men, without grief,
Who desire to go to the heaven,
    And yet love somewhat the world.
In like manner thou mightest
2040 Do much worship to thy nearest,
    And be saved.

MERIASEK.

Wealth of the world and sway,
And great riches, by my loyalty,
2044   Never have I loved them.
They are not to be trusted, but false.
Of them though thou hast many,
    Beware that thou confide not in them.

AGNATUS

2048 Na temptyogh na moy an den
reys yv the crist cuff colen
thy lel servye
na ve y vose guir sans
2052 mar lues merkyl dyblans
byth ny russe   [*finit*

COMES ROHANI

Ny vannef y annye
rag thym ny ammont defry
2056 meryasek me ath pesse
a wul vn dra ragovy
del oys ov goys
p. 81.   laddron mur us in povma
2060 lues den ov tustruya
grua then rena avodya
par del yv mur the galloys

Ny yl den mones then fer
2064 na vova robijs in suer
dustruys ha corff ha peth
certen feryov in breten
cafus y fensen certen
2068   ov gueres mar a mynneth

An wehes deth
in gortheren
an kynse feer
2072 han gela veth
mys est certen
orth ov deser
an viij^th deth
2076 han tresse mys gvyn gala
dugol myhal yv henna
in plu voala* neffrea
an keth feriovma a veth

MERIADOCUS

2080 Helma dis a veth grontis
poren del yv descrijs
dre grath du ha tra nahen
an ladron a veth pelleys
2084 ran the guel forthov treylys
mercy du mar crons goven

[*comes rohani trancit domum et
meriadocus expectat ibidem*

* leg. noala.

THE AGNATE.

2048 Tempt the man no more.
Need is Christ, dear heart,
   To serve him loyally.
If he were not a true saint
2052 So many miracles clearly
   He would never work.

THE EARL OF ROHAN.

I will not annoy him,
   For me it concerns not really.
2056 Meriasek, I would pray thee
   To do one thing for me.
     As thou art my blood.
Robbers many there are in this country,
2060 Many persons destroying :
Make those go away,
   As thy power is great.

No one can go to the fair
2064 Without being robbed surely,
   Ruined both body and wealth.
Certainly fairs in Brittany
I would have certainly
2068   If thou wouldst help me.

The sixth day,
   In July,
     The first fair,
2072 And the other will be,
   In the month of August certainly,
     By my desire.
     The eighth day,
2076 And the third month September,
Michael's feast-day is that.
In the parish of Noala ever
   These same fairs shall be.

MERIASEK.

2080 This to thee shall be granted
Just as is desired
   Through God's grace and nothing else.
The robbers shall be banished,
2084 Some turned to better ways,
   If they ask God's mercy.

   [The Earl of Rohan passes home and Meriasek
   waits in the same place.

p. 82.

PRIMUS EXULATOR

Nov mat*is* merugh adro
mar quelogh so mot y go
2088   de*n* ryb an coys ov quandra
gedyogh dymo quik y pors
eff angeveth god ys cors
    neb a covs erbyn raffna

Hic ignis venit super illos

SECUNDUS EXULATOR

2092 Out gony bras ha bye*n*
yma ol an coys gans tae*n*
    the lusu ython leskys
dufe warnan anfusy
2096 hennyv rag an devlugy
    a russyn oma in beys

TERTIUS EXULATOR

Ay tav an iovle theth lesky
praga pe*n*dryv an fesky
2100   us genes han terlemel
an golovder me a wor
nynsyv eff leme*n* an lor
    pan vsy ov trehevel

QUARTUS EXULATOR

2104 Out o^t fyyn ny
yma ov lesky
    an coys the vn tanges lel   *[horse aredy*
out o^t ny a veth skaldys
2108 alema fye uskys
    me a vyn mar a calla
p. 83. ha molleth du in gorel
pyma thym ov margh morel
2112   an iovle mur re*n* ancumbra
      [tranceat iiij^{tus} exulator super equum

PRIMUS EXULATOR

A me*r*yasek me*r*yasek
del ote sans galosek
    peys ragovy
2116 na veua lesk*is* in tan
ha the se*r*vont in certan
    me a veth bys venary

FIRST OUTLAW.

Now mates, look around !
If ye see, so mote I go,
2088   Any one wandering by the wood,
Guide his purse to me quick.
He shall have God's curse
    Who speaks against robbing.

Here fire comes upon them.

SECOND OUTLAW.

2092 Out ! woe's us ! great and small !
All the wood is on fire !
    We are burnt to ashes !
Misfortune has come on us :
2096 That is for the devilry
    That we have done here in the world.

THIRD OUTLAW.

Ah be silent ! the devil to burn thee !
Why, what is the hurry
2100   That is with thee, and the skipping ?
The light I know :
Is it not now the moon
    Since she is rising ?

FOURTH OUTLAW.

2104 Out, out, let us flee.
The wood is burning
    To a real blaze.   [*a horse ready.*
Out, out, we shall be scalded
2108 Hence fly forthwith
    I will if I can.
And God's curse on the work !
Where for me is my black horse ?
2112   May the great devil encumber him !
    [*Let the fourth outlaw go off on a horse.*

FIRST OUTLAW.

O Meriasek, Meriasek,
As thou art a mighty saint,
    Pray for me
2116 That I be not burnt in fire,
And thy servant certainly
    I will be for ever.

SECUNDUS EXULATOR

Meryasek sav vy heb flovs
2120 marsyv guir a glowys covs
    the voys galosek oma
thyso omry
y fannavy
2124   bys venary mar pewa   [*finit*

TERTIUS EXULATOR

Meryasek del oys guir sans
lemen prest sav ov bevnans
    ha thys y fanaff omry

QUINTUS EXULATOR

2128 me a greys in meryasek
y vones eff galosek
    servont dotho bethevy
ha rag ov fehas mosek
2132   mercy ihesu me a gry   [*finit*

PRIMUS EXULATOR

Gras the crist ha meryasek
sawys on ny glan ha tek
    the orth mys[ch]eff in torma
p. 84.   2136 mones dotho ny a vyn
hay deserya pur ylyn
    pesy crist dyny gava

                [*ad meriadocum in monte*

Meryasek lowene dys
2140 omma ython devethys
    rag pesy the cusel preyst
ny revue tus ongrasyas
ha re vsias hager gas
2144   raffna ladra pur lues feyst

Pan esen dethwyth in coys
ov mones sur a porpos
    the laddra tus purguyryon
2148 warnen y tuth bum a tan
ha luehes in pur certan
in hevelep leskis glan
    ny a vethe pur dyson

2152 Me a greys truethek
gueres thymo meryasek
    der henna y fuff sawys

SECOND OUTLAW.

Meriasek, save me without a flout,
2120 If it be true, as I have heard say,
    That thou art mighty here.
Give myself to thee
I will
2124   For ever if I live.

THIRD OUTLAW.

Meriasek, as thou art a true saint
Now quickly save my life,
    And to thee I will give myself.

FIFTH OUTLAW.

2128 I believe in Meriasek
That he is mighty,
    A servant to him I will be,
And for my stinking sin
2132   Mercy, Jesu, I cry.

FIRST OUTLAW.

Thanks to Christ and Meriasek,
Saved are we clean and fair
    From mischief this turn.
2136 We will go to him
And desire him right fairly
    To beseech Christ to forgive us.

          [To Meriasek on the mountain.

Meriasek, joy to thee!
2140 Here we are come
    To beseech thy counsel quickly.
We have been graceless folk,
And have used, an ugly case,
2144   To rob, to plunder very many indeed.

When we were on a day in the wood
Going surely on purpose
    To plunder full righteous folk
2148 On us came a blow of fire
And lightning in very certain.
Apparently clean burnt
    We were right surely

2152 I cried out piteously
' Help me, Meriasek!'
    By that I was saved.

ha part am felschyp gena
2156 ran in kerth re ruk feya
ran ny won pythens gyllys
maythovy ameys oma
ellas mar pethen dampnys

p. 85.

MERIADOCUS

2160 Pesugh mercy war ihesu
ha remembrogh agis du
guetyogh may fegh glan ȝesseys
na dreylogh the pegh na moy
2164 ha ragogh pur eredy
the ihesu crist me a beys

PRIMUS EXULATOR

A meryasek meryasek
an enevov bohosek
2168 kemer trueth mar kyl boys
na ve creya warnogh why
kellys ol y fyen ny
yowynk ha loys   [*finit*

MERIADOCUS

2172 Byth na gothugh in dysper
mercyabyl yv du ker
the vyns a vyn y pesy
pan us dywhy edrega
2176 y raff agis benyga
in nomine patris et filii
et spiritus sancti amen
the pup gruegh restorite
myns may hallogh pub termen

COMES ROHANI

2180 The ihesu rebo grasseys
hag inweth ȝᵉ veryasek
p. 86.   thyn ol ythyv coselheys
kefrys rych ha bohosek
2184 purguir a yll
lemen mones then feryov
an laddren pel mes an pov
gyllys yns purthyogeyll

2188 Grays the ihesu galosek
dre peiadov meryasek
oll yv helma

And part of my fellowship with me.
2156 Some away did flee,
 Some I know not where they are gone.
So that I am without here.
 Alas, if I should be damned!

MERIASEK.

2160 Ask mercy of Jesu,
And remember your God.
 Take care that you be clean confessed.
Turn not to sin any more.
2164 And for you very readily
 To Jesu Christ I will pray.

FIRST OUTLAW.

O Meriasek, Meriasek!
On the poor souls
2168 Take pity, if it can be.
Had there not been crying on thee,
We should all have been lost,
 Young and gray.

MERIASEK.

2172 Never fall into despair.
Merciful is dear God
 To as many as will beseech him.
Since you have repentance
2176 I will bless you
 In the name of the Father and the Son
 And of the Holy Ghost, amen.

To every one make restoration
 All that you can always.

THE EARL OF ROHAN.

2180 To Jesu be thanks,
 And likewise to Meriasek!
For us all is quieted.
 At the same time rich and poor
2184 Right truly may
Now go to the fairs.
The robbers far away from the country
 Are gone right certainly.

2188 Thanks to mighty Jesu,
Through Meriasek's prayer
 All this is.

an treffer a veth sensys

2192 meryasek as grontyeys
    gorthys rebo benytha
vi deth in mys gortheren
vn feer a veth in certen

2196 thum desyr in ketelma
in meys est an viij^res deth
an secund feer sur a veth
    sensys in pov benytha

2200 han tresse meys gvyngala
dugol myhall byth henna
    in plu wyn voala* sensys
ha meryasek benytha

2204   inna purguir campollys

p. 87.   *Hic Dux Cornubie pompabit dicens*

Me yv duk in oll kernow
indella ytho ov thays
hag vhel arluth in pov

2208 u tamer the pen an vlays
tregys off lemen heb wov
    berth in castel an dynas
    sur in peddre

2212 ha war an tyreth vhel
thym yma castel arel
a veth gelwys tyndagyel
    henna yv o[v]fen tregse

2216 Leferys yv thymmo vy
    bones in keverang penweth
den grassyes pur eredy
dres an mor dy eff a thueth

2220 nynsyv na pel
ov styward a glosugh why
covs annotho in tefry
    leferugh dym dyogel

p. 88.   SENESCALLUS DUCIS

2224 Clowys arluth galosek
eff yv gelwys meryasek
    den grassyes in y dethyov
gans pup ol ythyv kerys

2228 inweth del yv leferys
    dadder mur y ruk in pov

CAMERARIUS DUCIS

Arluth me a leuer guir
gallas henna the ken tyr

2232 nansyv sythyn tremenys

* leg. noala

The third fair shall be held :
2192   Meriasek has granted it.
      Worshipped be he ever.
Sixth day in the month July
A fair shall be certainly
2196   Thus according to my desire
In the month of August the eighth day
The second fair surely shall be
    Held in the country for ever.
2200   And the third month September
Michael's feast, that shall be
    Held in the blessed parish of Noala,
And Meriasek ever
2204   In them right truly talked of.

Here the Duke of Cornwall shall parade, saying

I am Duke in all Cornwall :
  So was my father,
And a high lord in the country
2208   From Tamar to the end of the kingdom.
I am dwelling now, without a lie,
  Within the castle of Dynas
    Surely in Pidar,
2212   And in the high land
I have another castle,
Which is called Tyntagel :
  That is my chief dwelling-seat.

2216   It is said to me
    That there is opposite (?) Penwith
A man gracious right truly,
Over the sea thither he came.
2220   He is not far.
My steward, have you heard
Speak of him really ?
  Tell me certainly.

THE DUKE'S STEWARD.

2224   I have heard, mighty lord.
He is called Meriasek,
  A man gracious in his days.
By every one he is loved
2228   Likewise as is said
  Much good he has done in the country.

THE DUKE'S CHAMBERLAIN.

Lord, I will say true
He has gone to another land
2232   Now it is a week past,

gans vn de*n* heb feladov
ny vue achy the kernov
in neb le vythol guelys

DUX

2236 Praga ytheth mes an pov
dremas o in y dethyov
ny glowys ken leferel
ny govsy mas honest*er*
2240 pur guir a fur a thadder
lues re ruk y gormel

CAMERARIUS DUCIS

Tevdar paga*n* ongrassyas
in povma eff re dyrhays
2244 del glovsugh ha nynsyv pel
ny vyn gothe vn cristyan
in y oges pur certen
marthys eff yv de*n* cruel
2248 me*r*yasek ganso lemen
helhys vue in kerth heb fael   [*finit*

p. 89.   DUX CORNUBIE

Out mylw* war an ky plos
prag na glowys helma kyns
2252 re*n* arluth the*n* beys am ros
me a ra pur cot y guyns
kyns ys dume*r*her the nos
eff a deerbyn trestyns
2256 hag a guayn pur sempellos
may kerna purguir y dyns

Bethugh p*ar*ys ov meyny
ny vanna alowe ky
2260 pur certe*n* achy thu*m* tyr
eff an p*r*eveth hag in tyn
avodia sur mar ny vyn
y woys a resek the*n* luyr

SENES[C]ALLUS DUCIS

2264 P*ar*ys on dywhy sur duk
mur a throk p*r*est eff re ruk
a pan duthe in povma
in menek in lestevdar
2268 yma y pe*n*plas heb mar
mur dotho ov resortya

By one man without fail
He has not been within Cornwall
Seen in any place at all.

THE DUKE.

2236 Why has he gone out of the country?
He was an honest man in his days.
I heard not other talk.
He spake not save decency.
2240 Right truly for much of his goodness
Many have praised him.

THE DUKE'S CHAMBERLAIN.

Teudar, a graceless pagan,
In this country he has landed,
2244 As you heard, and it is not long ago.
He will not endure a Christian
In his neighbourhood, right certainly;
A marvellous cruel man is he!
2248 Meriasek by him now
Has been hunted away, without fail.

THE DUKE OF CORNWALL.

Out a thousand times on the dirty hound!
Why have I not heard this before?
2252 By the Lord who gave me to the world,
I will make his wind right short.
Before it is Wednesday at night
He shall meet sadness,
2256 And shall gain a right simple loss,
So that he may right truly gnash his teeth.

Be ye ready, my household.
I will not allow a hound
2260 Right certainly within my land.
He shall prove it, and severely.
If he does not go off
His blood shall run to the floor.

THE DUKE'S STEWARD.

2264 Ready are we for you, sir Duke.
Much of evil now hath he done
Since he came into this country.
In Meneage, in Les-Teader,
2268 Is his chief place without doubt.
Many to him (are) resorting.

K

DUX CORNUBIAE

Kyn geffo eff myllyov cans
purguir ythons then mernans
2272   dre voth ihesu us avan
me a vyn gothfes praga
y tuthe sur then povma
      heb ov lessyans in certan
2276 ol warbarth duen alemma
      ov meny a luen golan

Dux descendit cum xx^{ti} armatoribus
[*w^t stremers*

p. 90.   DUX

Leferugh ov arlythy
pythyv guel thynny sensy
2280   the vetya gans an turant
mar calla y tebel far
drefen y voys sur heb mar
      erbyn fay crist dyspusant

SENESCALLUS

2284 Tregys vue in lestevdar
      honna yma in menek
sav plas aral sur heb mar
      us then tebel genesek
2288   berth in porder
honna veth gelwys goddren
ena purguir an poddren
      thotho prest re ruk harber

DUX

2292 The soyth ny a vyn sensy
      in hanov crist us avan
mar tryg in kernov defry
      ny a vet gans an belan
2296 ov baner dyspletyoghwy
      therago pur guir lemman
del goth the arluth worthy
me a vyn moys ahanan

[*ad tevdar*

SECUNDUS NUNCIUS *ad Tevdarum*

2300 Heyl tevdar emperour a rays
yma duk oma in vlays
      drehevys sur erthcbyn

DUKE OF CORNWALL.

Though he may have thousands of hundreds,
Right truly they shall come to the death
2272   Through the will of Jesu who is above.
I will know why
He came surely to the country
    Without my license certainly.
2276 All together let us còme hence,
    My household, with a full heart!

The Duke descends with twenty armed men
[with streamers.

THE DUKE.

Say, my lords,
What field is for us to hold
2280   To meet with the tyrant?
If I can, he will fare ill,
Because of his being surely, without doubt,
    Powerless against the faith of Christ.

STEWARD.

2284 He was dwelling in Les-Teader:
    This is in Meneage;
But another place surely without doubt
    The evil native has
2288   Within Powder,
This is called Godren:
There right truly the rotten fellow
    Has now made for himself a harbour.

THE DUKE.

2292 We will follow thee.
    In the name of Christ who is above.
If he dwells in Cornwall certainly
    We shall meet with the villain.
2296 My banner display ye
    Before me right truly now:
As becomes a worthy lord
    I will go hence.

[To Teudar.

THE SECOND MESSENGER *to Teudar.*

2300 Hail, Teudar, Emperor of grace!
A Duke is here in the kingdom
    Risen surely against thee,

ha ganso pur guir ost brays
2304 the vernans y fyn guelays
bostya a ra in certeyn

TEVDARUS IMPERATOR

Out warnotho an falge plos
me an deffy deth ha nos
2308 ree greff ovy erybyn
y a gren age barwov
tormentoris in arvov
dugh in rag guyfen vyleyn

p. 91.

PRIMUS TORTOR

[descendit ad teudar[um]

2312 Parys oll onn in arvov
y a schakyage barvov
neb a settya erthebyn
mar a peth reys sensy guel
2316 me a leuer dyogel
an iovle mur ny iust orthyn

TEVDARUS

The guel in hanov an iovle
duen heb nefre omsone
2320 y an prenvyth by my sovle
an duk hay dus rum ene
kyns gase weyll
yma parys dymmo lel
2324 pobyl omma dyogel
moy certen es xv myl

descendit cum xv armatoribus
[with stremers

Hic demon pompabit

p. 91a.

PRIMUS DEMON

Peys y say both fur and ner
golsowugh orth iubyter
2328 agis tassens an berth north
yma ov servons ov toys
belsebuc ny a vyn moys
thage gore in lel forth

And with him right truly a great host.
2304 Thy death he will see
He doth boast certainly.

TEUDAR THE EMPEROR.

Out on him, the false dirt!
I defy him day and night!
2308 Very strong am I against him.
They shall wag their beards.
Torturers in arms,
Come ye forward! Woe to him the villain!

FIRST TORTURER.

[He goes down to Teudar.

2312 Ready are we all in arms.
They shall shake their beards
Who set against thee.
If need be to hold a field,
2316 I say certainly
The great Devil will not joust against us.

TEUDAR.

To a field in the Devil's name!
Let us come without ever blessing ourselves!
2320 They shall pay for it, *par mon âme,*
The Duke and his folk, by my soul,
Before leaving work.
There is ready for me loyally
2324 People here clearly
More, certainly, than fifteen thousand.

He descends with fifteen armed men
[with streamers.

Here the Demon shall parade.

FIRST DEMON.

Peace I say both far and near.
Hearken ye to Jupiter
2328 Your holy father (?) from the north part!
My servants are coming.
Belsebuc, we will go
To put them on the right way.

II. BELSEBUK

2332 Mester henna yv grueys da
tevdar drok lor eff a ra
y confortya mar menyn
erybyn duen then tempel
2336 benytha ny welaff guel
es gul scherwynsy certyn

ad templum intret

TEVDARUS

Lowene dys du monfras   *[genuflectunt omnes*
me a vyn pesy the grays
2340   kyn moys the guell
byth ny garsen
gul da certen
na y predery dyogell

p. 91. b.   PRIMUS DEMON

2344 Tevdar wek manly omdok
ha byth na spar guthel drok
me ath venten
nynsa the ena the gol
2348 ragtho yma thymo tol
inweth rag the sovdrys ol
bethugh lowen

Sul voy ancov a rellogh
2352 the larchya preysys fethogh
kemendis wose helma

PRIMUS TORTOR

duen in kerth uskis lemen
ny reys dyn fors pendrellen
2356 mahum agen pev nefra

p. 91 *continued.*   SENESCALLUS

Ser duk me a weyl tevdar
ha parcel a throk coskar
pur thevrey orth y sewa
2360 covse ganso a vynnogh wy
ha govyn orto defry
in povma pendra wyla

BELSEBUC.

2332 Master, that is well done.
Teudar, evil enough he will do
    If we shall comfort him.
To meet him let us go to the temple.
2336 Never see I (aught) better
    Than doing evil certainly.

Let him go into the temple.

TEUDAR.

Joy to thee, god Monfras!   *[They all kneel.*
I will beseech thy grace,
2340   Before going a-field.
Never would I love
To do good, certainly,
    Nor to think it, surely.

FIRST DEMON.

2344 Sweet Teudar, bear thyself like a man,
And never spare to do evil.
    I will support thee.
Thy soul will not go to loss,
2348 For it I have a hole,
Likewise for all thy soldiers.
    Be ye joyous!

The more deaths ye do.
2352 The largelier shall ye be praised,
    (And) commended, after that.

FIRST TORTURER.

Let us come away at once now.
We need not care why we should go.
2356   Mahound will own us ever.

THE STEWARD.

Sir Duke, I see Teudar
And a parcel of evil retinue,
    Very seriously, following him.
2360 Do you wish to speak with him
And to ask of him seriously
    What he seeks in this country?

DUX CORNUBIAE

Manna purguir ov stywart
2364 kynthus inno tebel art
    byth ny vanna y thovtya
p. 92.   kynthusons ov thum̄wul creff
me a dava age grueff
2368   in age meske gruaff rovtia

                              [ad stallum

Ty turant a thyscregyans
    pendryv the kerth in povma
tytel na chalyng dyblans
2372   aberth mam na tas oma
    purguir nyth us
ty re wores mes an gluas
meryasek neb o dremas
2376   acontis certen a ʒus

TEVDARUS

Me ath wor gy mes an pov
    kyn moys avel meryasek
mar corthyyth an plos myn gov
2380   neb a thuk peynis anwek
    sur in grovs pren
a vethe gelwys ihesu
rag vyngia purguir me yv
2384   war y servons eff certen
devethys off ty myn reyv
    thage dyswul ol lemen

DUX

Ny seff henna yth galloys
2388   ty falge ky omschumunys
kynse me a scoyl the goys
ha ty a veth devenys
    avel losov
2392 rum ena the guthel covle
pagya mergh es by my sowle
    me a glowes in ʒ° pov
pendra deseff an map devle
2396   darvyngya war thuk kernov

p. 93.   ### TEVDARUS

Duk kernov hag oll y dus
indan ov threys me as glus
    poren kepar ha treysy

THE DUKE OF CORNWALL.

I will, right truly, my steward,
2364   Though in him is an evil art,
      Never will I fear him.
Though they are making themselves strong
I will handle their faces.
2368   In amongst them I will break.

Thou unbelieving tyrant!
    Why is thy way in this country?
Title nor claim, distinctly,
2372   On the side of father or mother here,
      Right truly, thou hast not.
Thou hast put out of the kingdom
Meriasek, who was an honest man
2376   Accounted certainly by folk.

TEUDAR.

I will put thee out of the country,
  Before going, like Meriasek,
If thou worshippest the dirty mouth of lies
2380   Who bore pains unsweet
      Surely on the cross-tree,
And who was called Jesus.
To take vengeance right truly am I
2384   On his servants certainly.
I am come, thou luckless (?) mouth,
    To undo you all now.

THE DUKE.

That stands not in thy power,
2388   Thou false, excommunicated hound!
Sooner will I spill thy blood,
    And thou shalt be minced
      Like herbs,
2392 By my soul, to make broth.
A girl's bastard thou wast, *par mon âme*,
  I have heard, in thy country.
What does the Devil's son desire?
2396   To take vengeance on a Duke of Cornwall?

TEUDAR.

Duke of Cornwall and all his folk,
Under my feet I will crush them
    Just like grains of sand.

2400 kynnago ov poscessyon
bras in meske sur ov nascyon
me ren moghheys eredy
conquerrour off
2404 corff da in proff
dovtijs in meske arlythy

DUX

Ny sensevy ath creffder
ty turant vn faven guk
2408 der an golen me ath ver
mar nynseth in kerth war nuk
quik mes am grond
predery a raff heb fal
2412 in the pov ythesta gal
peys gevyans warna losal
bo voyd am syght a pur hond

Py fyn alyon
2416 war crustunyon
omma deseves settya
me a ra ath pen crehy
may teverre an brehy
2420 ha pesy gueff ov metya

p. 94.

TEWDARUS

By my fay an we* besen
a latha margh a calla
indelle ty gargesen
2424 drok thymo ty a russa
a mennen vy
purguir sevel in cosel
na vanna mes ty losel
2428 yma myterneth ryel
a thue thum gueres defry

DUX

The vyterneth schumunys
theth gueres bohes a veth
2432 galwy dis bras ha munys
hag ol the varogyen keth
hath arlythy
me agis gorte in plen
2436 the crist del off servont len
hag ol ov fobyl defry

* leg. wel?

2400 Though my property was not
Large surely amongst my nation,
    I have greatened it already.
A conqueror am I,
2404 A good body in proof,
    Feared amongst lords.

THE DUKE.

I care not for thy might,
    Thou tyrant, one blind bean.
2408 Through the heart I will spit thee
    If thou go not away backwards
        Quick out of my ground.
I do think without fail
2412 In thy country thou wast a rascal.
Ask pardon of me, losel,
    Or get out of my sight, O very hound !

How will an alien
2416 On Christians
    Here desire to set ?
I will make of thy head a hash,
So that the juice (?) may drop,
2420   And thou wilt cry 'woe is me' to meet me.

TEUDAR.

By my faith, and well besene,
    If I could kill a horse.
So thou gudgeon,
2424   Ill to me thou wouldst do
        If I should like.
Right truly, stand quiet
I will not, but thou losel,
2428 There is a royal kingdom
    Will come to help me surely.

THE DUKE.

Thy accursed kingdom
    To thee shall be little help.
2432 Call to thee great and small,
    And all thy caitiff knights,
        And thy lords.
I will await you in the plain,
2436 As I am a loyal servant of Christ's,
    (I) and all my people, surely.

TEVDARUS

Ty vyl pen pyst
na gampol crist
2440   the ragovy
ha mar a qureth
ty a feth meth
    hath ost defry
2444 Plos marrek pour
    dar seposia
    prest a reta
omma settya orth emperour

p. 95.   DUX

2448 Ea ty falge nygythys
me ny won the voys genys
    in bysma the pastel dyr
na deseff ty allyon plos
2452 in ov hertons deth na nos
    ny rovtyyth pel gothfeth guir

Rag mellya gans tus vays
del o meryasek henways
2456   mur ty a far the lakka
by the dredful day off dome
me a leuer dys ty grome
    mas pur sempel nyth sensa

TEVDARUS

2460 Ser duk ty a nagh the fay
bo neyl presner thymmovy
    eseth kens haneth the nos
mytern alwar ha pygys
2464 mytern margh ryel kefrys
mytern casvelyn gelwys
    gans sokyr thym us ov tos

DUX

Dens an rena pan vynnans
2468   omma y a veth bohays
byth ny schappyons heb mernans
    re thu arluth mur a rays
kynfy omma m[y]llyov cans
2472   ny a vyn ages gortays
in hanov crist thyn yma wans
    orth escar crist batalyays

TEUDAR.

Thou vile blockhead,
Prate not of Christ
2440   Before me!
And if thou dost
Thou shalt have shame,
    And thy host surely.
2444 Very foul knight,
    Wilt thou think
    Readily
Here to set (thyself) against an Emperor?

THE DUKE.

2448 Yea, thou false scoundrel,
I know not that thou wast born.
    In this world to break up deer (?)
Do not desire, thou dirty alien.
2452 In my heritage, day or night,
    Thou shalt not assemble longer, know for true.

For meddling with good folk,
As Meriasek was called,
2456   Thou shalt fare much the worse.
By the dreadful day of doom
I say to thee, thou groom,
    Good, very frankly, I hold thee not.

TEUDAR.

2460 Sir Duke, thou shalt deny thy faith,
Or else a prisoner of mine
    Thou shalt be before this very night.
King Alwar and Pygys,
2464 King Margh Ryel, also
The king called Casvelyn
    With succour are coming to me.

THE DUKE.

Let those come when they will,
2468   Here they shall be a small matter.
Never will they escape without death,
    By God, great Lord of grace,
Though there be here thousands of hundreds
    We will await you.
In Christ's name we have a desire
    Against Christ's enemy to do battle.

TEVDARUS

Cryst ha ty me a thefy
2476 hag omma ol agis fay
 atlyan kepar del ogh
rag mennes thymo settia
ov sovdrys gruegh heb lettya
2480 then crustunyon pennov trogh

DUX

Dus rag mar quyk del vynny
in hanov crist a vercy
 theth gortheby parys off
2484 ov sovdrys duen warnetha
pur thefry kyns tremena
 ahanan y a perth coff

 gonnys] *Hic praeliabunt*

TEVDARUS

Ov sovdrys dregh* thymo margh [*horse aredy*
2488 na felle sur nynsus pargh†
 dare ov fobyl yv marov
ha me tebelwolijs
da ythomleth a feyys
2492 an duk yv corff heb parov

DUX

Ho sovdoryon lemmen ho
galles an turant then fo
 nynso abel thum perthy
2496 darum y bobyl yv marov
gorthyans the crist caradov
 grontia dym an vyctory [*ascendit*

Peys warbarth myns os omma
2500 bevnans meryasek yma
 parte thyugh hythyv disquethys
dugh an II. a dermen
han remenant in certen
2504 dre gras du a veth guelys

Evugh oll gans an guary
ny a vyn agis pesy
 a luen golon

---

* The corrector appears to have made this *keregh* leg. *kergh* ' fetch thou.'
† MS. *paragh.*

TEUDAR.

Christ and thee I defy,
2476 And here all your faith,
  Castaways as you are!
For wishing to set on me,
My soldiers, without hindrance, make
2480   For the Christians broken heads.

THE DUKE.

Come on as quick as thou wilt!
In the name of Christ of mercy
  I am ready to answer thee.
2484 My soldiers, let us come upon them!
Right surely before passing away
  Of us they shall bear remembrance.

  Guns.]   *Here they shall fight.*

TEUDAR.

My soldiers, bring me a horse!   [*a horse ready.*
2488 No longer surely now is there sparing.
  Ruin! my people are dead,
And I ill-wounded.
Fighting well I have fled:
2492   The Duke is a person without peer.

THE DUKE.

Ho, soldiers, now ho!
The tyrant has gone to flight:
  He is now not able to bear me.
2496 Through me his people are dead.
Worship to loveable Christ
  For granting me the victory!   [*he goes up.*

Peace altogether all that are here!
2500 Meriasek's Life is
  In part to you set forth to-day.
Come ye on the second day in time,
And the remainder, certainly,
2504   Through God's grace shall be seen.

Drink ye all with the play,
We will beseech you
  With a full heart.

2508 wy ag*is* beth gor ha gruek
banneth c*ri*st ha me*r*yasek
banneth maria cambron
pybugh menstrels colonnek
2512 may hyllyn donsia dyson

p. 98.

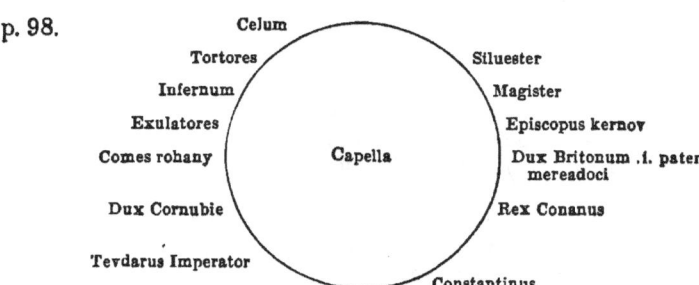

p. 99.

In secunda die Constantinus Imperator hic pompabit dicens

Ithoff gelwys costentyn
in rome chyff cyte an beys
empe*r*our curunys certyn
2516 ha der syluest*er* treylys
the voys crystyen
me a comond der ov gluas
naha dewov nagyv vas
2520 ha gorthya c*ri*st lue*n* a ras
age*n* pre*n*nas in grovs pren

Hic comes Globus cecus incipit dicens

A thu asoma grefijs
rag na wela tra in beys
2524 pendra dale ol ov rechys
ledyogh vy the veryasek
me re glowes galosek
y vose in y ve*r*clys
2528 thymo mar myn boys methek
inta y feth rewardys

ARMIGER DUCIS GLOBI

Bys dotho me agys led
dre voth ihe*s*u ny a sped
2532 ganso age*n* nygysyov

2508   Ye shall have, man and woman,
The blessing of Christ and Meriasek,
   The blessing of Mary of Camborne.
Pipe ye, hearty minstrels,
2512   That we may be able to dance forthwith.

Heaven.
Torturers.
Hell.
Outlaws.
The Earl of Rohan.
The Duke of Cornwall.
Emperor Teudar.
The Chapel.
Silvester.
The Master.
The Bishop of Kernou.
The Duke of Brittany, i.e. Meriasek's father.
King Conan.
Constantine.

*On the second day Emperor Constantine shall here parade,
saying,*

   I am called Constantine.
   In Rome chief city of the world
   Emperor crowned certainly,
2516   And by Silvester converted
    To be a Christian.
   I order throughout my kingdom
   Denial of gods that are not good
2520   And worship of Christ full of grace
    Who redeemed us on the cross-tree.

Here the blind Earl Globus begins, saying,

   O God, I am grieved
   For I see not aught on earth.
2524   What avails all my wealth ?
   Lead ye me to Meriasek.
   I have heard that he
    Is mighty in his miracles.
2528 If he will be leech to me
    He shall be well rewarded.

A SQUIRE.

   Unto him I will lead you.
   Through Jesu's will we shall speed
2532   By him our errands.

L

duen scon inban then meneth
ha why covsugh arluth freth
   dotho agis galarov

tranceat ad montem Mereadoci

[*And hys squyer ledys hym   and a staff yn hys
  handde*

p: 100.

COMES

2536 Arluth neff rum gueresa
ha yehes thym re grontya

MEREADOCUS

Arluth a ruk moyr ha tyr
  pup vrol rum gueresa
2540 ha roy thym in forth a guir
  ov bevnans oma gedya
ihesu arluth ortheff myr
  hath lel gras dymo grontya
2544 ihesu pup vr ol ov desyr
  yv in bysma the plesia

COMES

Meriasek lowena dys
  densa ath conuersascon
2548 purguir ythoys acontys
  hag in meske ol the nasconn
henwys oys pronter grassijs
  the ryche ha bohosogyon
2552 parys certen ath guereys
  the socra othomogyon

Me yv den dal nyth wela
  kyn covseff orthys der reff
2556 the pesy me a vynsa
  hag in ov gallus mar seff
  the aquyttya

p. 101. mar mynnes gul dym guelas
2560 fout syght numbus ommeras
lemen mar qureth ov gueras
  thys ny fyl peth an bysma

MERIADOCUS

A peth an beys num dur man
2564 the kyns sur na rych na guan
  awos peth me ny socra
rag nynsyv mas tarosvan
  ha pur sempel the cara

Let us come at once up to the mountain,
And you, strong lord, tell
To him your ailments.

Let him pass to Meriasek's mountain.
[And his squire leads him. And a staff in his
hand.

THE EARL.

2536 May Heaven's Lord help me,
And grant health to me !

MERIASEK.

May the Lord who made sea and land
Always help me,
2540 And grant me in the way of truth
To guide my life here.
Lord Jesu, look at me,
And grant me thy loyal grace !
2544 Jesu, always my desire
Is in this world to please thee.

THE EARL.

Meriasek, joy to thee !
A good man of thy converse
2548 Right truly thou art accounted,
And amongst all thy nation
Art named a gracious priest.
To rich and poor,
2552 Ready surely with thy help
To succour the needy.

I am a blind man that sees thee not.
Before I presume to speak to thee
2556 I would beseech thee,
And if it shall stand in my power,
Will repay thee,
If thou wilt make me see.
2560 In default of sight I am not able to help myself.
Now if thou canst help me
Thou shalt not lack the wealth of this world.

MERIASEK.

Of the wealth of the world nought concerns me.
2564 Neither rich nor weak the sooner
On account of wealth will I succour,
For it is nothing but a phantom,
And it is very foolish to love it.

L 2

COMES

2568 Mur a varth yv genavy
na gerte rychyth an beys
bewe pel ny eltegy
heb pyth na denvyth genys
2572 der rychyth pur eredy
den a veth degemerys
in ban in mesk arlythy
ha ganse prest enorys

2576 Govyn a myns a vynny
meryasek the ortheff vy
ha ny fellyth annotha
kyn teseryas punsov cans
2580 mar qureth dym gueles dyblans
gans our pur sur me ath pea

MERIADOCUS

Nynsyv the denvyth guertha
ov map grays du war an beys
2584 yma guel forth es honna
mar a pethy prederys

p. 102.   COMES

Ry peth dyso thym ny vern
vnw¹ gueles a callen
2588 sensy quarel orth mytern
purdefry my ny dovtsen
na russen nes
guel vya gene the wyr
2592 prest gueles es x puns tyr
rag nefre kyn rollen des

MERIADOCUS

Oll the promes hath teryov
guethy lemen avel kyns
2596 me a vyn in ov dythyov
gul warlergh crist pen an syns

COMES

Me ath peys a luengolon
ty the vynnes ov sawya
2600 rag kerense an passconn
a thuk ihesu in bysma

THE EARL.

2568 Much wonder have I
  That thou lovest not the riches of the world.
  Live long thou couldst not
  Without wealth, nor (could) any one born.
2572 Through riches right readily
  One will be accepted
  Up amongst lords
  And by them quickly honoured.

2576 Ask all that thou wishest,
  Meriasek, of me,
  And thou shalt not lack thereof.
  Though thou shouldst desire an hundred pounds
2580 If thou makest me see distinctly
  With gold right surely I will pay thee.

MERIASEK.

It is not to any one to purchase.
  My son, God's grace on the world.   .
2584 There is a better way than this
  If it be considered.

THE EARL.

To give wealth to thee concerns me not.
  Once if I could see
2588 To hold a quarrel with a king
  Certainly I should not fear,
  Nor should I make alliance.
  Better were it with me truly
2592 Now to see than though ten pounds (worth of) land
  For ever I should give to thee.

MERIASEK.

All thy promise and thy lands
  Keep them now as before.
2596 I will, in my days,
  Do according to Christ, the head of the saints.

THE EARL.

I beseech thee with a full heart
  That thou wouldst save me
2600 For love of the Passion
  Which Jesus bore in this world.

scor*gis* gans an ȝethewon
kentrewys treys ha dula
2604 gans gu lym in tenewon
del russons y y guana

Der an golon
y woys dyson
2608 may tevera
gueres de*n* dal
oma heb fal
orth ihe*s*u rag kere*n*sa

MERIADOCUS

2612 Orth ihe*s*u rag kere*n*se
a qurelles opery kyns
guereses ty a vye
oll ath rychyth me a syns
2616 nebes an fa   [*genuflectit*
p. 103.   ihe*s*u cr*i*st lue*n* a ve*r*cy
ihe*s*u cr*i*st y syght grua dry
de*n* denma del yth pesa

COMES [*genuflectit*

2620 Ihe*s*u arluth galosek
rebo gorthys benytha
han sans glorijs me*r*yasek
ru*m* sawyas vy in torma
2624 me a wyl leme*n* in tek
bythqueth ny welys cler*r*a
del wothen letris ha lek
lel se*r*vont du yv helma

OBSESSUS

[*y˙ devyll aredy by hys syde*

2628 A gueresvy me*r*yasek
orth ihe*s*u rag kere*n*sa
me yv vexijs anhethek
gans tebel sper*i*s oma
2632 nu*m*bus bewa
eff am keme*r* gans schor*i*s
may wothaffse*n* boys lesk*i*s
le greff es pe*r*thy orta

Scourged by the Jews,
  Nailed, feet and two hands,
2604 With a sharp spear (in) the side
  As they did pierce him

Through the heart,
His blood quickly
2608   That it might drop.
Heal a blind man
Here without fail
  For love towards Jesu!

MERIASEK.

2612 For love towards Jesu
  If thou wouldst act before,
Cured thou wouldst be.
  All of thy riches I hold
2616   Less than a bean.   [*he kneels.*
Jesu Christ, full of mercy,
Jesu Christ, his sight bring
  To this man, as I beseech thee!

THE EARL   [*kneels.*

2620 May Jesu, mighty Lord,
  Be worshipped ever,
And the glorious saint Meriasek,
  Who salved me this turn.
2624 I see now beautifully,
  Never have I seen clearer.
As we know, lettered and lay,
  A loyal servant of God is this (man).

THE DEMONIAC

[*the devil ready by his side.*

2628 O help me, Meriasek,
  For love towards Jesu!
I am vexed (and) loathsome.
  By an evil spirit here
2632   I have not life.
He seizes me with shivering fits (?)
So that I would endure to be burnt:
  A lesser grief than to bear up against them.

SURDUS

2636 Me yv den na yl clowas
meryasek ty yv dremas
　　ov breys thym yma ov ton
y halses prest ov gueras
2640 rag kerense crist map ras
　　myr thynny bohosogyon　　　　*[genuflectit*

MERIADOCUS

Ihesu crist der the vercy
　　mar sus drok sperys ogas
2644 ihesu gorre thy teythy
　　hag omma darber zehas
　　then ij denma
p. 104.　may fo guelys
2648 ov boys in beys
　　orth the servya

DEMON　　　　*[vlulat en[er]goumenus*

Out o' warnes meryasek
ty yv thymo molothek
2652 　orth ov domhel dres an pov ·
genes prest me numbus creys
wath me a ra moys deseys
　rag atty dyso myngov

OBSESSUS

2656 The ihesu rebo grasseys
an drok sperys avodys
　　yma sur the ortheff vy
sav off numbus galarov
2660 meryasek in ov dythyov
　　sensys off mur dysogy　　　　*[ffinit*

SURDUS

Ha my a clov
　　mar tha del reys
2664 in ov dethyov
　　ythoff sensys
　　　the veryasek
　　dretho sawys
2668 ha gueresys
　　ython purdek　　　　*[ffinit*

A DEAF MAN.

2636 I am one who cannot hear.
Meriasek, thou art a worthy man,
My judgment to me is bearing
That thou couldst at once heal me.
2640 For love of Christ, son of grace,
Look at us, poor (fellows).   [*He kneels.*

MERIASEK.

Jesu Christ, through thy mercy,
If there be an evil spirit at hand
2644 Jesu, put him to his faculties,
And here prepare healing
For these two men.
So that it may be seen
2648 That I am on earth
Serving thee.

THE DEMON   [*the demoniac howleth.*

Out, out on thee, Meriasek!
Thou art to me accursed
2652 Driving me through the country.
By thee now I have not strength,
Yet I will go, disease
To sow for thee, thou mouth of lies.

THE DEMONIAC.

2656 To Jesu be thanks!
The evil spirit gone forth
Is surely from me.
Whole am I, I have not ills.
2660 Meriasek, in my days
I am greatly bound to thee.

THE DEAF MAN.

And I hear
As well as need (be).
2664 In my days
I am bound
To Meriasek.
Through him healed
2668 And cured
We are right fairly.

COMES GLOBUS

Meryasek gorthys reby
genes confortis onny
2672 ese in *mur* a ponfos
ha dreys sur the lowena
ny a beys rag venytha
 crist re sensa the gallos

p. 105.

MERIADOCUS

2676 Ov flehys wek eugh why dre
ov banneth genogh neffre
 na letyogh vy am servys
ha guetyogh the du grassee
2680 eff re ruk agis sawye
 adar my cresugh pup preys
  [*tranceunt omnes domum*

Hic Comes venetensis pompabit

Me yv ʒurle in venetens
arluth mur ov denyte
2684 then arluth du murworthyens
 ha grays thym ʒy ventine
 re tharbarre
epscop an pov yv marov
2688 then colgy heb feladov
 me a vyn moys aleme
reys yv thym meres hythov
agen epscop thynny pyv a ve

ARMIGER COMITIS* VENETENSIS

2692 Ser arluth ny a genogh
hebogh why sur na menogh
 ny sped mater in povma
yma rych ha bohosek
2696 ov teserya meryasek
 epscop pur guir may fova [*descendit*

p. 106.   COMES VENETENSIS
     [*ad decanum in collegio† in placea*

Ser deyn lowene dywy
ha the oll agys colgy
2700 me re duth sav guel aveys
rag gothfes purthyogel
pyv a veth epscop in lel
 omma lemen dewesys

* MS. comes   † MS. colegia

EARL GLOBUS.

Meriasek, worshipped be thou!
By thee comforted are we
2672 Who were in much trouble,
And brought surely to joy.
We will pray for ever
  May Christ keep thy power!

MERIASEK.

2676 My sweet children, go ye home.
My blessing with you ever!
  Do not hinder me in my service.
And take care to give thanks to God.
2680 He hath healed you
  Through (?) me, believe ye always.

         [All pass home.

Here the Earl of Vannes shall parade.

I am earl in Vannes.
  A lord, great my dignity.
2684 To the Lord God, great worship,
  And grace to me to maintain it.
   May he vouchsafe!
The bishop of the country is dead:
2688 To the college without fail
  I will go hence.
Needful is it for me to see to-day
  Our bishop for us who shall be.

A SQUIRE OF THE EARL OF VANNES.

2692 Sir lord, we will go with you.
Without you surely not often
  Speeds a matter in this country.
Rich and poor are
2696 Desiring Meriasek
  That he be bishop right truly *[he goes down.*

THE EARL OF VANNES
  [to the dean in the college on the stage.

Sir Dean, joy to thee,
And to all your college.
2700 I have come, saving better advice.
To know right certainly
Who shall be bishop loyally
  Here now chosen?

DECANUS· [*in placea*

2704 Ser ʒurle ov arluth worthy
oma wolcum sur owhy
    peys da on ag*is* aveys
rag gothfos pur eredy
2708 pyv a vo epscop thynny
    in guelle p*r*eys

COMES VENETENSIS

Yma oll an come*n* voys
gans me*r*yasek ov cul noyys
2712   may fo epscop eredy
ha me ny won de*n* byth wel
pyv a vyn ken leferel
    gorthebugh o*m*ma dynny
            [*Comes trancit domum*

CANONICUS

2716 Ny yv certen lowenek
rag cafus dyn me*r*yasek
    the voys revler
a the*n*sa nynson tollys
2720 danvenogh rag y vollys
    ov arluth ker

p. 107.   COMES VENETENSIS

Dus in rag ov masege*r*
ke thym the pap selueste*r*
2724   laue*r* boys an guelhevyn
a vreten* orth y pesy
rag me*r*yasek de*n* worthy
epscop in venete*n*sy
2728   y cafus p*r*est y fe*n*syn

NUNCIUS PRIMUS *ad comes* (sic) *venetensis*

Ser ʒurle ny vethugh tollys
the dre y troff y vollys
    bys oma ny letya pel
2732 mones a raff
uskis ha schaff
    genogh fa*r*wel

* MS. a vrete*r*.

THE DEAN [*on the stage.*

2704 Sir Earl, my worthy lord,
Here welcome surely are ye.
Well satisfied shall we be with your advice
To know right readily
2708 Who should be bishop for us
In the shortest time.

THE EARL OF VANNES.

All the common voice is
With Meriasek making a noise
2712 That he be bishop readily,
And I know not any one better.
Whoso will say otherwise
Answer ye here to us.
[*the Earl goes home.*

THE CANON.

2716 We are certainly joyous
To find for us Meriasek.
To be ruler.
In the goodman we are not deceived:
2720 Send ye for his bulls,
My dear lord.

THE EARL OF VANNES.

Come forward, my messenger!
Go for me to Pope Silvester,
2724 Say that the chiefs
Of Brittany are beseeching him
For Meriasek, a worthy man.
Bishop of Vannes,
2728 Have him at once we would.

FIRST MESSENGER *to the Earl of Vannes.*

Sir Earl, you shall not be deceived,
Home I will bring his bulls,
Even here I will not delay longer.
2732 I will go
Quickly and rapidly.
To you farewell.

SILVESTER

Gallus ha confort an tas
2736   rebo genen pup termen
ihesu an map luen a ras
sokyr ny mo ha meten
an sperys sans benygas
2740   y gras genen may keffen
maria mam ha guerhas
the vercy du peys ragoen

Mercy du prest yv parys
2744   the vap den mar an wyla
nynsyv y voth boys kelys
an peth a ruk the prenna
p. 108.   insol bethugh glan ȝesseys
2748   avodyogh pegh in bysma
ha rag an pehas us grueys
kemerogh luen edrega
ha bethugh war
2752   na dreylogh ȝe pegh na moy
ha why a thue sur then ioy
us in neff nangeves par

PRIMUS NUNCIUS   [ad silvestrem

Sylvester gorthyans dywhy
2756   oma danvenys ovy
a vreten* pur eredy
rag weles sur arluth wek
gallus may fo meryasek
2760   epscop sacrys purdefry
in venetens† cyte dek
helmyv both an arlythy

SILVESTER

Wolcum ythos ov map wek
2764   den grassyes yv meryasek
del glowys y acontia
y vollys a veth screfys
ha waree grueys dis parys
2768   may hylly prest lafuria

        [bollys aredy.

CARDINALE   [to yᵉ masyger

Yma an bollys parys
maseger kemery dis
der lescyens ov arluth da

---

* MS. vrereten   † MS. vetenens

SILVESTER.

The might and the comfort of the Father
2736　　Be with us always!
Jesu, the Son full of grace
　　Succour us evening (?) and morning!
The holy blessed Spirit
2740　　His grace with us that we may have,
Mary, Mother and Virgin,
　　To God's mercy pray for us.

God's mercy is ever ready
2744　　For the son of man if he seeks it.
It is not His will that
　　What he has redeemed should be lost.
Up! be ye clean confessed,
2748　　Avoid ye sin in this world,
And for the sin that is done
　　Take full repentance,
　　　And be ye wary,
2752　Turn unto sin no more,
And ye shall surely come to the joy
　　That is in heaven (and) that hath no equal.

FIRST MESSENGER　　　　　　[to Silvester.

Silvester, worship to you!
2756　Here am I sent
　　From Brittany very readily
To seek surely, sweet lord,
Power that Meriasek be
2760　　Consecrated bishop right earnestly
In Vannes, a fair city.
　　This is the will of the lords.

SILVESTER.

Welcome art thou, sweet son!
2764　A gracious man is Meriasek,
　　As I have heard him accounted.
His bulls shall be written
And anon made ready for thee
2768　　So that thou mayst at once go onward.

　　　　　　　　　　　　　[bulls ready.

A CARDINAL　　　　[to the Messenger.

The bulls are ready.
Messenger, take them to thee
　　By licence of my good lord.

2772 yma notijs
sur ha covsis
mur thadder an keth denna

p. 109.   **PRIMUS NUNCIUS**

Ov arluth dywhy mur grays
2776 mar uskis why the vynnays
spedia sur ov negysyov
kumyas pesa
rag moys lema
2780 troha ham pov

SILVESTER

Banneth crist rebo genes
dynerugh arlythy an gluaes
thymo vy ha meryasek
2784 den grascyes ef a veth lel
byth nystufons guel bugel
in age oys gor na gruek

NUNCIUS   [*ad comitem venitensem*

Heyl ser ȝurle in agis tour
2788 ov negesyov spedijs dour
the porpos yma gena
kemerugh thygh an bollys
meryasek pan gampollys
2792 an pap a ruk y presia

COMES VENETENSIS

Maseger wolcum ythos
lemmen ens tus then guelfos
the kerhes dyn meryasek
2796 dotho degogh lytherov
del ma guelheven an pov
orth y exaltya purdek

p. 110.   **DECANUS**

Arluth henna a veth grueys
2800 duen alemma gans mur greys
the veryasek
yma eff prest in guylfos
eff a thue mes a ponfos
2804 ganso mar plek

2772 There is noted
Surely and spoken
    Much goodness of that same man.

FIRST MESSENGER.

My lord, to you much thanks,
2776 So quickly that thou wouldst
    Speed surely my errands.
Leave I pray
To go hence
2780   To my province.

SILVESTER.

Christ's blessing be with thee!
Greet ye the lords of the country
    For me, and Meriasek.
2784 A gracious man he will be loyally.
Never will they have a better shepherd
    In their age, man nor woman.

THE MESSENGER [to the Earl of Vannes.

Hail, sir earl, in your tower!
2788 My errands sped vehemently
    According to (your) purpose are by me.
Take to you the bulls:
When I spoke of Meriasek
2792   The Pope did praise him.

THE EARL OF VANNES.

Messenger, welcome art thou.
Now let folk go to the wilderness
    To seek for us Meriasek.
2796 To him bear ye letters
As the chiefs of the country are
    Exalting him right fairly.

THE DEAN.

Lord, that shall be done.
2800 Let us come hence with much might
    To Meriasek.
He is at present in a wilderness.
He will come out of trouble
2804   If he pleases.

[*ad montem ad meriadocum*

Lowene d*is* meryasek
at oma d*is* lyther tek
   lemen redya
2808 an arlythy ol y myens
rag boys epscop venitens
   purguir orth the deseria

MERIADOCUS

Mur grays ol then arlythy
2812 ha thyugh a chenons worthy
   ny vannaff an dynyte
na benythe cafus cur
na charge vyth in bysma sur
2816   hedre vevhen benythe

CANONICUS

Meryasek nynsos den fur
bevnans ryel a feth sur
   pan veste epscop worthy
2820 iij cans puns gyllyth speyna
in blethen ha moy inta
   the bollis parys yma
   nynseth in cost eredy

p. 111.   ### MERIADOCUS

2824 Vn conduconn sur owhy
kepar ha lues defry
   hythyv an dus sans eglos
pan lafuryens rag benefys
2828 ware y feth govynnys
   py lues puns a yl bos
   anethy grueys
ny remembrons y an charych
2832 a reys dethe ry har lych
   therag crist pan deer then vrueys

Myns angeves charge a cur
remembrogh* helma lemen
2836 eff a ree reken in sur
an enevov neb termen
   grugh attendia
mar peth prevys dyogel
2840 in gethna fovt in bugel
   go eff doys then keth chargna

* MS. remenbrogh.

Joy to thee Meriasek!
Lo, here for thee a fair letter
   Now to read.
2808 That the lords all
To be bishop of Vannes
   Right truly are desiring thee.

MERIASEK.

Much thanks to all the lords,
2812 And to you, O worthy canons!
   I wish not the dignity:
Nor ever to have a cure,
Or any charge in this world surely,
2816   While I am alive, ever.

A CANON.

Meriasek, thou art not a wise man.
A royal life thou shalt have surely
   When thou mayst be a worthy bishop.
2820 Three hundred pounds thou wilt be able to spend
In a year, and more well.
Thy bulls are prepared
   Thou wilt not go into cost readily.

MERIASEK.

2824 The same condition surely are ye
Even as many certainly
   To-day of the folk of holy Church
When they labour for a benefice
2828 Anon it will be asked
   How many pounds can be
     Made thereof?
They remember not the charge
2832 Of the need to them to give a lengthy list
   Before Christ when they come to the Judgment.

All that have charge of a cure,
   Remember ye this now,
2836 He will cause to reckon surely
   The souls every time:
     Consider ye:
If there be proved certainly
2840 On that day fault in the Shepherd,
   Woe is him to come to that same charge.

M 2

The harhe a vo an rol
the pelle why a wor ol
2844   hy a veth prest ov redya
nefre me ny fanna cur
marnes a vn ena sur
    du roy thym y lel revlya

DECANUS

2848 Ov breder duen ny the dre
ny vyn an den ma cole
    dotho orth neb a vyn da

                    [ad comes (sic) venetensis

ser ʒurle ny vyn meryasek
2852 thynny ny bones tasek
    na cafus cur benytha

                [ascendit et expectat ibidem

p. 112.   COMES VENETENSIS

Soweth prendreny dotha
mur a varth yv annotha
2856   vodya sur an dynyte
ny a vyn ompredery
forth rag y treyla defry
    ken plesijs me ny vethe

Hic pompabit episcopus kernov si placet

EPISCOPUS KERNOV

2860 Gelwys off epscop kernov
in breten heb feladov
    parlet worthy
the venitens* mannaff moys
2864 ena y fensen ov boys
    purguir gans an arlythy

CROSSER EPISCOPI KERNOV

Yma ena mur the gul
besy yv cafus cusul
2868   a tus fur a velogh why
pyv a vo epscop sacrys
meryasek yma notis
    boys dotho an ro defry   [finit
                            [descendit
                [hic pompabit secundus episcopus

                * MS. vetinens

The lengthier the roll shall be,
The longer, you all know,
2844   It shall be ever a-reading.
Never do I wish a cure
Unless of one soul surely.
    God grant to me to rule it loyally!

THE DEAN.

2848 My brethren, let us go home.
This man will not hearken
    To one who wishes well to him.

                [To the Earl of Vannes.

Sir earl, Meriasek will not
2852 To us be fatherly,
    Nor ever take a cure.

        [He goes up and waits in the same place.

EARL OF VANNES.

Alas, what shall we do to him?
Much marvel is thereat
2856   To reject surely the dignity:
We will bethink us
Of a way to turn him really,
    Otherwise I shall not be pleased.

Here the bishop of Kernou shall parade if he likes.

BISHOP OF KERNOU.

2860 I am called bishop of Kernou,
In Brittany without fail
    A worthy prelate.
To Vannes I will go;
2864 There I should like to be
    Right truly with the lords.

THE BISHOP OF KERNOU'S CROZIER-BEARER.

There is much to do there.
Need is to take counsel
2868   Of wise folk, see ye?
Who shall be bishop?
Meriasek, it is noted
    That to him the gift is certainly.

              [He goes down.
        [Here a second bishop shall parade.

EPISCOPUS SECUNDUS

2872 Ov crosser duen alemma
mur a weyl the gul yma
war epscop venetensi
meryasek yv dewesys
2876 sav eff ny vyn del glowys
y receva eredy

p. 113.　　　SECUNDUS CROSSER

Ser arluth by sen iowan
my an kemer purlowan
2880　　mar mynner dym y profia
hag a rose noblennov
appen sur an colmennov
ny vya reys ov dynnya　　　　[finit
[descendit secundus episcopus
[descendit comes globus

COMES GLOBUS

2884 Ser epscop kernov bon iour
an cowethes peseff dour
the venetens* moys a regh

EPISCOPUS KERNOV

Wolcum ser ʒurle be thys day
2888 wolcum ser epscop worthy
wolcum yv myns us genegh

SECUNDUS EPISCOPUS

Ser ʒurle hag epscop kernov
mur grays dyugh heb feladov
2892　　in vn forth kelmys onny
in venetens
yma dyblens
mur the gul del glowys vy

COMES GLOBUS　[ad comitem venitensem

2896 Ser ʒurle lowene dywhy
ha reverens then hole colgy
bras ha byen
ny re duth oma adre
2900 in govcnek exaltye
meryasek in pur certen

* MS. venetenens.

SECOND BISHOP.

2872 My crozier-bearer, let us come hence :
Much of work to do there is
   On the bishop of Vannes.
Meriasek is chosen,
2876 But he will not, as I heard,
   Receive it readily.

SECOND CROZIER-BEARER.

Sir lord, by Saint Jovian,
I will take it right gladly,
2880   If it be wished for me to prove it.
And I would put nobles
At the end surely of the halters,
   It would not be needful to entice (?) me.

EARL GLOBUS.

Sir bishop of Kernou, *bonjour.*
2884 The company I beseech earnestly
   That ye will go to Vannes.

BISHOP OF KERNOU.

Welcome, sir Earl, by this day !
Welcome, worthy sir bishop !
   Welcome are all that are with you.

SECOND BISHOP.

Sir Earl and bishop of Kernou,
Many thanks to you without fail.
2892   On one way are we bound.
In Vannes
There is clearly
   Much to do as I have heard.

EARL GLOBUS [*to the Earl of Vannes.*

2896 Sir Earl, joy to thee,
And reverence to the whole college,
   Great and small !
We have come here from home
2900 In the desire to exalt
   Meriasek very certainly.

p. 114.

COMES VENETENSIS

Wolcum ser ʒurle caradov
wolcum owhy epscobov

2904   mur a anneys gyllys on
meryasek yv dewesys
the vones epscop sacrys
    sav eff ren nahas dyson

[descendunt omnes cum comes (sic) *ventensis*

EPISCOPUS KERNOW

2908 The dre mar tuth y vollys
epscop eff a veth sacrys
   du dufen ken
prag na vyn y kemeras

2912 dretho y hyl gul gueras
   ha les the ol y ehen

SECUNDUS EPISCOPUS

Dotho wath bethens covsys
mar a kylle boys treylys

2916   then dynyte
densa dy conuersasconn
sur in mesk ol y nascon
   ny a wor guir y vose

COMES GLOBUS

2920 Heb na herre lafarov
ny a vyn heb feladov
   moys then teller may meve
hag alena sur y dry

2924 den beneges ha worthy
   yv in meske age hense

p. 115.

EPISCOPUS KERNOV

Henna ol ny a assent
duen alemma verement

2928   brays ha byen
tus hen guelhevyn an pov
agen attent why a clov
   leyk ha lyen

        tranceat ad heremum [in monte

SECUNDUS EPISCOPUS

2932 Oma yma meryasek
ser ʒurle arluth galosek
   covsugh why dothe kynsa

THE EARL OF VANNES.

Welcome, loveable sir Earl!
Welcome are ye, bishops!
2904   Very ill at ease have we become.
Meriasek is chosen
To be consecrated bishop,
      But he refused us at once.

      [All go down with the Earl of Vannes.

THE BISHOP OF KERNOU.

2908 If his bulls have come home
He will be consecrated bishop.
      God forbid (aught) else!
Why will he not take it?
2912 Thereby he might help
      And benefit all his race.

SECOND BISHOP.

To him again let it be spoken
If he can be turned
2916   To the dignity:
A good man of his converse
Surely amongst all his nation
      I know truly that he is.

EARL GLOBUS.

2920 Without any longer words
We will, without fail,
      Go to the place where he is,
And thence surely bring him.
2924 A man blessed and worthy
      He is amongst their chiefs.

THE BISHOP OF KERNOU.

To that we all assent:
Let us come hence, verily,
2928   Great and small,
Old folk, chiefs of the country,
Our attempt ye shall hear,
      Lay and learned.

      Let him pass to the hermitage [on the mountain.

SECOND BISHOP.

2932 Here is Meriasek,
Sir Earl, mighty lord,
      Speak you to him first,

mar a mynna dre dect*er*
2936 dones gene*n* heb awer
trueth yv y dystempra

COMES VENETENSIS [*ad meriadocum*

Lowene d*is* me*r*yasek
o*m*ma avel bohosek
2940 solla deth ty re vewas
lemme*n* der the vvelder
exaltijs the reelder
ty yv dremas rag the voas

COMES GLOBUS

2944 De*n*sa ath conue*r*sasco*nn*
ty yv in meske the nascon
ha sevys an gois worthy
nytheseth purguir ragoys
2948 oma trege in ponfoys
rag henna dus gene*n*ny

p. 116. SECUNDUS EPISCOPUS

The vollys dufe the dre
in venetenes the sacre
2952 epscop gallus thyn yma
henna yv both oll an pov
ty a yl in the dethyov
purguir boys se*n*sis detha

MERIADOCUS

2956 Na govsugh an dynyte
rag kere*n*se c*r*ist avan
epscop ny vethe neffre
na cur ny vanna certan
2960 a vap de*n*vyth in bysme
mas ov ene ov honan
arlythy arlithy eugh dre
na letyogh ov devoco*nn*

EPISCOPUS KERNOW

2964 Na wele covs gere*n*nov
hag orthe*n* guthel te*n*nov
gans an pap pan yv ornys
mynny gy kyn na vynny
2968 ty a in kerth gene*n* ny
hag oma gays the cumyys

If he will through fairness
2936 Come with us without grief.
    A pity it is to ruffle him.

THE EARL OF VANNES *to Meriasek*

Joy to thee, Meriasek
Here like a poor man
2940   For a long time thou hast lived.
Now through thy humility
Exalted to royalty
    Thou art for that thou art excellent.

EARL GLOBUS.

2944 A good man of thy converse
Thou art among thy nation,
    And raised of the worthy blood.
Not, right truly, for thee is it meet
2948 Here to dwell in trouble,
    Therefore come thou with us.

SECOND BISHOP.

Thy bulls have come home.
In Vannes to consecrate thee
2952   Bishop we have power.
That is the wish of all the country.
Thou mayest in thy days
    Right truly be bound to them.

MERIASEK.

2956 Talk ye not of the dignity,
    For love of Christ above!
Bishop I would never be
    Nor, certainly, do I wish a cure
2960 Of a son of any man in this world
    Save my own soul.
Lords, lords, go ye home,
    Hinder not my devotion !

THE BISHOP OF KERNOU.

2964 Seek not to talk words
And against us to pull,
    When it is ordered by the Pope.
(Though) thou wilt, though thou wilt not
2968 Thou shalt go away with us,
    And here leave thy height (?)

MERIADOCUS

[*meryasek yledyt*

Maria wyn gueres vy
maria the orthys gy
2972   erbyn ov both ledijs off
maria mam ha guerhes
maria da y wothes
    an charg peys da my nynsoff

p. 117.   COMES VENETENSIS

2976 Meryasek nynsoys de*n* fur
reys yv the ran cafus cur
    oma sur an enevov
le may fo bugel medel
2980 an lowern pur thyogel
    a leghya an dewysyov

Vnferheys kep*ar* del on
berth in eglos sent sampson
2984   bethens eff *consecratis*
gans worschyp ha revvte
nynsyv helme mas levte
    m*e*ryasek na veth s*err*ys

MERIADOCUS

[*yn y' deyn ys church*

2988 Rag kere*n*se an pasco*nn*
    a thuk ih*e*su ragon ny
kentrewys gans ʒethewon
    treys ha dule eredy
2992 guesk*is* gu in y golon
    may reses goys y guythy
cure*n* sp*er*n dre an grogon
    an dryn a hethes defry
2996   thy ompenyon
rag y gere*n*se leme*n*
agys pesy me a vye*n*
epscop benytha na ven
3000   a thu orth an charg ny von

p. 118.   EPISCOPUS KERNOW

Na govs thyn geryov vfer
dus oma ese yth cheer
    guyske the dylles yth kerhyn
3004 gene*n* ty a veth taklays
del goth the epscop a rays
    tra ny fyl dyso certeyn

[*her meryasek weryth a yowne*

MERIASEK.

[*Meriasek led.*

Blessed Mary, help me!
Mary, from thee
2972   Against my will I am led.
Mary, Mother and Virgin,
Mary, well thou knowest
    With the charge well satisfied I am not.

THE EARL OF VANNES.

2976 Meriasek, thou art not a wise man.
Need is for some to take the cure
    Here surely of the souls.
In the place where there is a soft shepherd
2980 The fox, right certainly,
    Will lessen the sheep.

One-minded as we are,
Within the church of Saint Sampson
2984   Let him be consecrated
With worship and sway.
This is naught save loyalty,
    Meriasek, be not angered.

MERIASEK.

[*in the Dean's Church.*

2988 For love of the Passion
    Which Jesu bore for us,
Nailed by the Jews
    Feet and hands,
2992 A lance thrust into his heart
    So that the blood of his veins ran,
A crown of thorns through his skull,
    The thorns reached surely
2996   To his brains:
For love of him now
I will beseech thee
That I be not a bishop.
3000   O God, of the charge I know not!

BISHOP OF KERNOU.

Speak not to us vain words.
Come thou here, sit in thy chair:
    Put on thy robe around thee:
3004 By us shalt thou be arrayed
As becomes a bishop of grace.
    Aught will not fail thee certainly.

[*Here Meriasek wears a gown.*

SECUNDUS EPISCOPUS

Sens the vagyl in the leff
3008 in hanov crist us in neff
ha maria guirhes pur
[*bagyll of syluer & myter aredy*

settyn muter war y ben
ny a yll bones lowen
3012 y thoys then cur

EPISCOPUS KERNOW

Lemmen gruen y venyga
ihesu crist map maria
reth gedya del vo plesijs
3016 lemen pen oys theth nasconn
tus nobil installasconn
deth gore yv devethys

COMES VENETENSIS

Lemmen oll ny yv plesijs
3020 meryasek y voys sacrys
epscop thynny
pensevyk yv thy nasconn
mentenour fay crustunyon
3024 socour the lues huny

p. 119   ### MERIADOCUS EPISCOPUS

An dynnyte thymo vs reys
ythevel gena y voys
schame sur moy es honester
3028 peys da du thym dustuny
nynsoff y cafus defry
a ioy an bysme numduer

NUDUS INFIRMUS

Du regys sawya tus vays
3032 rag kerense an pasconn
a porthes crist map guirhays
gueskis gu in y golon
treys ha dule kentreweys
3036 berth in grovs inter ladron
gans curen sperne curuneys
may hethons thy ompynyon
purguir an dreyn

SECOND BISHOP.

Hold thy crozier in thy hand.
3008 In the name of Christ, who is in heaven,
    And Mary, a pure virgin,
        [*A crozier of silver and a mitre ready.*

Let us set the mitre on his head.
We may be glad
3012   Of his coming to the cure.

BISHOP OF KERNOU.

Now let us bless him.
May Jesu Christ, Son of Mary,
    Guide thee as he shall be pleased.
3016 Now thou art head to thy nation.
Noble folk of (the) installation,
    An excellent day is come.

THE EARL OF VANNES.

Now we are all well pleased
3020 That Meriasek is consecrated
    Bishop for us.
Prince he is to his nation,
Upholder of the Christians' faith,
3024   Succour to many a one.

MERIASEK THE BISHOP.

The dignity that is given to me
Seems to me to be
    A shame surely more than an honour.
3028 Well satisfied, God be my witness,
I am not to have it really;
    For joy of this world I care not.

A NAKED SICK MAN.

God save you, good people!
3032   For love of the Passion
Which Christ, a Virgin's son, bore,
    A lance thrust into his heart,
Feet and hands nailed
3036   On a cross between thieves,
With a crown of thorns crowned,
    So that to his brains
        Right truly the thorns entered.

3040 lemen rag y gerense
regh thym queth rag ov huthe
me yv noth han guyns yv ʒeyn

COMES VENETENSIS

A thermas cry war the gam
3044 nynsyv onest thys heb nam
dones the rag arlythy
ha ty noth the corff ol trogh
me ny welys na menogh
3048 moy podrek ay esely

NUDUS

A rag oll an golyov
a thuk crist cleth ha dyov
the vap den rag saluasconn
3052 ov corff vy yv antythy
pedrys squattis ov guythy
numcar neb lues map bron

p. 120.
Menogh gans yrgh ha clehy
3056 me re vue in mes dre nos
rewys an doyr pur defry
ov golyov luen a plos
prest ov sclaldya*
3060 ny gar den ry thym guely
podrethek am esely
drefen purguir ov bosa

MERIADOCUS EPISCOPUS

Ty a feth purguir delles
3064 kynthellen vy prest inhoth
trueth mur yv the gueles
pedrys ʒ° kyk avel poth

NUDUS

Mur yv sur ov galarov
3068 ha feynt off heb feladov
mensen cafus dyweth tek
ny vyn mernans ov gueles
yma orth ov goheles
3072 drefen ov boys anhethek

MERIADOCUS EPISCOPUS

Ihesu re grontya ʒehes
thyso oma a dremaes
kefrys corff hag esely

* leg. scaldya?

3040 Now for love of him
Give ye me a garment to cover me,
    I am naked and the wind is cold.

THE EARL OF VANNES.

O worthy man, cry on thy way,
3044 It is not honourable for thee without exception
    To come before lords:
And thou naked (and) thy body all broken.
I have not seen often
3048   (One) more putrid in his limbs.

THE NAKED MAN.

O for all the wounds
Which Christ bore, left and right,
    For salvation to the son of man!
3052 My body is powerless,
Rotten, stricken are my veins
    Not any son of a breast loves me.

Often with hail and ice
3056   I have been out through night,
The ground frozen right earnestly.
    My wounds full of filth
    Always inflaming.
3060 No one likes to give me a bed,
Stinking in my limbs
    Because, right truly, I am.

BISHOP MERIASEK.

Thou shalt right truly have raiment,
3064   Though I (myself) should now go nakedly.
Great pity it is to see thee,
    Thy flesh putrid like rot.

THE NAKED MAN.

Great surely are my sorrows,
3068 And faint am I without fail,
    I would fain have a fair end.
Death will not see me.
It is avoiding me
3072   Because of my being loathsome.

BISHOP MERIASEK.

May Jesu grant healing
To thee here, O worthy man,
    Likewise body and limbs!

3076 rag den̄del dyso kefyans
ihesu arluth a selwyans
 sav an den̄ma heb ely
kem̄mer queth dresos dyblans
3080 omconfortya may hylly
    [*a govn or mantell apon Nudus*

NUDUS

Ihesu arluth galosek
ren̄ tala dis meryasek
 sav yv thymo pup esel
3084 war ov corff nynsus goly
an kyk poder eredy
 sav ha dealer yv lel

p. 121.   COMES VENETENSIS

Gorthyans dyso meryasek
3088 ny wothyan mer galosek
 the vote sur in bysma
worthy oys then̄ dynyte
ny a vyn mones the dre
3092 pup ol ay du a lem̄ma
    [*tranceat domum et cometis*

MERIADOCUS EPISCOPUS

Banneth du genogh rebo
an dynnyte us dymmo
 reys oma sur drethogh why
3096 me an grontse dyogel
lowen̄he the den̄ arel
 du dustuny

    tunc tranceant domum omnes

PRIMUS LAZARUS

Arluth an neff pendra raff
3100 rag certen̄ my yv mar claff
 ny gar map den̄ ov gueles
del re glowys meryasek
a wereses tus bohosek
3104 panak vo age deses
mones dotho colon̄nek
 man̄naff the weles guercs

3076   For gaining to thee affection,
       Jesu, lord of salvation,
          Heal this man without a salve !
       Take raiment over thee clearly
3080   So that thou mayst comfort thyself.
          [A gown or mantle upon the naked man.

THE NAKED MAN.

       May Jesu (the) mighty lord
       Repay this to thee, Meriasek !
          Healed for me is every limb,
3084   On my body is not a wound,
       The putrid flesh already
          Whole and diseaseless it is truly.

THE EARL OF VANNES.

       Honour to thee, Meriasek !
3088   I knew not that thou wast
         So mighty surely in this world.
       Worthy art thou of the dignity.
       We will go home
3092   Every one on his side hence.
         [Let him go home, and the Earl's (people).

BISHOP MERIASEK.

       God's blessing be with you !
       The dignity that is to me
          Given here surely by you,
3096   I would grant it
       Gladly to another man,
         God (be my) witness.

          Then let all go home.

FIRST LEPER.

       Lord of the heaven, what shall I do ?
3100   For certainly I am so sick
         No son of man loves to look on me.
       As I have heard, Meriasek
       Has healed poor folk,
3104   Whatever be their disease :
       Go to him heartily
         I will to seek help.

               N 2

SECUNDUS LAZARUS [ad meriadocum

Meryasek dursona dys
3108　ny yv ij then debertheys
　　　ny reys thyugh y leferel
　rag kerense crist avan
　ny ages pesse certan
3112　　　gul gueres dyn dyogel

p. 122.　　　　CAPELLANUS MERIADOCI

Sevugh ues a denewen
nynsyv purguir rag clevyen
　dones in fays arlythy
3116　thyugh cothe sevel abel
ha gortes pur thyogel
　　alusyen an den worthy　　　　　　　[finit

MERIADOCUS EPISCOPUS

A na moy ov chaplen wek
3120　na repreff tus vohosek
　dymo a vo devethys
parusse ovy dethy
es then brasse arlythy
3124　　us in gluascour thymo creys

Clevyon pendra govsugh why
us nygis dyugh ortheff vy
　leferugh in hanov du

PRIMUS LAZARUS

3128　Rag kerense arluth neff
gueres dyn orth agen gref
　　clevyon deberthys ny yv
notyys yma
3132　the voys densa
　　heweres prest orth tus du

MERIADOCUS EPISCOPUS [genuflectit

Maria myternes neff
　peys gena the crist a rays
3136　maria orth age greff
　an othomogyan guerays
maria del yth peseff
　sav an rema corff ha fays
3140　maria a wonetheff
　dywhy re wrontya zehays

SECOND LEPER [*to Meriasek.*

Meriasek, a great blessing to thee !
3108 We are two separated men,
Needs not to say it to you.
For love of Christ above
We would pray you certainly
3112 To heal us surely.

MERIASEK'S CHAPLAIN.

Stand ye without on one side !
It is not truly for lepers
To come in the face of lords.
3116 You it behoves to stand afar
And await certainly
The worthy man's alms.

BISHOP MERIASEK.

Ah no more, my sweet chaplain,
3120 Reprove poor folk
That may be come to me.
More ready am I for them
Than for the greatest lords
3124 That are in the kingdom, believe me.

Lepers, what say you ?
Have you an errand with me ?
Speak in God's name.

FIRST LEPER.

3128 For love of the lord of heaven
Help us from our grief.
Separated lepers are we.
It is noted
3132 That thou art a good man,
Helpful always towards God's folk.

BISHOP MERIASEK [*kneels.*

Mary, Queen of heaven,
Pray with me to Christ of grace,
3136 Mary, from their grief
Help the needy ones.
Mary, as I beseech thee,
Heal these, body and face.
3140 May Mary, whom I serve,
To you grant healing !

p. 123.

PRIMUS LAZARUS

The ihesu rebo grasseys
ov cow^t ty yv sawys
3144   cler ha tek knesen ha fays   [*finit*

SECUNDUS LAZARUS

Indella ythoys thegy
teka den nyth welys vy
     na clerra the ihesu grays
3148 meryasek reverons dywhy
     in guythres den benygays.   [*finit*

MERIADOCUS EPISCOPUS

Ov flehys eugh why de dre
ha thymmo na regh grasse
3152   mas only the crist avan
cresugh helma ov flehas
ihesu us ol ov queras
     ha creff ha guan   [*tranceat*

Hic pompabit Rex Massen

3156 Guelwys off mytern massen
     arluth bolde in ov dethyov
then guylfoys in purcerten
     me a vyn mones deyow
3160   prest the helghya
honter grua parys the kuen
ham meyny oll in tyen
kefrys lek ha mab lyen
3164   parusugh the voys gena

p. 124.

VENATORES REGIS

Arluth ny a veth parys
mylguen ha rethys* kefrys
     yma thym stoff annetha
3168 kyn settyen oma karov
dystogh y fye marov
     cresugh henna   [*finit*

Hic filius Mulieris cuiusdam ut invenitur in miraculis de beato mereadoco pompabit dicens

The den yonk ythyv dufer
3172   bones in mesk arlythy
ena eff a deske dadder
ha manhot pur eredy
may fo the guel

* MS. rechys

FIRST LEPER.

To Jesu be thanks!
My comrade, thou art healed,
3144   Clear and fair, skin and face.

SECOND LEPER.

So thou art, thou.
Fairer man I never saw thee,
3148   Nor clearer, to Jesu thanks!
Meriasek, reverence to you,
In work a blessed man.

BISHOP MERIASEK.

My children, go ye home,
And give not thanks to me,
3152   But only to Christ above.
Believe ye this, my children,
That Jesu is all helping
Both strong and weak.   [*Let him go off.*

Here King Massen shall parade.

3156   I am called King Massen,
A lord bold in my days.
To the wilderness very certainly
I will go on Thursday,
3160   Ready to hunt.
Hunter, make ready thy hounds,
And my household altogether,
As well layman as student,
3164   Prepare ye to go with me.

THE KING'S HUNTERS.

Lord, we shall be ready.
Greyhounds and nets likewise,
I have wealth of them.
3168   If here we set on a hart,
Forthwith he would be dead,
Believe ye this.

*Here the son of a certain woman (as is found in 'the
Miracles of Blessed Meriasek') shall parade, saying,*

To a young man it is a duty
3172   To be amongst lords,
There he will learn goodness
And manhood right readily
So that he may be the better.

3176 me a vyn mones heb bern
lemen the corte an mytern
ov mam wek genogh farwel
[*descendit*

MULIER .i. MATER EIUS

Ov map banneth maria
3180 genes rebo
guel plesijs me a vya
so mot y go
ty the drega
3184 in tre oma genevy
maria mam a vercy
me a vyn moys the pesy
kekefrys thagen socra
ad ecclesiam tranceat

3188 Maria lowene dis
ha gorthyans bys venytha
maria wyn beth guereys
ha socour thym in bysma
p. 125. 3192 maria numbus flehys
marnes vn map thum cherya
maria wek myr thy leys
ol ov threst warnes yma

FILIUS [*ad regem massen*

3196 Heyl dyugh ov arluth mytern
thyugh oma y tuth heb bern
kepar del yv ov dute
mar mynnogh oma neb preys
3200 thymo comendya servys
awos arveth me an gruae

REX

Wolcum oys ov servont len
then guylfoys mones lemen
3204 ny a vyn sur ʒᵉ sportya
kemerens pup y arvov
yma drok turant in pov
ny garsen orto metya
[*descendit cum armatoribus*

Hic Tyrannus pompabit dicens

3208 Me yv turant heb parov
in dan an hovle pensevyk
pan veua fol ha garov
nynsus in beys genesyk
3212 thym asetya

3176 I will go without grief
Now to the court of the king.
  My sweet mother farewell to you!
       [He goes down.

    THE WOMAN i.e. HIS MOTHER.

My son, Mary's blessing
3180   Be with thee.
Well pleased I should be,
  So mote I go,
    That thou shouldst dwell
3184 At home here with me.
Mary, mother of mercy
I will go to pray
  Likewise to succour us.
    [Let her go to the church.
3188 Mary, joy to thee
  And worship for ever!
Blessed Mary, be help
  And succour to me in this world
3192 Mary, I have not children
  Save only one son to cherish me.
Sweet Mary, see to his benefit
  All my trust is in thee.

    THE SON   [to *King Massen.*

3196 Hail to you, my lord king,
To you here I have come without grief
  As is my duty.
If you will, here, at any time
3200 To me entrust service
  For wages I will do it.

    THE KING.

Welcome are you, my leal servant.
Go to the wilderness now
3204   We will surely to sport.
Let every one take his arms,
There is an evil tyrant in the country
  I should not like to meet with him.
    [He goes down with armed men.

  Here the Tyrant shall parade, saying,

3208 I am a tyrant without equal,
  Prince under the sun.
Though he be mad and rough
  There is none in the world born
3212   To set against me.

moys the[n] guelfos me a vyn
the sportya purguir lemyn
kefrys brosyen ha kemyn
3216   parusugh the voys gena

p. 126.   PRIMUS MILES TYRANNI

Ov arluth a fur galloys
parys rag moys then guelfoys
    ny yv genogh alema
3220 agis greons yv lescijs
ha ny warbarth hernessijs
    cansov in arvov oma   [*finit*

SECUNDUS MILES TYRANNI

Yma oma kuen munys
3224 v lon bowyn dufunys
    y a depse in ij deth
lonk ylo ha lap keryn
scurel wyrly ky melyn
3228   blak bert labol ky degueth
        [*finit. dessendat*

REX

Nov honter quik myr adro
mar quelyth game ioy reth vo
    dulle the kuen desempys
3232 me a weyll busch brays a dus
annethe yma thym schus
    age bones ongrassyeys
        [*y⁰ hert aredy yn y⁰ wode*

SECUNDUS VENATOR REGIS

Hethov me a weyll carov
3236 pur* uskis y feth marov
    awoys ovn a then genys
ser kyng na vethugh dyswar
yma an turant heb mar
3240   er agis pyn drehevys
    yn pur certen

p. 127.   REX

Genen y feth gorthebys
gorten oma ov sovdrys
3244   ha warbarth omparuson
        [*and y⁰ hert yhontyd*

* MS. parur

I will go to the wilderness
To sport right truly now :
Likewise great persons and common
3216   Prepare ye to go with me.

FIRST SOLDIER OF THE TYRANT.

My lord of great power,
Ready to go to the wilderness
     Are we with you hence.
3220 Your greyhounds are leashed
And we together harnessed
     Hundreds here in arms.

SECOND SOLDIER OF THE TYRANT.

Here are little hounds
3224 Five loins of beef minced
     They would eat in two days
Lonk ylo and *Lap Keryn,*
Scurel wyrly a yellow hound,
3228   Blackbird, *Lalol* a workaday hound.
                [*Let him go down.*

THE KING.

Now hunter, quick, look around !
If thou seest game joy mayst thou have.
     Let go thy hounds at once.
3232 I see a great flock of folk
Of them I have fear
     That they are graceless.
              [*The hart ready in the wood.*

THE KING'S SECOND HUNTER.

Peace : I see a hart
3236 Right soon he will be dead.
     Notwithstanding fear of man born.
Sir king, be ye not unwary.
The tyrant is without doubt
3240   Against you arisen
     Very certainly.

THE KING.

By us he shall be answered.
Let us wait here, my soldiers,
     And together let us prepare ourselves.
             [*and the hart hunted.*

Hic tortores pompabunt

PRIMUS TORTOR

Cowethe na vethen lent
galles purguir an turent
   then guelfoys del glowys vy
3248 war y lergh guel yv mones
ken sur ny a veth blamyes
   ha kerethys eredy

SECUNDUS TORTOR

Thenny mar a cruk donfen
3252 agen part yv in certen
   warnotho sur attendia
ethe adre me ny won
agen mav plosek caugyan
3256   eff a alse aspya

TERTIUS TORTOR

Danvenen ny agen mav
guas pur uskis in meske ix
   the vothfes marseth adre
3260 ha dens eff thagen guarnya
yma ov quan rewardya
   y servysy rum ene

PRIMUS TORTOR

Hen na wer thyn bones lent
3264 ny yllyn pee agen rent
   the guel awos y wagis
mar ny veth thyn arluth guel
ny venen bones na pel
3268   by my sovle dotho pagys

p. 128.   SECUNDUS TORTOR

Ty vav scherevwa* del oys
myr an turant then guelfoys
   mar a mynna lafurya
3272 ha dus thagen guarnya ny
may hyllen pur eredy
   moys ganso thy confortya

TERTIUS TORTOR

Gueyt pel na veth heb doys dyn
3276 duen ny glebyn agen meyn
   lemen cowethe gentyl

* MS. stherevwn

Here the torturers shall parade.

FIRST TORTURER.

Comrades, we should not be slack :
The tyrant right truly has gone
　　To the wilderness as I have heard.
3248 After him it is better to go,
Else surely we shall be blamed
　　And chastised readily.

SECOND TORTURER.

To us if he hath sent
3252 Our part is certainly
　　On him to attend.
(Whether) he has gone homewards I know not.
Our boy, dirty hog,
3256 　　He might spy.

THIRD TORTURER.

Let us send our boy,
A lad, very quickly, amongst nine,
　　To know if he has gone home :
3260 And let him come to warn us.
He is rewarding poorly
　　His servants, by my soul.

FIRST TORTURER.

This helps us not, to be slack,
3264 We cannot pay our rent
　　The better because of his wages.
If he is not a better lord to us
We will not be any longer,
3268 　　By my soul, pages of his.

SECOND TORTURER.

Thou boy, most rascally as thou art,
See the tyrant, to the wilderness
　　If he will go onwards,
3272 And come thou to us to warn us,
That we may right readily
　　Go with him to comfort him.

THIRD TORTURER.

Beware, he will not be far without coming to us.
3276 Let us come, let us wet our mouths,
　　Now, gentle comrades.

in kerth galles tobesy
molleth du war y vody
3280   scherevwa yv in meske myl
[*iij tortores tranceant in tento filius* (sic)
mulieris iuxta

CALO

Wel an negys a veth grueys
the lowenha a*gis* breys
    dretho na ve   [*descendat*
3284   ser turant agys pagys
sur ny vynnons fovt wagys
    vn stap lafurye adre

TYRANNUS

Dar dufe hy the henna
3288   thage herhes marsama
    me as pee indan one*n*
may teffons thymo pur schaff
martese*n* gans keher claff
3292   dethe a pup tenewen
dyso gy y comondyaff
    wele dyn pob y welen

p. 129.   CALO

War ov forth hyr
3296   s*er* turant floyr
    honnyv marthys cusel da
atta guelynny pa*r*ys
ha na sparyovgh bethens peys
3300   rag dysky dethe tou*n*tya

TYRANNUS   [*ad tentum tortores*

Hov ser*is* pyv us intre
nyth heb oy atte o*mm*e
    malbe yeman in harber
3304   py halles an rema moys
re vahom du a galloys
    moghheys thymo ov awer

CALO

Me a*gis* gor bys detha
3308   in tave*r*n sur ov eva
    y mons pur ruth age myn

Away Tobias has gone,
God's curse on his body!
₃₂₈₀   Most rascally he is amongst a thousand.
      [*Let the three torturers pass into the tent of*
       the Woman's Son hard by.

THE DRUDGE.

So the errand shall be done
That your mind the gladder
     Thereby shall not be.   [*let him go down.*
₃₂₈₄ Sir tyrant, your pages
Surely will not for want of wages
     One step go on from home.

THE TYRANT.

Harm! will it come to that?
₃₂₈₈ To fetch them if I am,
     I will pay them under ash,
So that they may come to me very quickly
Perhaps with a sore stroke (?)
₃₂₉₂   To them on every side.
To thee I command
     See for us every one his rod.

THE DRUDGE.

On my long way,
₃₂₉₆ Sir flower of tyrants,
     This is wondrous good counsel.
Behold rods ready
And spare ye not: let them be paid
₃₃₀₀   For teaching them to teaze.

TYRANT [*at the torturers' tent.*

How sirs, who is it that is at home?
A nest without an egg, lo here!
    .... servant in harbour.
₃₃₀₄ Where could these have gone?
By Mahound, god of power,
     Greatened for me (is) my grief.

THE DRUDGE.

I will put you even to them.
₃₃₀₈ In a tavern surely drinking
     Their mouths are very red.

arluth gesugh vy the govs
ornugh ragthe pob y bovs
3312   may fo claff age duklyn

clamat ille in alio tento

Hov mestresy us lemyk
me a leu*er* the plemyk
    thywy nowothov nowyth
3316 guelheys yv ages nygys
by my fay y feth wa*gis*
    ha henna wy a clowyth
marsus dagre*n*
3320 dymo leme*n*
    yste*n*nogh oma an pyth

p. 130.   PRIMUS TORTOR

A wolcu*m* the dre gargese*n*
pendra leu*er* an podren
3324   a reys dym mones dotho
dus nes hag assy an poyt
thysogy eff a cost groyt
    kyns dybert so mot y go

SECUNDUS TORTOR

3328 By god ny re eves ree
yma bohes tus the pee
    molleth du thage*n* mest*er*
raghyl yv in y pemont
3332 argya orto ny ammont
    ythese*n* pel a theller

TERTIUS TORTOR

Ty vav prag na ruste dre
don age*n* wagys ome
3336   byth ny yllyn soweny
boys age*n* gober hep pee
ix nobyl a calame
    a russe sokyr thynny

TYRANNUS

3340 Wel wel me a bee an scot
ha warbeyn kylly ov hot
    by my sovle ny warth mas ran
lem*m*e*n* tobesy gueras
bys may fons ov teharas
    the gerthes gays an guelan

Lord, allow ye me to speak,
Order for them every one his bout
3312   That their buttocks may be sore.

He shouts in another tent.

How Masters, is there a sup?
I will tell uprightly*
     To you new news.
3316 Your errand is shewn.
By my faith there will be wages
     And that ye shall hear.
If there be a drop
3320 For me now,
     Reach out here the thing.

FIRST TORTURER.

Ah, welcome home, gudgeon!
What does the stinkard say?
3324   Is there need for me to go to him?
Come nearer and try the pot:
To thee it shall cost a groat
     Before parting, so mote I go.

SECOND TORTURER.

3328 By God, we have drunk overmuch.
There are few people to pay,
     God's curse to our master!
A rascal is he in his payment.
3332 To argue with him avails not.
     We are far behind.

THIRD TORTURER.

Thou slave, why didst thou not
Bring home our wages here?
3336   Never can we thrive
That our hire is without being paid.
Nine nobles on the calends of May
     Would have helped us.

THE TYRANT.

3340 Well, well, I will pay the shot,
And, on pain of losing my hood,
     By my soul, a good part will not laugh.
Now, Tobias, help
3344 Till they be apologizing.
     Let the rod go along!

* lit. ' to plummet,' *d'aplomb, ad perpendiculum.*

Tyrannus et calo verberant tortores

p. 131.

PRIMUS TORTOR

Dar ena ythesogh why
molleth‚du the tobesy
3348   eff re ruk agen tolla
a ser arluth faverugh ny
nebes esen ov teby
    y fethe hy in forma

SECUNDUS TORTOR

3352 Ser arluth na cronk na moy
trogh yv agen esely
    benithe ny vethen vays
myscheff war gorff tobesy
3356 eff revue treytour thynny
    gony ellas

TERTIUS TORTOR

Arluth gays thym ov bevnans
me a vyn pesy gevyans
3360   boys mar thyek yth keuer
molleth du the corff ov mav
mar uskis ytheth y pav
    thyugh rag gul thynny bysmer

TYRANNUS

3364 Lemmen ythogh rewardis
ha mar tuff thagis kerheys
    arta sur why a far guel
dugh genevy desempys
3368   alemma then guelfos snel

p. 132.

DEMON

Peys y hot both wylde and tame
y say monfras ys my name
benythe numbethe schame
3372   awoys gul drok
yma thymo servysy
orth ov gorthya pur vesy
    in dyweth a thue ӡum lok

SECUNDUS DEMON

3376 Der the ingynnys hath hus
sotel oys ov tolla tus
    sav me yv gueyth

The tyrant and the drudge beat the torturers.

FIRST TORTURER.

Ruin ! are ye there ?
God's curse to Tobias :
3348   He has deceived us.
Ah, sir lord, favour us !
We were not thinking at all
      That it would be in this way.

SECOND TORTURER.

3352 Sir lord, beat no more !
Broken are our limbs :
      Never shall we be well.
Mischief on Tobias' body !
3356 He has been a traitor to us.
      Woe is us, alas !

THIRD TORTURER.

Lord, leave me my life !
I will beseech forgiveness
3360   For being so sluggish as regards thee.
God's curse to my slave's body !
So quickly went his foot
      To you to do us injury.

THE TYRANT.

3364 Now you are rewarded !
And if I come to fetch you
      Again, surely you will fare better.
Come with me forthwith
3368   Hence to the wilderness, quickly.

DEMON.

Peace I order, both wild and tame.
I say Monfras is my name.
Never had I shame
3372   On account of doing evil.
I have servants
Worshipping me right busily :
      In the end they will come to my jail.

SECOND DEMON.

3376 Through thy engines and thy magic
Subtle art thou, deceiving folk,
      But I am worse.

O 2

ov hanov yv schyrlywyt
3380 ahaneff neb a ra fyt
me an aquyt in gode feyth

PRIMUS DEMON

Duen ny lemmen then tempel
an turant a vyn cowel
3384 gul sakyrfeys
may hallo guthel moy drok
myryn orto vn golok
kyn na vo hy rag y leys

[*descendat ad templum*

TYRANNUS

3388 Seris dugh oll in tempel
nynsyv helma du sempel
y terfen y enora

[*genuflectunt omnes*

omma pen tarov schylwyn
3392 offrynnya sur me a vyn
tan 5°gy map ydama

p. 133.   ### PRIMUS TORTOR

Thum du ny vanna boys gorth
mahum kemer dys pen horth
3396 gorovrys y gernygov
na gymer meth am present
lemen pan ywe messent
me an set ryb the frygov

SECUNDUS TORTOR

3400 Thum du offrynnyaff pen margh
tan ha gore in the argh
present worthy
yma orto skyrennov
3404 eff a dall denerennov*
rag baban a welogh why

TERTIUS TORTOR

Thum du iovyn benygas
me a offren iij bran vrays
3408 marthys rond age mellov
y a dall denerov vj
me as kerhes purguir de
war geyn margh mes an hellov

* leg. deneren nov ?

My name is Shirlywit.
3380 With me whoso will match
I will pay him off in good faith.

FIRST DEMON.

Let us come now to the temple.
The tyrant will completely
3384   Make sacrifice
So that he may do more evil.
Let us look at him one look,
    Though that be not for his advantage.

[he descends to the temple.

TYRANT.

3388 Sirs, come ye all into the temple!
This is not a foolish god:
    He deserves to be honoured.

[All kneel.

Here a white-naped bull's head
3392 Offer surely I will.
    Take, to thee a son am I.

FIRST TORTURER.

To my god I will not be adverse.
Mahound, take to thee a ram's head,
3396   Gilded his little horns.
Take no shame of my present,
Now since it is well-scented
    I will set it by thy nostrils.

SECOND TORTURER.

3400 To my god I offer a horse's head,
Take, and put in thy chest
    A worthy present.
There are on it frontals.
3404 It is worth nine pence
    For a bauble (?) you see.

THIRD TORTURER.

To my god, blessed Jove,
I will offer three ravens,
3408   Wondrous round are their limbs.
They are worth sixpence.
I fetched them right truly for him
    On a horse's back out of the marshes.

CALO

₃₄₁₂ Thum du iovyn in y fath
me a offren lawen cath
ny yl boys guel legessa
me as droys a voruelys
₃₄₁₆ le may fue an iovle elys
degens ytte om hascra
pen bogh ha gaver pelys
ov du lemen thyn grassa

[*et cantant omnes tortores*

p. 134.

DEMON

₃₄₂₀ Me agis son an barth cleth
drok hag anfusy inweth
guetyogh vsia
ha pyle bohosogyan
₃₄₂₄ molothov kentrevogyan
thywhy sowyny a ra   [*finit*

PRIMUS TORTOR

Nov lemen duen ygyn forth
agen tassens an barth north
₃₄₂₈ re roys thynny
purguir y venedycconn
ha pyle bohosogyon
y commondias thyn defry   [*finit*

SECUNDUS TORTOR

₃₄₃₂ Yma debren thov ij vregh
mar bel bones heb gul pegh
duen alema
mar sus treytour
₃₄₃₆ byth moy feytour
a vynner the dalhenna   [*finit*

TERTIUS TORTOR

Ny reys thyn fors py thellen
rag bener re thewellen
₃₄₄₀ menogh y rer y pesy
gans agen kerens nessa
ha wath oll the lowenha
pup vr oll y fethenny   [*finit*

THE DRUDGE.

3412 To my god, Jove, in his face
I will offer a tom-cat:
   There cannot be better to catch mice.
I have brought it from Morville
3416 A place where the devil has been anointed (?).
   Let him take, behold them in my bosom,
A buck's head and a skinned goat.
   My god, now thank us.

        [*And all the torturers sing.*

THE DEMON.

3420 I will sain you from the left side.
Evil and misfortune likewise
   Take care to use,
And to pillage poor men.
3424 Curses of neighbours
   Will make you thrive.

FIRST TORTURER.

Now at present let us come on our way.
Our holy father from the north part
3428   Has given to us
Right truly his blessing,
And to pillage poor men
   Has commanded us really.

SECOND TORTURER.

3432 There is an itch to my two arms
So long to be without committing sin.
   Let us come hence.
If there be a traitor,
3436 Ever more a scoundrel,
   He would be laid hold of.

THIRD TORTURER.

Needs not for us to care where we go,
For never may we return!
3440   Often will he be besought
By our nearest kinsmen,
And yet all the gladder
   Always we shall be.

SECUNDUS VENATOR REGIS

3444 Arluth me ages guarnyas
fetel ese turant brays
er *agis* pyn drehevys
attense enos in prays
3448 ha ganso ost brays ervys   [*finit*

p. 135.   REX

Pup ol tennens thy arvov
ny a gren agen barvov
mar ny omthegen the guel
3452 an turant yv ongrassyas
menogh y car ewyas
ha guerrya purthyogel

Sav bytegyns
3456 in spyt thy dyns
me an gorthyb gans reson
ha mar a myn
mellya *certyn*
3460 a wysk gu in y golon
[*ad stallum w^e ij stremeres*

TYRANNUS

Hov serrys pan a aray
leferugh thym w'out nay
pyv a ros dywhy lescyans
3464 rag dones in ov grond vy
the helghya best arlythy
gorthebugh war beyn mernans

REX

Ser turant ke war the gam
3468 bythqueth ny vue map the vam
genys wath then eretons
saff in neys na veth re tont
me yv prest arluth an gront
3472 nansyv blethynnyov vgons

p. 136.   TYRANNUS

Ser prence yv why us omma
guel vya dyugh omdenna
a dermen ha pesy grath
3476 mar a tuen ha debatya
mas an nyyl party omma
ov teberth purguir ny warth

SECOND KING'S HUNTSMAN.

3444 Lord, I have warned you
How there was a great tyrant
Risen against you.
Behold him there in the meadow
3448 And with him a great host armed.

THE KING.

Let every one draw to his arms.
We will shake our beards
If we do not bear ourselves the better.
3452 The tyrant is graceless.
Often he likes moving
And making war very certainly.

But nevertheless
3456 In spite of his teeth
I will answer him with reason,
And if he will
Meddle certainly
3460 Thrust a spear into his heart.

[*To the stall with two streamers.*

THE TYRANT.

How sirs, what an array!
Tell ye to me without nay,
Who has given to you license
3464 To come into my ground
To hunt lords' beasts?
Answer on pain of death.

THE KING.

Sir tyrant, go thy way:
3468 Never has there been a son of thy mother
Born yet to the heritage.
Stand nearer, be not too lofty,
I am now lord of the ground
3472 It is now twenty years.

TYRANT.

Sir Prince, is it you that are here?
Better were it for you to withdraw
In time and to beseech grace.
3476 If we come and fight,
Well one of the two parties here
At parting truly will not laugh.

Nov by hym that iudas solde
3480 ny senseff ath geryov bolde
vn faven kuk
byth nynsoff the omager
na der reson vyth danger
3484 dyso ny ruk

Thymo quarel
mar pottyth lel
a falsury
3488 the aquyttya
kyn moys lema
me a ra gans lendury

TYRANNUS

Ty falge horsen [n]am brag vy
3492 avond tellek theth cregy
hath chettis plos
me am beth goys the colon
scollys omma war an ton
3496 kyns hy bos nos

p. 137.   REX

Ny seff henna yth galloys
ty nag ongrassyas del oys
mentenour a thyscregyans
3500 ren arluth crist a vercy
me nyth sense guel es ky
denagh the tebelvryans

Bo me a vyn
3504 scollya the lyn
oma war ton
byth na wyle
neb ur braggye
3508 an crustunyon

TYRANNUS

Fy dis hag oll theth nasconn
fy mylwyth then crustunyon
denagh the fay
3512 bo ty ha myns us genas
a vyrwe omma re satnas
der beyn ha mur anfusy

THE KING.

Now by Him that Judas sold,
3480 I care not for thy bold words
One blind bean.
Never am I thy vassal,
Nor through any reason lordship
3484 For thee have I made.

On me a quarrel
Of falsehood
If thou really puttest,
3488 Repay thee,
Before going hence,
I will with usury.

THE TYRANT.

Thou false whoreson, insult me not
3492 A halter with a hole (?) to hang thee
And thy foul chits!
I shall have blood of thy heart
Spilt here on the meadow
3496 Before it be night.

THE KING.

That stands not in thy power,
Thou, ungracious as thou art!
Upholder of unbelief!
3500 By the Lord Christ of mercy,
I hold thee not better than a hound.
Deny thine evil privilege,

Or I will
3504 Spill thy blood
Here on meadow.
Never seek
At any time to insult
3508 The Christians.

THE TYRANT.

Fie on thee and all thy nation!
Fie a thousand times on the Christians!
Deny thy faith,
3512 Or thou and all that are with thee
Shall die here, by Satan!
Through pain and much misfortune.

REX

Nefre ny nehyn an fay
3516 awos ovn ahanes gy
nag ʒethov ongrassyas
rag mentons fay crustunyon
oma parys war an ton
3520 ny dovtya y voys treas

p. 138.   TYRANNUS

O! o' o'* bemont ectour
ens lemen pup thy arvov
an iovle agis acectour
3524 rebo pan vowhy marrov
mar quregh fynsya
sesyogh thymmo an prevyon
falge plosethes crustunyon
3528 then dour gansa

REX

Why a gren agis barvov
treytours kyn gul indella
yma parys tus arvov
3532 thagis gortheby oma
dugh pan vynnogh
sovdrys dehesugh detha
the ʒethov sur obaya
3536 nefre ny vanna orthogh

                              Hic praeliabunt

REX MASSEN

Out gony reys yv feya
bo neyl marov on oma
intorma ny yv rewan
3540 yma ran sur kemerys
gans an ʒethov ongrassys
a thu fetel veth lemman   [finit
                              [tranceat domum

TYRANNUS

Wel far yov sovdrys ryel
3544 an remyv fyys abel
us nag onen vyth sesijs

* The original scribe wrote *Out charlys* over which the corrector placed O' o' o'

THE KING.

Never will we deny our faith
3516   For fear of thee,
      No! graceless Jew!
To maintain the faith of Christians
Here ready on the meadow
3520   I fear not that it should be tried.

THE TYRANT.

Out, out, out, Beaumont, Hector,
  Let every one go now to his arms.
The devil be your attendant
3524   When you are dead
      If you flinch (?).
Seize for me the worms,
False, foul Christians,
3528   To the ground with them!

THE KING.

Ye shall shake your beards,
  Traitors, before doing so.
Ready are armed people
3532   To answer you here
      Come when ye will.
Soldiers, strike at them.
A Jew obey surely
3536   Never will I for you.

               [Here they shall fight.

KING MASSEN.

Out, woe is us, need is to flee!
Or else dead are we here.
  This turn we are too weak.
3540 Some surely are taken
By the graceless Jew.
    O God, how will it be now?

               [Let him pass home.

THE TYRANT.

Well fare you, royal soldiers,
3544 These are fled afar.
    Is never a one seized?

TERTIUS MILES TYRANNI

Va vn den yonk at oma   [capiat filius mulieris
me re ruk sur y sesia
3548   ser turont gothfeth thym grays   [finit

p. 139.   TYRANNUS

Nov wel far the gentel knyght*
eff a pee purguir y wyght
a our kyn boys dylyfrys
3552   hag a nagh pelle y fay
bo in preson eredy
pedry y ra in stockys

FILIUS

Henna yv an pyth na raff
3556   ihesu crist ny denahaff
awoys a ylly dym gul
wath in dyspyt war the dyns
me a worth kepar ha kyns
3560   neb a ruk an gol han sul

TYRANNUS

Wel wel mar nynseth ay nagh
in preson ty a in bagh
ho why geylers dugh omma
3564   gorugh helma in preson
mar ny nagh crist map maryon
ena pedry† eff a ra
                    [ascendit in curro‡ suo

CARCERARIUS

Ser turant the voth y ren
3568   dus in rag oma ty then
in preson the growetha   [ad Filius
ty re fue napyth redovnt   mulieris
moys the serry an turant
3572   lemen ty a oyl henna

p. 140.   GARCON

Ny a vyn y carhara
purguir na ala guaya
na luff na troys
3576   gogy pan vus ov perthy
oma ty a ra pedry
ny feth na deves na boys

* MS. kynght   † MS. predry   ‡ MS. turro.

THIRD SOLDIER OF THE TYRANT.

There is a young man, lo here!   *[let him take the*
I have surely seized him.   *Woman's Son.*
3548   Sir tyrant, give thanks to me.

THE TYRANT.

Now well fare thee, gentle knight.
He shall pay right truly his weight
     Of gold before being delivered,
3552 And shall further deny his faith,
Or in prison readily
     He shall rot in (the) stocks.

THE SON.

That is the thing I will not do:
3556 Jesu Christ I will not deny
     Because of what thou mayst do to me.
Still in spite of thy teeth
I will worship even as before
3560   Him that made the holiday and the Sunday

THE TYRANT.

Well, well, if thou wilt not go from refusing him
Into prison thou shalt go in short.
     Ho ye gaolers, come here!
3564 Put ye this man into prison,
If he denies not Christ, Son of Mary,
     There he shall rot.
         [He goes up in his chariot.

A GAOLER.

Sir tyrant, thy will we shall do.
3568 Come forward here thou man,
     In prison to lie.
Thou hast been somewhat (?) too lofty,   *[to the*
To go to anger the tyrant.   *Woman's Son.*
3572   Now thou wilt bewail that.

A BOY.

We will imprison him,
Right truly so that move
     Can neither hand nor foot.
3576 Woe to thee when thou wast parting!
Here thou shalt rot:
     Thou shalt have neither drink nor food.

PRIMUS NUNCIUS [*ad matrem Filius*

Heyl dyso a venen tha
3580   me ath war*n* pr*est* a vn dra
    the vap yma kemerys
  gans an turant ongrassyas
  me ny won ragtho ellas
3584   pendra veth grueys   [*finit*

MULIER

Ellas ov hole*n* yv trogh
ellas thym nynsese flogh
    mas eff na co*n*fort in beys
3588   maria gonys a raff
  thy fesy gans cole*n* claff
    rag ov map me a vyn moys

[*tranceat ad eclesiam beate marie. genuflectit*
  et expectat ibidem

Maria mam ha guerhes
3592   me a vyn the lue*n*besy
maria ov map gueres
    ha restoria thymo vy
maria me reth cervyes
3596   thu*m* gallus bythqueth defry
maria wyn rag ov les
    y colme*n*nov grua te*r*ry
maria mar a mynnes
3600   delyfrys bya surly

p. 141.   TYRANNUS

Hov geylers golsovugh wy
    me a charg war beyn tenna *
boys na dewes na regh ry
3604 .   the*n* guas a ruk vy orna
the pr*e*son pur eredy
    an vorov ru*m* lel ena
me a vyn pr*e*st y cregy
3608   y quartrona hay de*n*na

CARCERARIUS [*ad tyrannum*

Arluth the voth a veth grueys
eff nefre ny veth goleys
    me a wor the guir henna
3612   mar peth cregys an vorov
vastya boys heb feladov
    ny vene*n* adro dotha

* MS. ten*n*na

MESSENGER [*to the Son's mother.*

Hail to thee, O good woman!
3580 I warn thee at once of one thing.
Thy son is taken
By the ungracious tyrant.
I know not for him, alas,
3584 What will be done.

THE WOMAN.

Alas, my heart is broken!
Alas, to me there is no child
But he, nor comfort in the world.
3588 Mary I do serve:
To beseech her with a sick heart
For my son, I will go.

[*Let her pass to the church of the Blessed Mary.
She kneels and waits in the same place.*

Mary, Mother and Maid,
3592 I will beseech thee fully,
Mary, help my son,
And restore him to me.
Mary, I have served thee
3596 According to my power ever earnestly,
Blessed Mary, for my good
Break his bonds.
Mary, if thou wouldst,
3600 He would be delivered surely.

TYRANT.

How gaolers, hearken ye!
I charge on pain of drawing,
Neither food nor drink give ye
3604 To the lad whom I ordered
To prison right readily.
To-morrow, by my loyal soul,
I will hang him,
3608 Quarter him, and draw him.

GAOLER [*to the tyrant.*

Lord, thy will shall be done.
He shall never be loosed,
I know that of a truth.
3612 If he be hung to-morrow,
Waste food without fail
I would not about him.

MULIER

Maria me reth pesys
3616 rag ov map sur lues guyth
maria wath ny vynsys
 thymo vy gul confort vyth
maria me a weyl neys
3620 am creya vy fors ny reyth
maria mercy mar suys
 in nos praga nam clowyth

Maria nynsus nahen
3624 ny ammont ov peiadov
maria ov map certen
 yma in tyn colmennov
maria creys thym lemen
3628 rag ov flogh an caradov
maria the vap byen
 gene dre ytha hythov

p. 142. Maria ater the vregh
3632 dulle thym the vap ihesu
awoys ovn peryl na pegh
 eff a dre gena hythyv
 dus dus a vaby
3636 farwel genes maria
ny vanna the annya
 oma na moy ov pesy
       tranceat domum [*cum ihesu*

Ihesu crist lowene dys
3640 purker ty a veth guythys [*cofyr aredy*
 avel ov flogh ov honyn
hag in quethov fyn malys
in ov cofyr sur gorys
3644 oma alwethys certeyn
lemen me yv lowenheys
 moys the powes me a vyn

MARIA [*in celo dicit*

Ihesus ov map caradov
3648 myns us grueys heb feladov
 dalour y wothes certen
ha pendra us in golon
confort thum cervons dyson
3652 boys y carsen

THE WOMAN.

Mary, I have besought thee
3616   For my son surely many times.
Mary, yet thou hast not willed
    To do me any comfort.
Mary, I see again
3620   For my crying thou carest not,
Mary, if there be mercy,
    Why dost thou not hear me to-night ?

Mary, it is not otherwise :
3624   My prayer avails not.
Mary, my son certainly
    Is in strait bonds.
Mary, believe me now,
3628   For my son, the loveable,
Mary, thy little Son
    With me home shall go to-day.

Mary, outside of thy arm,
3632   Let come to me thy son Jesu.
Notwithstanding fear of peril or sin,
    He shall go home with me to-day.
    Come, come, O baby !
3636 Farewell to thee, Mary,
I will not annoy thee
    Here praying more.

                [Let her go home with Jesu.

Jesu Christ, joy to thee !
3640 Full dearly thou shalt be kept   *[A coffer ready.*
    Like my own child,
And swaddled in fine clothes,
Put into my coffer
3644   Here locked surely.
Now I am gladdened :
    I will go to rest.

MARY *says in heaven.*

Jesus, my loveable Son,
3648 All that is done, without fail,
    Well enough thou knowest certainly,
And what is in the heart.
Comfort to my servants at once
3652   I should like to be.

IHESUS

A vam grua del vy plesijs
neb ath worth a veth esijs
   kyn fensi polge ov cortes
p. 143. 3656 theth servont myr
grua the desyr
   ha both the vreyes

      [*descendit maria cum ij angelis
        ad carcerem*

MARIA

A then yonk fetel esta
3660 mur yv the lavyr oma
   heb y dyndyl
sav a vo in bevnans da
grays du purguir the henna
3664   in dyweth certen ny fyl

FILIUS

Ihesu arluth thum gueres
byth ny alla omheres
   dyegrys off gans gvynder
3668 ny won rum caredevder
pendra yv an golevder
   us adro thym heb awer

MARIA

Omconfort drefe warvan
3672 kynthos gyllys feynt ha guan
   wath ty a veth confortys
in nos na gymer dyglon
me ath dylerff an preson
3676   oma y tuth rag the leys

p. 144.   FILIUS

Grovs crist benedicite
pyv re duth thymo ome
   han darasov ol degeys
3680 nos tevle ytho nam nygen
ha lemen sur golvygyen
   adro thym yma cothys
hag yma forme a vynen
3684   myternes pur in y greys

JESUS.

O mother, do as thou mayst be pleased.
Whoever worships thee shall be eased
  Though they be tarrying a moment.
3656 To thy servant look,
Do thy desire, .
  And the will of thy mind.

    [*Mary descends with two angels
      to the prison.*

MARY.

O young man, how art thou ?
3660 Great is thy labour here
  Without deserving it.
But he who shall be in the good life,
God's grace right truly to that (man)
3664   At the end certainly shall not fail.

THE SON.

Lord Jesu, to help me !
I cannot help myself.
  Blinded am I by whiteness.
3668 I know not, by my loveableness,
What is the radiance
  That is around me without grief.

MARY.

Comfort thyself, rise up !
3672 Though thou art become faint and weak
  Yet thou wilt be comforted.
To-night lose not heart: *
I will deliver thee from the prison.
3676   Here I have come for thy good.

THE SON.

O cross of Christ, benedicite !
Who has come to me here,
  And the doors all shut ?
3680 A dark night now, to me not otherwise,
And now surely radiance
  Around me is fallen,
And there is a form of a woman,
3684   A queen, right in the midst of it.

    * lit. 'take not unheart.'

MARIA

Dore in mes the garov
the orthys an carharov
   prest me a den
3688 ha dyso an darasow
vgoreff heb feladow
nynsus dyalwethy gov
   am guyth certen

3692 Lemen ov map ke theth vam
ha lafer dethy heb nam
   maria theth delyfrya
ha spesly lauer dethy
3696 drens hy ov map dymovy
ha gruens ov servia deyly
   arta awose helma

p. 145.   FILIUS MULIERIS

Maria gorthys reby
3700 maria guyff nynsen vy
   genes the vones ledijs
maria thyso mur grays
maria na ve the rays
3704   gon guyr y fyen dyswreys

MARIA

Ov banneth genes heb nam
ham banneth y roff theth vam
   lauer in delle dethy
3708 kyn thevely dethy pel
ov boys heb y clowes lel
   ny vennen y ankevy   [*finit*
    [*tranceat maria ad celum*

CARCERARIUS

Out gony mata sa ban
3712 haneth oll an beys gans tan
yma purguir han presan
   ov colowhy
me a greys boys grueys forth lan
3716   ena defry

GARCON

An presnour in kerth galleys
han darasov oll degeys
   pyv an iovle revue oma

MARY.

Bring out thy legs :
From thee the fetters
    At once I will draw,
3688 And for thee the doors
Open without fail.
There are not false keys
    In my keeping certainly.

3692 Now, my son, go to thy mother,
And say to her without error
    That Mary delivered thee,
And specially say to her,
3696 Let her bring my Son to me,
And let her serve me daily
    Again after this.

THE WOMAN'S SON.

Mary, worshipped be thou!
3700 Mary, worthy I was not
    By thee to be guided.
Mary, to thee much thanks !
Mary, (if) thy grace were not
3704   I know truly I should be undone.

MARY.

My blessing (be) with thee, without exception,
And my blessing I give to thy mother :
    Say thus to her ;
3708 Though it should seem that far from her
I am without hearing her loyally,
    I will not forget her.

[Let Mary pass to heaven.

THE GAOLER.

Out, woe's us, mate, stand up !
3712 To-night all the world with fire
Is right truly, and the prison
    A-blazing.
I believe that a clear way is made
3716   There really.

THE BOY.

The prisoner has gone away,
And the doors all closed.
    Who the devil has been here ?

3720 duen then turant leferyn
a molleth du in gegyn
at oma sur drog athla

p. 146.   CARCERARIUS [ad tyrannum

A ser turant gony gony
3724 an presner in kerth defry
galles eff haneth in nos
golovder ganso revue
bythqueth moy ovn numdarfe
3728   re thu am ros   [finit

TYRANNUS

Out govy harov harov
py ma ov fresner feyys
why a feth purguir marov
3732   mara sywe dyenkys
rum lel ena
an horsens revue methov
ha re ases tus an pov
3736   me a wor thy delyvrya

GARCON

Ay turant ke war the gam
molleth du the vap the vam
yma ree ov leferel
3740 heb ty vyth nag ovlya
delyfrys der varia
fetel ywa dyogel
hagis boys wy de vlamya
3744   war vohogo[g]yon cruel   [finit
                                          [yerde aredy

TYRANNUS

Ay dar indelle vethy
mal myscheff regis doga
ov sclandra mar mynnogh why
3748   ha leferel ov bosa
omma cruel
why an prevᵗ du in test
have that me agis lest
3752   rag desky drok thym covsel   [finit
verberat eos

3720 Let us come to the tyrant: let us say:
O God's curse in the kitchen,*
See here surely an evil outlaw.

THE GAOLER *to the tyrant.*

O sir tyrant, woe's us, woe's us!
3724 The prisoner away really
He has gone this very night
Radiance was with him,
Never had I greater fear,
3728 By God who made me!

THE TYRANT.

Out woe's me, haro, haro!
Where has my prisoner fled?
You shall be right truly dead
3732 If he has escaped
By my loyal soul!
The whoresons were drunk,
And allowed the people of the country,
3736 I know, to deliver him.

THE BOY.

O tyrant, go on thy way!
God's curse to thy mother's son!
Some are saying,
3740 Without any oath or howling (?),
Delivered by Mary
As he is certainly,
And that you are to blame,
3744 To the poor men cruel.

[*a staff ready.*

THE TYRANT.

Ah, ruin, will they be so?
May ill mischief bear you off!
If you will slander me,
3748 And say that I am
Here cruel,
You shall prove it, God in witness!
Have that! I will hinder you
3752 From teaching (folk) to speak ill of me.

he beats them.

* lit. in the kitchen.

p. 147.

FILIUS

Hebasca thywhy ov mam
  mur reverons the varia
thynny prest y fye cam
3756   mar ny rellen y gorthya
  in guelhe preys
hy re ruk ov delyfrya
mes a preson mam kerra
3760   le may theua drokhendelys

MULIER

Maria rebo* gorthys
dasvewys yv ov sperys
  ov map the gueles oma
3764 fetel vusta delyfrys
laver thymo me ath peys
  ov map kerra

FILIUS

Maria thymo in nos
3768   purguir a thueth then preson
gans golov ha mur a tros
  in coske bo dufen dyson
  ny won esen
3772 hy purguir am degolmas
han dares dym egoras
hag vfel am comondyas
  thum mam the dre may thellen

3776 Inmethy lauer theth vam
me theth delyfrye heb nam
  sav thymo restoryans hy
ov map henna nynsyv cam
3780   pan vsy y flogh dethy   [finit

p. 148.

MULIER

The varya wyn mur grays
a vyna hy the guerays
  in dyweth ny veth tollys
3784 y flogh me a gemerays
the orth y yamach a rays
  drefen nages restorijs
  thymo gensy
3788 marthys claff o ov holon
an flogh then ymach dyson
  me a vyn don eredy

* perhaps revo.

THE SON.   *[he goes up to his mother*

Sweetness (?) to you, my mother,
 Much reverence to Mary!
For us ever it would be wrong
3756 If we did not worship her
  In best time.
She has delivered me
Out of prison, dearest mother,
3760 A place where I was evilly handled.

THE WOMAN.

Mary be worshipped!
My spirit is revived
 To see my son here!
3764 How wast thou delivered!
Tell me, I beseech thee,
 My dearest son.

THE SON.

Mary to me at night
3768 Right truly came to the prison
With light and much noise.
  Asleep or awake
  I know not whether I was.
3772 She right truly unchained me,
And opened the door for me,
And gently bade me
  To go home to my mother.

3776 She said: 'tell thy mother
That I have delivered thee without exception,
  But to me let her restore
My son: that is not wrong
3780 Since she has her (own) son.'

THE WOMAN.

To blessed Mary much thanks!
If she will help thee,
 At the end thou wilt not be deceived.
3784 Her child I took
From her image of grace
  Because thou wert not restored
  To me by her.
3788 Wondrous sick was my heart.
The child to the image at once
  I will bear readily,

Ha mos quik bys in eglos
3792 oma atte guythys clos
  y aperia ny vynnys
maria lowene *dis*
maria dyso m*ur* grays
3796   ov map dym dry pan vynsys
  [*descendit ad ecclesiam beate marie cum ihesu*

Maria kem*er* the flogh
maria re vuff relogh
  in the gever
3800 sav m*er*cy y raff pesy
hag onen ath s*er*vysy
  nefre bethe heb awer*

    [*finit tranceat domum*
    [*demens et paterfamilias paratus*

p. 149.   DEMENS   [*forling and suagynk*

Out warnogh wy falge guesyon
3804 prag y russugh ov kelmy
ag*is* pennov myllusyon
 me a ra age therry

    PATERFAMILIAS

Lau*er* purguir mar kyllyth
3808 henna lem*en* y fyllyth
  rag pur fast ythos chenys
the veryasek me a vyn
the wore purguir lemyn
3812   mar kyllyth bones sawys

    DEMENS

Lau*er* thymo lagasek
pendrama gans m*er*yasek
  mar guir an iovle theth lesky

    PATERFAMILIAS

3816 Meryasek dyugh lowena
de*n* mes ay revle us gena
  ha t*us* re ruk ov heskey
may relle*n* y dry oma
3820   the voys socrys genogh wy

* Here the scribe writes *ffinit hec pagina.*

And go quick to the church.
3792 Lo here it is, wrapt close :
   I would not open it.
Mary, joy to thee !
Mary, to thee much thanks,
3796   Since thou wouldst bring me my son.

[*She goes down with the image of Jesus to the church*
   of blessed Mary.

Mary, take thy child,
Mary, I have been overlax
   Regarding thee.
3800 But mercy I beseech,
And one of thy servants
   Ever I shall be without grief.

             [*Let her go home.*
        [*A madman and a head of a family ready.*

A MADMAN *hurling and swagging.* *

Out on you, ye false fellows !
3804   Why have you bound me ?
Your lousy heads
   I will break them.

HEAD OF A FAMILY.

Talk right truly if thou canst.
3808 That now thou shalt lack,
   For right fast thou art chained.
To Meriasek I will
Put thee right truly now
3812   If thou canst be healed.

THE MADMAN.

Tell me, thou big-eyed,
What thing is with Meriasek ?
   So truly the devil burn thee !

THE HEAD OF A FAMILY.

3816 Meriasek, joy to thee !
A man out of his mind is with me,
   And folk have advised me
That I should bring him here
3820   To be succoured by you.

---

* *Furl,* to throw, to hurL One that falls down with some violence and noise is said to come down with a swag. Kennett cited Halliwell, s. v. *swag.*

MERIADOCUS EPISCOPUS

Ihesu arluth us avan
re werese creff ha guan
   trewethek syght yv helma
3824 gueles den yonk tek certan
   cheynys in keth vanerma

p. 150.   DEMENS

Awoys ov bones cheynys
a tefes dym nebes neys
3828   me a pylse the pen blogh
hag a russa
dyso oma
   garrow pur trogh

MERIADOCUS [genuflectit

3832 Ihesu arluth me ath peys
   gueres omma an denma
ihesu crist arluth grassyeys
   thy skyans lemen drofa
3836 ihesu arluth map guerheys
   y envy gor the orta
ihesu gront na ven nehys
   ha peys gene maria

3840 Gorta ty then dym omma
in hanov map maria
   me a vyn the degelmy
neb a yl hag a ylly
3844 ressawhyagy heb yly
   amen warbarth gruen pesy

DEMENS

The crist ihesus murworthyans
ha thys meryasek nefra
3848 cryst thym re dros ov skyans
   drethos meryasek oma
meryasek in ov bevnans
me a vyn prest the servya
3852 meryasek dyso reverans
   sensys ovy theth gorthya   [finit

p. 151.   MERIADOCUS

Thum oratry moys manna
the besy war varia
3856   prest ov gueres

BISHOP MERIASEK.

May Jesu, lord that art above,
Aid strong and weak!
 A piteous sight is this.
3824 To see a young man, fair certainly,
 Chained in this same manner.

THE MADMAN.

Because of my being chained,
If thou wouldst come to me somewhat nearer,
3828 I would peel thy blockhead,
And I would make
For thee here
 Legs all broken.

MERIASEK [*kneels.*

3832 Jesu, Lord, I beseech thee
 Help here this man.
Jesu Christ, gracious Lord,
 To his wits now bring him.
3836 Jesu, Lord, son of a virgin,
 His enemy put from him!
Jesu, grant that I be not denied,
 And beseech with me, Mary.

3840 Wait, thou man, for me here:
In the name of Mary's Son
 I will unbind thee.
May he who can, and who will,
3844 Heal thee without salve!
 Amen together let us pray!

THE MADMAN.

To Christ Jesu, much honour,
 And to thee, Meriasek, ever!
3848 Christ has brought me my wits
 Through thee, Meriasek, here.
Meriasek, in my life
 I will always serve thee.
3852 Meriasek, to thee reverence!
 Bound am I to honour thee.   [*he ends.*

MERIASEK.

To my oratory I will go
To pray to Mary
3856 Always to help me,

ha thum guythe pup seson
omma the orth temptasconn
 ha the orth pup drok covsy(s)
   [ad oratorium genuflectit

3860 Ihesus arluth luen a ras
 gorthyans dys ha lowena
ihesu arluth in pup plas
 guyth ov ena heb mostya
3864   ham corff·kefrys
maria gvyn guyrhes pur
maria beth ov socur
maria a gara mur
3868   the du ker peys rag ov leys

   IHS.

Ov eleth ker eugh then beys
susten an neff bethens reys
 the veryasek
3872 megys y feth gans ov grays
benyges yv in pup plays
 y oberov dym a plek

p. 152.   (MI)CHAEL

Ihesu de voth a veth grueys
3876 dotho eff ythen uskys
genen y feth confortis
 in forth wella
dotho megyans
3880 degen dyblans
 the orth an formyer guella
   Descendunt [*organs or syngyng*

   GABRIEL

Meryasek lowena dis
crist ker regyn danvoneys
3884 oma prest theth confortya
kyn theses ov thyr penys
oma ty a veth megys
 gans boys eleth in torma

Sumens cibum cum laudibus diuinis epulis
 quotidie sentit se refectum

  MERIADOCUS [*genuflectit*
3888 Ihesu arluth nor ha neff
 pup vrol rebo* gorthys
ihesu crist nynsefeth greff
 in bysma ath lel wonys

   * perhaps *revo.*

And to keep me at every season
Here from temptation,
    And from every evil thought.

              [He kneels at the oratory.

3860 Jesus, Lord, full of grace
    Worship to thee and joy
Jesu, Lord in every place,
    Keep my soul without corruption,
3864   And my body likewise.
Blessed Mary, pure virgin,
Mary be my succour!
Mary, whom I love much,
3868   To dear God pray on my behalf.

JESUS.

My angels dear, go ye to the world.
Let the food of heaven be given
    To Meriasek.
3872 Nourished he shall be with my grace,
Blessed he is in every place,
    His works are pleasing to me.

MICHAEL.

Jesus, thy will shall be done,
3876 To him we shall go quickly,
By us he shall be comforted,
    The best way.
Nourishment to him
3880 Let us bear clearly
    From the best Creator.

       They descend.   *[Organs or singing.*

GABRIEL.

Meriasek, joy to thee!
Dear Christ hath sent us
3884   Here now to comfort thee.
Though thou art at three penances
Here thou shalt be nourished
    With angels' food this turn.

*Taking sustenance with praises of God, every day he feels
    himself recruited with sumptuous food.*

MERIASEK   *[kneels.*

3888 Jesu, Lord of earth and heaven
    Always be worshipped,
Jesu Christ, there will not be grief
    In this world from thy loyal service.

Q

3892 ihesu dyso y crasseeff
 gans boys neff pan of megys
ihesu arluth ny dovtyeff
 kyn fen treddeth ov penys

p. 153. *Hic dux .i. primus Magus pompabit*

3896 Me yv arluth heb parov
 duk inweth astronymer
the helghya heb feladov
 the prince par del yv dufer
3900 moys me a vyn
ha geneff cowethe da
an epscop purguir a thuea
 the certen plas er ov fyn

DUX .i. SECUNDUS MAGUS

3904 Besy yv thyn bones war
yma dragon vras heb mar
 ꞏ in caff oma rebon ny
mar a tuny er y fyn
3908 marov on bras ha byyn
 da yv boys fur eredy

VENATOR [*ducibus magos*

Yma oma tus arvov
hag archers gans guaregov
3912 abel purguir dy latha
me thovtya gans ov huen
marnes y a vo ree luen
 kyns es dybarth y squerdya

     [*descendit cum armatores*

Hic episcopus poly pompabit

3916 Me yv epscop a theveys
 ha parlet mur ov rasov
y tethewys nansyv meys
 mones inhans then prasov
p. 154. 3920 erbyn duk magus a breys
den fur in y worthebov
ov crosyer ota parys
 lemen thum gormennadov

CROSSER EPISCOPI POLI

3924 Me yv parys arluth da
sav guan revle yma oma
 na yllyn lefya kyn moys

3892 Jesu, to thee I give thanks.
 Since by heaven's food I am fed,
Jesu, Lord, I fear not
 Though I be three days at penance.

Here a Duke, to wit, the first Magician, shall parade.

3896 I am a lord without peers,
 A duke, likewise an astronomer.
To hunt without fail
 As it is a duty for a prince
3900 I will go,
And with me comrades good.
The bishop right truly he will come
 To a certain place to meet me.

A DUKE, to wit, THE SECOND MAGICIAN.

3904 Need it is for us to be wary.
There is a great dragon without doubt
 In a cave here by us.
If we come against her
3908 Dead are we great and small.
 It is well to be wise readily.

HUNTSMAN [*to the Dukes the Magi.*

Here there are armed folk,
And archers with bows
3912 From afar right truly to slay her.
I fear not with my hounds,
Unless they shall be too full
 Before parting to tear her.

    [*he goes down with armed men.*

Here the bishop of Pola shall parade.

3916 I am a bishop exactly (?)
 And a prelate, great my graces.
I have promised, it is now a month,
 To go down to the meadows
3920 To meet Duke Magus of price,
 A man wise in his answers.
My crucifer, art thou ready
 Now according to my orders ?

THE BISHOP OF POLA'S CRUCIFER.

3824 I am ready, good lord.
 But a bad rule is here
  That we may not dine before going.

gvak yv thym an pengasen
3928 a molleth du in gegen
schant yv an dewes han boys
Descendunt

EPISCOPUS POLI

Heyl dyugh duk nobil magus
me ham crosser presagus
3932 reduth dywy ȝ· sportya
na wethen ree then ternans
rag yma dragon dyblans
hag onen vras sur omma

PRIMUS DUX MAGUS

3936 Noov wolcum ffadyr byschyp
ny thue dragon me a dyp
oges thynny
mar thue in syght me an gor
3940 yma omma pobil lor
rag y latha eredy

[*her y dragon aredy in y· place*

p. 155.   ### SECUNDUS DUX MAGUS

Na drestiyn ny the henna
arlythy duen alema
3944 attahy sur defethys
out drethy bethen marov
gans flam tan mes ay ganov
nys gorta myl den ervys

[*her a gonn yn y dragon ys movthe aredy & fyr*

PRIMUS DUX

3948 Hov dehesugh warnethy
nansus ran lenkis gonsy

[*sum of y· sovdrys y sowlyd*

pythyv an iovle a reny
mahom reges ancumbra
3952 in agen meske ov scumbla
avel wy mark attahy

EPISCOPUS POLI

A gony gony fyen
ken marov bras ha byen
3956 re corff mahum on oma

Empty have I the end of the paunch (?).

3928 O God's curse in the kitchen,
Scant is the drink and the food.

[*They go down.*

BISHOP OF POLA.

Hail to you, noble Duke Magus !
I and my crozier-bearer, Praesagus,

3932 Have come to you to sport.
Let us not keep overmuch to the low land,
For there is a dragon clearly,
And a big one, surely here.

FIRST DUKE MAGUS.

3936 Now welcome, father bishop !
The dragon will not come I think
Near to us.
If she come in sight, I know it,

3940 Here there are people enough
To slay her readily.

[*Here the dragon ready in the open space*

SECOND DUKE MAGUS.

Let us not trust to that.
Lords, let us come hence !

3944 Behold her surely unconquered !
Out ! by her we shall be dead
With flame of fire out of her mouth.
A thousand armed men abide her not.

[*Here a gun ready in the dragon's mouth and fire.*

FIRST DUKE.

3948 How, strike at her !
Now are some swallowed by her !

[*Some of the soldiers swallowed.*

What the devil shall we do ?
May Mahound cumber you !

3952 Amongst us dunging
Like water, mark ! behold her !

THE BISHOP OF POLA.

Ah woe's us, woe's us ! let us flee
Else dead, great and small,

3956 By Mahound's body, we are here.

duen then emperour costentyn
ha dotho eff leveryn
y vryans eff yv helma

PRIMUS DUX [*ad constantinum*

3960 Heyl ser emperour costentyn
ha warnes ny a cry out
deswreys yv an pov lemyn
ha der the wryens heb dovt
3964   lues marov

p. 156.

an dragon vrays us in caff
vn den the gerthes ay saff
ny gas nan lathe heb wov

EPISCOPUS POLI

3968 Bythqueth ny vue vays in pov
aban vys crystyan heb wov
molleth du war ath treylas
ny glowys gans den genys
3972 a worthya crist nygythys
bythqueth the faria in fays

CONSTANTINUS

Arlythy eugh wy war gam
crist ha maria y vam
3976   dua rag agen gueras
dus oma ov maseger
ha kergh uskys sylvester
the covs gena a fur spas

NUNCIUS [*ad constantinum*

3980 Costentyn arluth somper
me a doro syluester
oma dywy an vorov
ny goske welen indan droys
3984 na nefre ny debre boys
er na govsen orth y ganov

[*ad syluestrem*

Siluester lowena dys
then emperour dones uskys
3988   reys yv thywy in certeyn
rag ef a vyn covs orthys
pur wyr lemmyn   [*finit*

Let us come to the emperor Constantine,
And to him let us tell,
His lordship is this.

FIRST DUKE *to Constantine.*

3960 Hail, sir emperor Constantine!
And on thee we cry out.
Undone is the country now,
And throughout thy lordship without doubt
3964 Many dead.
The great dragon that is in a cave
One man to go from his standing
She will not let without killing him truly.

BISHOP OF POLA.

3968 Never has there been good in the country
Since thou becamest a christian without a lie.
God's curse on him who converted thee!
I have not heard that any one born
3972 Who worshipt evil Christ
Ever fared well.

CONSTANTINE.

Lords, go your way.
Christ and Mary his Mother
3976 Will come to help us.
Come here, my messenger,
And fetch quickly Silvester
To speak with me for a short space.

MESSENGER *to Constantine.*

3980 Constantine, lord without equal,
I will bring Silvester
Here to you to-morrow.
A rod shall not sleep under foot,
3984 Nor ever shall I eat food.
Until I speak at his mouth.

[To Silvester.

Silvester, joy to thee!
To the emperor to come forthwith
3988 Need is for you certainly,
For he will speak to thee
Right truly now.

p. 157. SILVESTER *[descendit siluester*

The constentyn me a due
3992 thy comondment benythe
       eff yv arluth mur y nel
                                [ad constantinum
ser emperour dyugh lowene
oma prest me re dufe
3996   ha ny vynnys lettya pel

IMPERATOR CONSTANTINUS

Ima oma sur dragon
ov latha pobil dyson
       heb numbyr sur del clowa
4000 tovlel a rons warnavy
bones an causer defry
       begythys rag ov bosa
                         *[descendit constantinus**

SYLUESTER

Dre voth crist arluth avan
4004 an dragan me a ra guan
       dregen in pov na relle
may welle myns us in rome
ihesu crist a bev ry dome
4008   ha gul kepar del vynne

PRIMUS DUX *magus*

Cans den lethys war ov feth
nav re vue sur in vn geth
       prest gensy hy
4012 mar qureth y ouercummya
the crist ny a vyn treyla
       var off ny yllyth defry

SYLVESTER

Thum peiadov alema
4016   mones a vanna rygthy   *[genuflectit*

IHC.

Pedyr lemen thymo kea
the syluester eredy
p. 158. gueyt in tek y confortye
4020   ha gans henne y desky

                * MS. constautinum.

SILVESTER. [*Silvester goes down.*

To Constantine I will come
3992 According to his command ever
He is lord: great his might.

[*To Constantine.*

Sir Emperor, joy to you!
Here at once I have come
3996 And I would not hinder long.

EMPEROR CONSTANTINE.

There is here surely a dragon.
Slaying people
Without number surely, as I hear,
4000 They do cast on me
That I am the causer really
For my being baptized.

[*Constantine goes down.*

SILVESTER.

Through the will of Lord Christ above
4004 The dragon I will pierce
So that she may not do hurt in the country.
So that all that are in Rome may see
Jesus Christ owns the (right of) giving doom,
4008 And doth as he will.

FIRST DUKE MAGUS.

A hundred men slain, on my faith,
Now were surely in one day
By her.
4012 If thou canst overcome her
To Christ we will turn.
I am aware that thou wilt not be able really.

SILVESTER.

According to my prayer hence
4016 I would go before her. [*he kneels.*

JESUS.

Peter, now for me go
To Silvester readily.
Take care fairly to comfort him,
4020 And therewithal to teach him.

an dragon y ra fethe
der ov gallus defry*
ytheseff orth y care
4024 ny vanna y ankevy

PETRUS

Arluth the voth me a ra
syluester scon y guarnya
  an dragon nangeffo ovn
4028 eff as led avel on doff
ha der gallus du in proff
  as comond then dysert dovn
descendit petrus [solus ad syluestrem in placea

Syluester wek beth lowen
4032 crist a vyn orthys certen
  fethe purguir an dragon
the ij chaplen kemery
genes thegy eredy
4036   ha gueres ad du dyson

SYLVESTER

Arluth neff rum gueresa
me ny won thum confortia
  pyv us oma devethys
4040 mur yv gallus crist avan
ha trestia a raff certan
  pup vr ol eff thum guereys

PETRUS

Me yv the crist abostel
4044 ha pedyr ov hanov lel
  na thovt dysset in matter†

p. 159 Then dragonn covs in delma
ihesu crist map maria
4048   ha genys a lel werheys
a fue marov in grovs pren
hag anclethys in beth men
  then tresse deth dasserrys
4052 assendijs then neff inban
deth brus eff a thue certan
  thagen brusy kyk in kneys

* The scribe wrote *eredy* which the corrector has struck out substituting *defry*.
† At least three lines are here wanting.

The dragon he will vanquish
　Through my power readily.
I am loving him,
4024　　I will not forget him.

PETER.

Lord, thy will I shall do,
(And) Silvester at once warn him
　Of the dragon that he should not have fear.
4028　He will lead her like a tame lamb,
And through God's power in proof
　Will command her to the deep desert.

Peter descends [alone to Silvester in the open space.

Silvester sweet, be glad!
4032　Christ will for thee certainly
　　Defeat right truly the dragon.
Thy two chaplains, take them
With thee to her readily,
4036　　And help from thy God at once.

SILVESTER.

Lord of heaven help me!
I know not to comfort me
　Who is come here.
4040　Great is the power of Christ above,
And I do trust certainly
　　That always he will help me.

PETER.

I am an apostle of Christ's,
4044　And Peter is my loyal name:
　　Fear not deceit in the matter.

To the dragon speak thus:
" Jesu Christ, son of Mary,
4048　　And born of a loyal virgin,
Has been dead on the crosstree,
And buried in a tomb of stone,
　　On the third day he arose,
4052　Ascended up to heaven.
On Doomsday he will come certainly,
　　To judge us, flesh in skin.

in y hanov ty dragon
4056 in mes oma thymo duys

Syne an grovs kymer genys
ha ty as led del vynneys
      poren theth voth 3° honen
4060 ihesu a vyn daguereys
      rag the voys y servont len

SYLVESTER

Benyges rebo an preys
me a vyn mones uskys
4064 then dragon sur alemma   [descendit
dugh gene ov dev chaplen
syne an grovs theragon scoen
degeugh aberth maria

                [a crosse aredy ffor primus
                 capellanus seluestris

PRIMUS CAPELLANUS SILVESTRIS

4068 Me a thek pur guir an grovs
hav cowyth inweth heb flovs
      degens lantern gans golov
dovn yv an caff may ma hy
4072 cans pas del glowys ha moy
      crist guyth ny orth tewolgow

                [secundus capellanus beryth
                 y° lantern

p. 160.   PRIMUS DUX .i. MAGUS

Serys duen ny the veras
pan dyweth an thragon vras
4076   a ra syluester lemen
ny grese vy mas pystry
y wore gul eredy
      thagen tolla pur certen

SYLVESTER [genuflectit

4080 In hanov map maria
ihesu crist ythyv henna
      a fue marov anclethyys
dasserrys then tresse deth
4084 then neff assendias inweth

In his name, thou dragon,
4056   Come out here to me."

The sign of the cross take with thee
And thou wilt lead her as thou wishest,
    Right according to thy own will.
4060 Jesu will help (thee) well,
    For that thou art his faithful servant.

SILVESTER.

Blessed be the time !
I will go forthwith
4064   To the dragon surely hence.
Come with me, my two chaplains :
The sign of the cross before us
    Bear ye on behalf of Mary.

          [A cross ready for Silvester's
               first chaplain.

SILVESTER'S FIRST CHAPLAIN.

4068 I will bear right truly the cross,
And my comrade likewise, without flout,
    Let him bear the lantern with a light :
Deep is the cave where she is,
4072 An hundred paces, as I have heard, and more.
    Christ keep us from darkness !

          [The second chaplain bears
              the lantern.

FIRST DUKE i.e. MAGUS.

Sirs, let us come to see
What end of the great dragon
4076   Silvester will make now.
I believe that nought save magic
He can do readily,
    To deceive us right certainly.

SILVESTER *kneels.*

4080 In the name of Mary's Son,
Jesu Christ is that,
    Who has been dead, buried,
Raised on the third day,
4084 To heaven he ascended likewise

an berth dyov the du tays
deth brus eff a thue purfeth
the vrusi an drok han mays

4088 In y hanov dus in mes
par del yv gorhemynnes
gans crist dymo in bysma

[*exiuit de spelunca*

PRIMUS DUX .i. MAGUS

atta an dragon ov toys
4092 war theller guel yv dyn moys
o^t marov ythoff omma
pur guir gans hy anel poys
benytha vays ny vetha

[*cadat in terrore monstri*

SECUNDUS DUX .i. MAGUS

4096 Hy rum lathes gans hy gvyns
re vahum wek pen an sens
alemma numbus gvaya
govy na vuma war kyns
4100 hager dyweth yv helma   [*finit*
[*cadat in terrore monstri*

p. 161.   SILVESTER

Gorta oma ty dragon
in hanov crist cuff colon
me a vyn the thalhenna
4104 hath ledya kepar hag on
der gallus du in delma

CONSTANTINUS

Syluester gorthys reby
ty re proves eredy
4108 boys crist pen an arlythy
thymo othem o hena
seris pendra govsughwy
den benyges yv helma

EPISCOPUS POLY

4112 Yma omma tus varov
mar kyllons heb feladov
thage bevnans bones dreys

On the right side of God (the) Father.
On Doomsday he will come perfect
To judge the bad and the good.

4088 In His name come forth,
Even as is commanded
By Christ to me in this world.

[She issued from the cave.

FIRST DUKE i.e. MAGUS.

Behold the dragon coming!
4092 Back it is better for us to go.
Out! I am dead here!
Right truly by her heavy breath.
Never shall I be well.

*[Let him fall down in fear of
the monster.*

SECOND DUKE i.e. MAGUS.

4096 She has killed me with her wind.
By sweet Mahound, the chief of the saints,
Hence I cannot move.
Woe 's me, I was not wary before!
4100 An ugly end is this.

*[Let him fall down in fear of
the monster.*

SILVESTER.

Stay here, thou dragon!
In the name of Christ, the loveable heart,
I will lay hold of thee,
4104 And lead thee like a lamb,
Through God's power, so.

CONSTANTINE.

Silvester, praised be thou!
Thou hast proven readily
4108 That Christ is the head of the lords.
Need to me was that.
Sirs, what say you?
A blessed man is this.

BISHOP OF POLA.

4112 Here there are dead folk.
If they can, without fail,
To their life be brought,

cavs thynny eff a vya
4116 in ihesu map marya
the cresy byen ha brays

SILUESTER

Ihesu arluth creff ha guan
ihesu an dusma leman
4120 vsy war dor omgellys
gront dethe sevel in yagh
mar a syns fur y a nagh
in vrna tebel wythreys*

[*Surrexit ij^us ducibus et omnes*

PRIMUS DUX .i. MAGUS

4124 Syluester gorthys reby
in crist me a vyn cresy
du a vercy y vosa
p. 162. an dragon yv tebelvest
4128 me a vyn pesy baptist
ha gorthya map maria   [*finit*

EPISCOPUS POLI

Thum skyans pan oma dreys
me a vyn boys begythys
4132 gorthya ihesu benitha
an falge dragon tebel preff
ny gara gueles y grueff
desawer vest yv honna

SILVESTER

4136 Na berthuth ovn annethy
dre gras ihesu us avan
then dysert me as gor hy
then le na relle dregan
4140 in hanov crist a vercy
me ath worhemyn dragan
then guylfos quik mathylly
avoyd ʒᵉ orthef leman
4144 drok nefre gueyt na rylly
the vest na den creff na guan
na byth moy na ʒᵉwylly
war beyn ancov ty belan

* MS. looks *voythreys*.

Cause to us it would be
4116 In Jesus, son of Mary,
To believe, small and great.

SILVESTER.

Jesus, Lord of strong and weak,
Jesus, this folk now
4120 That are on earth overthrown,
Grant to them to stand up whole.
If they be wise, they will reject
In that hour evil-doing.
[*The two dukes arise and all.*

FIRST DUKE i.e. MAGUS.

4124 Silvester, worshipt be thou !
In Christ I will believe
That he is God of mercy.
The dragon is an evil beast.
4128 I will beseech a baptizer,
And worship Mary's Son.

BISHOP OF POLA.

To my wits since I am brought,
I will be baptized
4132 (And) worship Jesus always.
The false dragon, evil worm,
I like not to see her face.
An unsavoury beast is that !

SILVESTER.

4136 Do not bear fear of her.
Through grace of Jesus who is above,
To the desert I will put her,
To the place where she cannot do evil.
4140 In the name of Christ of mercy
I command thee, dragon,
That thou go quick to the wilderness.
Out of the way from me now !
4144 Take care that thou never do evil
To beast, nor man, strong nor weak,
That thou never more return
On pain of death, thou villain.

R

EPISCOPUS POLY

4148 In kerth sur galles holma
oll rome yv sensys nefra
the enora syluester
grua scon agen begythya
4152 opynguelys yv omma
nagus du mas ihesu ker   [*finit*

[*holy water aredy*

p. 163.   SYLVESTER

Me agys beseth warbarth
oma lemen kyns dybarth
4156   in nomine patris et* filij
et spiritus sancti amen
lemen ov mebyen lyen
ware thum palys duen ny   [*finit*

SECUNDUS CAPOLLANUS SILVESTER

4160 Purys on the voys genogh
ny a ra bohes venogh
syluester servys dywhy
gorthyans the crist in torma
4164 lues enaff sur oma
drethogh sawys us defry   [*finit*

CONSTANTINUS

Gorthyans the crist a selwans
der syluester in torma
4168 pobyl rome orth ij vernans
delyfrys ythyns oma
kynsol a debel cregyans
lues den dreys in forth da
4172 ha ny ol guythys dyblans
orth an dragon preff an pla

Duen ny oll gans procession
thy curte syluester dysonn
4176   gruen y gora
dotho oll ython sensys
lues oma deworijs
gans an dragon ongrassijs
4180   na ve eff sur a vya   [*finit*

[*ad palacium pape procesconant*

* MS. *ef*

BISHOP OF POLA.

4148 Away surely this is gone.
All Rome is bound ever
    To honour Silvester.
Forthwith do thou baptize us.
4152 Openly seen is here
    That there is no God save dear Jesus.

[*Holy water ready.*

SILVESTER.

I will baptize you together,
Here now before parting,
4156   In the name of the Father and the Son
And of the Holy Ghost, amen.
Now, my sons of learning,
    Anon to my palace let us come.

SILVESTER'S SECOND CHAPLAIN.

4160 Ready are we to go with thee.
We will often do a little,
    Silvester, of service to you.
Worship to Christ at this turn !
4164 Many souls surely here
    Through you are healed really.

CONSTANTINE.

Worship to Christ of salvation !
    Through Silvester this turn
4168 Rome's people from two deaths
    Are here delivered,
First of all from evil belief
    Many a one brought on a good road,
4172 And we all clearly preserved
    From the dragon, the worm of the plague.

Let us all come with a procession.
To his court forthwith Silvester
4176   Let us put him.
To him we are all bound :
Many here devoured
    By the graceless dragon,
4180   Were he not, surely would have been.

[*They go in procession to the
Pope's palace.*

R 2

LANGUIDUS vel CONTRACTUS

A thu assoma grefijs
mans ov esely a heys
  mas orth dev croyth ny gerthaff
4184 assoff guan hag anhethek
kelmys off the vryasek
  sav ny von pur in metyaff

Me re vue in mes dres nos
4188 mur ov anwys ham ponfos
  pan veth lues ov cosca
in pollov prest omhelys
ov ij lyn ham kyk squerdys
4192   sevel am saff ny alla

Devethys ythoff then plays
dorsona thys a thremays
  rag kerense ihesu wek
4196 lauer dym a then grassyes
  py caffsenua meryasek

MERIADOCUS

Ov covs genes at eva
pendra vynta annotha
4200   lauer in scon
me a garsa
in norvysma
pup vr socra
4204   bohogogyon

CONTRACTUS

Me yv cropyl podrethek
devethys dys meryasek
  purothomek the du gras
p. 165. 4208 rag kerense an pasconn
a porthes ihesu ragonn
  meryasek grua thym gueras

Numbus esel nag yv mans
4212 ha pur vr* yma mernans
  in beys orth ov gohelas
numbus kerthes mas sklynkya
ny gar namur in bysma
4216   doys in ov syght nam guelas
noth off avel best oma
  war lur ov pedrevanas   [genuflectit

* leg. pup ur or pur guir.

A FEEBLE MAN, OR A CRIPPLE.

O God, I am grieved !
Maimed are my limbs for a long time :
   Except on two crutches I walk not.
4184 I am weak and loathsome.
Bound am I to Meriasek,
   But I know not when I shall meet him.

I have been out during night.
4188 Great my chilliness and my trouble
   When many are sleeping.
In pools quite overturned.
My two knees and my flesh torn.
4192   I cannot stand up.

I am come to the place.
A blessing to thee, O worthy sir !
   For love of sweet Jesus,
Tell me, O gracious man,
4196   Where I may find Meriasek.

MERIASEK.

Speaking with thee, behold him.
What thing wouldst thou of him ?
4200   Say forthwith.
I should like
In this world
Always to succour
4204   Poor people.

THE CRIPPLE.

I am a rotten cripple
Come to thee, Meriasek,
   Right needy, thanks to God.
4208 For love of the Passion
Which Jesus bore for us,
   Meriasek, help me !

I have not a limb that is not maimed,
4212 And always death is shunning me
   In the world.
I cannot walk but slink.
Not much in this world loves
4216   To come into my sight or to see me.
Naked am I, like a beast here
   On the ground crawling.

MERIADOCUS

Ihesu a ruk neff ha nor
4220 me a peys omma in clor
re therbara dis ȝehes
mones ha doys may hylly
kepar del yl heb yly
4224 sawya oll the esely
a pup galer ha cleves

Ihesu yv agen savyur
retrehava the war lur
4228 maria reth weresa
ha re grontya
y both mar pea
ȝehes thyso in torma

CONTRACTUS

4232 Arluth assoff lowenheys
grassaff ȝe crist a vercy
ha thys meryasek kefrys
restorijs ov esely
4236 yv thym heb wov
kerthes me a yl
lemen heb peryl
yagh ha pur salov

p. 166. MERIADOCUS EPISCOPUS

4240 The ihesu rebo grassees
the guyske kymer dylles
lemen densa yth kerhen
ha tan dis dewes ha boys
4244 grasse the crist a galloys
eff yv the vethek certen

CONTRACTUS

Ihesu avan
map guerhes* splan
4248 thyugh ren tala
meryasek wek
then bohosek
parys owhy the socra

MERIADOCUS   [in oratorio iacebat

4252 Dugh why thym ov bredereth
corff ov arluth del deleth
hythyv me re recevas

* MS. grurhes.

MERIASEK.

May Jesus, who made heaven and earth,
4220 I beseech here gently
  Provide healing for thee,
To go and come that thou mayst,
As he can without a salve
4224 Heal all thy limbs
  From every disease and illness.

Jesus is our Saviour.
May he raise thee up from the ground !
4228   May Mary help thee !
And grant,
If it be her will,
  Healing to thee at this turn !

THE CRIPPLE.

4232 Lord, I am rejoiced.
  I give thanks to Christ of mercy
And to thee, Meriasek, likewise.
  My limbs restored
4236   Are to me without a lie.
I can walk
Now without peril,
  Healed and quite whole.

BISHOP MERIASEK.

4240 To Jesus be thanks !
For clothing take raiment
  Now, good man, around thee,
And take thou to thee drink and food.
4244 Give thanks to Christ of power :
  He is thy leech certainly.

THE CRIPPLE.

May Jesus above,
Son of a bright virgin ;
4248   Repay it to you !
Sweet Meriasek,
To the poor man
  Ready are you to give succour.

MERIASEK   [*he was lying in the oratory.*

4252 Come ye to me, my brethren.
My Lord's Body as one ought,
  To-day I have received.

reys yv dyberth otyweth
4256   kyn fo tek an gowethas
The ihesu rebo grasseys
gans mernans me yv tuchys
    reys yv mones an bysma
4260 bredereth vsyogh dader
han vohosogyen pub vr
    bethugh sokyr an rena

DECANUS   [ad meriadocum

Arluth fetel vyth dynny
4264 mar teberthyth eredy
    meryasek the orthen
me a wor in guir heb mar
benytho arluth ath par
4268   pur thefry nygynbethen

p. 167.   MERIADOCUS

Yma an preys ov nesse
the crist me a vyn grasse
    thym y thadder in bysma
4272 zesseys vnctis communijs*
off lemen the ihesu grays
the orth crist lel map guirhas
    rag ov servesy in beas
4276   war thu pesy me a ra   [genuflectit
Neb am gorth vy in bysma
    ihesu arluth gront dethy
gallus boys zesseys oma
4280   kyns es merwel eredy
corff crist inweth receva
    vngijs gans henna defry
then vlas neff age ena
4284   may thella purguir then ioy

In le may feua gorthys
    peseff rag an keth rena
maystefons y luen zeheys
4288   pesy warnaff a rella
ha sawys a pup cleveys
    aberth an corff han ena
susten maystefons kefrys
4292   ha lor pegans the vewa

In kernov me ambeth chy
    ryb maria a cambron
tnam wyles neb a thue dy
4296   me as aquit purdyson
    kyn fo ov corff in ken le
        * MS. seems connuijs

Need is it to part at last,
4256   Though fair be the companionship.

To Jesus be thanks!
By death I am touched.
    Need is it to go from this world.
4260 Brethren, practise goodness,
And the poor people always,
    Be ye the succour of those.

THE DEAN *to Meriasek.*

Lord, how will it be to us
4264 If thou departest already,
    Meriasek, from us?
I know truly, without doubt,
Never a lord equal to thee
4268   Certainly shall we have.

MERIASEK.

The time is drawing nigh.
To Christ I will give thanks
    For his goodness to me in this world.
4272 Confessed, anointed, houseled
Am I now, thanks to Jesu.
From Christ, loyal son of a virgin,
For my servants in the world,
4276   On God, I do pray.   *[he kneels.*

Whoever shall honour me in this world,
    Jesu, Lord, grant to them
Power of being confessed here
4280   Before dying readily,
Christ's Body likewise to receive,
    Anointed therewith certainly,
To heaven's kingdom that their soul
4284   May go right truly to the joy.

In the place wherein I may be honoured
    I pray for those same
That they may have full confession
4288   If they should pray to me,
And be healed of every disease
    Within the body and the soul.
Sustenance that they may have likewise.
4292   And enough pittance for living.

In Cornwall I shall have a house
    By Mary of Camborne.
To see me whoever comes thither
4296   I will absolve him at once,
    Though my body be in another place.

in keth plasna neb a beys
gans ihesu y feth clowys
4300 hay petyconn colenwys
lafyll purguir mar pcthe

p. 168.
Ov gol a veth suer
in mes metheven
4304 an kynsa guener
rag nefre certen
ov banneth vy
gans banneth crist pen an sens
4308 the kemmys ov gol a sens
y pese bys venary

CANONICUS

Meryasek fetel esogh
adar medelheys brays ogh*
4312 bethugh a cher
ny a yl boys morethek†
war the lergh ha herethek
mar seth the orthen in suer

MERIADOCUS

4316 Du guener crist ihesu ker ,
a ruk merwel ragon ny
maythoff lowen du guener
dascor ov ena defry
4320 thum selwadour
ha du guener rag henna
bethens ov gol vy nefra
sensys gans ov flehys dour

4324 Bredereth dugh nes omma
in tokyn a gerensa
amma thyugh ol mc a vyn
in hanov map maria
4328 in vvelder deberthyn

in manus tuas domine
spiritum meum commendo

Et sic emisit spiritum

[*ye holy goste aredy ffro hevyn to fett
ye sowle and ye sovle aredy*

p. 169.
IHS.

Ov eleth nygyogh then nor
4332 thc kerhes thymo pur clour
oma eneff meryasck

---

* MS. seems *adar medelhe ys braysogh*   † MS. seems *merethek*

In that same place whoever shall pray,
By Jesus he will be heard,
4300 And his petition fulfilled
    If it be, truly, right lawful.

My festival shall be surely
    In the month of June,
4304 The first Friday
    For ever certainly.
    My blessing,
With the blessing of Christ, the head of the saints,
4308 For as many as keep my festival
    I beseech for ever.

A CANON.

Meriasek, how are you ?
Alas ! you are greatly weakened.
4312   Be you of cheer.
We may be mournful
After thee, and yearning,
    If thou goest from us surely.

MERIASEK.

4316 On Friday, dear Christ Jesu,
    Did die for us,
So that I may be glad on Friday
    To yield up my soul
4320   To my Saviour.
And on Friday therefore
Be my festival ever
    Held by my brave children.

4324 Brethren, draw nearer here.
In token of love
    I will kiss you all
In the name of Mary's son.
4328   In humility let us part.

Into thy hands, O Lord,
I commend my spirit.

        And so he sent forth his spirit.
        [*The Holy Ghost ready from heaven*
        to fetch the soul, and the soul ready.

JESUS.

My angels, fly to the earth,
4332 To fetch me very gently
    Here Meriasek's soul.

myns a deserias gront*is*
yma dotho war an beys
4336   y van*er* o da ha tek

MICHAEL

Ihesu eff re the*n*delas
in gluas neff bones treges
    ʒiso y fue se*r*vont lel
4340 the volnogeth
p*ar* del deleth
    ny a ra snell   [*finit*
    [*yᵉ holy goste aredy and yᵉ
    sovle aredy*

GABRIEL

Meryasek beth lowe*n*
4344 myns a deserijs ce*r*te*n*
    thys yv grontys
the*n* neff ty a
the lowena
4348   rag trega in ioy a beys   [*finit*

EPISCOPUS KERNOV

Ov crossyer me re glowes
boys me*r*yasek yn newores*
    moys ʒy veres me a vyn
4352 mar sywe byv bo marov
y cowyth heb feladov
me a greys in ov dythyov
    ny wela sur in bretyn   [*descendit*

p. 170.   ### COMES VENETENSIS

4356 Morethek off rag vn dra
meryasek del glowa
    yma sur war y vasken
dugh gena ov marogyon
4360 thy wore in doyr dyson
    ny a vyn mones lemmen   [*descendit*

SECUNDUS EPISCOPUS.

Yma sur an arlythy
the veryasek eredy
4364   ov moys thy wore in doyr
du kcme*r* wᵗ ay ena
ny veth arel an p*ar*na
    in trogel in brete*n* suyr
    descendunt

* MS. ynne wores.

All he desired granted
Is to him in the world.
4336 His way of life was good and fair.

MICHAEL.

Jesu, he has deserved
To dwell in heaven's kingdom.
To thee he has been a loyal servant.
4340 Thy will
Even as is meet
We will do swiftly.
*[The Holy Ghost ready and
the soul ready.*

GABRIEL.

Meriasek, be glad.
4344 All that thou desiredst certainly
To thee is granted.
To the heaven thou shalt go
To gladness
4348 To dwell in joy for ever.

BISHOP OF KERNOU.

My cross-bearer, I have heard
That Meriasek is *in extremis* (?).
I will go to see him
4352 If he be alive or dead.
His comrade without fail
I believe in my days
I shall not see in Brittany. *[he goes down.*

EARL OF VANNES.

4356 Mournful am I for one thing.
Meriasek, as I hear,
Is surely on his bier.
Come with me, my knights,
4360 To put him into the ground at once
We will go now. *[he goes down.*

SECOND BISHOP.

The lords are surely
To Meriasek readily
4364 Going, to put him into earth.
God, take care of his soul!
There will not be another like that
In a body in Brittany surely. *[he goes down.*

COMES VENETENSIS.

4368 Lowena dyugh arlythy
meryasek an den worthy
   del glowa yv tremenis
thy wore in doyr purguir
4372 del grese kelmys ogh suyr
   ha ny kefrys

EPISCOPUS KERNOV

Ea ser ȝurle eredy
par del ove den worthy
4376   agen part yv
mones purguir gans reverans
thy wore in doyr dywans
   eff o lel servont ihesu

p. 171.
[descendit comes globus

SECUNDUS EPISCOPUS

4380 Lowena dywhy ha ras
peys* da off an cowethas
   in torma pur eredy
tremenys yv meryasek
4384 ihesu arluth galosek
   thy ena re grontya ioy

GLOBUS COMES

Eff o purguir den worthy
ay genesygeth defry
4388   del wothen ol in breten
ha moy worthy y vryans
yv the kemendya dyblans
del welys vy experyans
4392   gonethys ganso certen

Dal y fueff lues blythen
methek vythol ny gefen
   a alho gul dym gueres
4396 pan duthe prest dotho eff
der gallus crist mytern [n]eff
   ov golek thym restoryes
ha gras the ihesu heb greff
4400   meryasek am sawyes

* MS. seems poys

THE EARL OF VANNES.

4368 Joy to you, lords!
Meriasek the worthy man,
 As I hear, is passed away.
To put him into earth right truly,
4372 As I believe, ye are surely bound
 And we likewise.

BISHOP OF KERNOU.

Yea, sir earl, readily,
As I am a worthy man,
4376 Our part is
To go right truly with reverence
To put him into earth quickly.
 He was a loyal servant of Jesus.
 [*Earl Globus goes down.*

SECOND BISHOP.

4380 Joy to you and grace!
Well satisfied am I with the company.
 At this time right readily.
Departed is Meriasek.
4384 May Jesus, mighty Lord,
 Grant joy to his soul!

EARL GLOBUS.

He was right truly a worthy man
From his birth really,
4388 As we all know in Brittany,
And most worthy his privilege
Is to be commended clearly,
As I saw a proof
4392 Wrought by him certainly.

Blind was I many years:
Any leech I got not
 Who could work me a cure.
4396 When I came here to him,
Through the might of Christ, king of heaven,
 My sight he restored to me,
And, thanks to Jesus without grief,
4400 Meriasek healed me.

p. 172.

EPISCOPUS KERNOV

Luyes den yma sensys
the veryasek sur in beys
neffre *pu*rguir ȝy gorthya
4404 rag me an creys sans in neff
purthefry y vones eff
warlergh y ober oma

COMES VENETENSIS   [*ad decanum*

Du re sawya an colgy
4408 ser deyn leferugh thynny
yv me*r*yasek tremenis
notijs in pov sur yma
boys y eneff an bysma
4412 del greseff the ioy gylles

DECANUS

Arluth eff yv tremenys
y eneff gans an drensys
creseff y voys
4416 teka dyweth in bysma
ny glowys de*n* ru*m* lovta
ȝe guthel na yonk na loys

CANONICUS

Y leferys offe*r*e*n*
4420 du guene*r* vette*n* certe*n*
glorijs ha tek
warlergh henna lefer*is*
gans ancov y voys tuchys
4424 grays the ih*e*su galosek

[*y*e *processyon aredy and
ij sansours*

p. 173.

DECANUS

The orth c*r*ist y ruk pesy
certe*n* desyr eredy
the keneve*r* an gorthya
4428 thotho eff agen gelwys
ha thynny a comondyas
doys oll dotho the amma

THE BISHOP OF KERNOU.

Many men are bound
To Meriasek surely in the world
Ever surely to worship him,
4404 For I believe, a saint in heaven
Full surely that he is
After his work here.

THE EARL OF VANNES *to the dean.*

May God save the college!
4408 Sir Dean, say you to us
Is Meriasek passed away?
Noted in the country surely it is
That his soul from this world,
4412 As I believe, has gone to joy.

THE DEAN.

Lord, he has passed away.
His soul with the Trinity
I believe that it is.
4416 Fairer end in this world
I have not heard, by my loyalty,
That any one has made, young or gray.

THE CANON.

He said mass
4420 On Friday morning certainly
Glorious and fair,
After that he said
By death that he was touched.
4424 Thanks to mighty Jesus.

[*The procession ready and two censers.*

THE DEAN.

Of Christ he did beseech
Certainly (the) desire readily
For whoever should worship him.
4428 To him he called us,
And us he commanded
To come all to him to kiss him.

s

Y ij luff y trehevys
4432 war guir thu mercy creyays
ha then neff eff a verays
lowenek in syght thynny
an vers in manus tuas
4436 ys leferis heb powas
pan o hy due eredy
y eneff y tascoras
then tays du luen a vercy

CANONICUS

4440 Ny wor mas ran pur thyson
in beys y conuersasconn
kyn wyske pan tek aveys
in y nesse hevys ruen
4444 pup deth y weska certen
na noys vyth ny ree poweys
in hotheys na lyynnyov
marnes in cala garov
4448 hyr ny vethe y huenneys

p. 174.   DECANUS

Havel o ov corthy crist
prest orth sen iowen baptyst
guyn na syder ny vsya
4452 mylwyth in nos purcertyn
ythe the pen y ij lyn
ihesu crist rag y worthya

Ha mylw⁴ purguir in geth
4456 war ben y ij lyn purfeth
y fynna moys awoys greff
may ruk y ij lyn hothfy
mar vras scantlor y hylly
4460 trewythyov kerthes'ay saeff

CANONICUS

Neffrev pesy bo redya
in eglos eff a vetha
marnes dadder ny govsy
4464 megys vue gans boys eleth
ken ny grese in god feth
y halse bewe defry   [finit

His two hands he upraised.
4432 On the true God he cried mercy,
And to the heaven he looked,
Joyous in our sight.
The verse *In manus tuas*
4436 He said it without pausing.
When it was ended readily,
His soul he resigned
To the Father God full of mercy.

THE CANON.

4440 A good part, right surely, knows not
His converse in the world.
Though he wore fair cloth outside
Next him a shirt of horsehair
4444 Every day he wore certainly.
Any night he rested not
In blankets (?) nor sheets.
Unless in rough straw
4448 Long used not to be his slumber.

THE DEAN.

Like he was in worshipping Christ
Quite to Saint John Baptist.
Wine nor cider he used not.
4452 A thousand times at night right certainly
He went on the end of his two knees,
Jesus Christ, to worship him.

And a thousand times right truly in the day
4456 On the end of his two knees perfectly
He would go on account of mortification.
So that his knees swelled
So great that hardly could he
4460 At times (?) walk from his standing.

THE CANON.

Always praying or reading
In church he used to be.
Aught save goodness he said not.
4464 Nourished was he with angels' food,
Else I believe in good faith
He could not have lived really.

s 2

COMES VENETENSIS

Assyv helma mur a col
4468 in breten sur thynny oll
    mestresy mar sogh parys
mones deglos ny a vyn
thy anclethyes in certyn
4472   an corff uskys

p. 175.

DECANUS

Pup travle oma yv parys
an cur yma arays
    del goth erbyn den worthy
4476 an pov fast ymons ov toys
kerys o gans yonk ha loys
    in bysma dres arlythy   ;

COMES VENETENSIS

I tendeles y cara
4480 lues den guan in bysma
    pur guir eff a confortyas
dal ha bother evrethyon
palgy ha dyvers clevyon
4484   ny wothen covs mar luas

DECANUS

Duen in kerth in hanov du
ha maria mam ihesu
    gueresugh orth an geler
4488 may hyllen moys in eglos
cryst roy thynny deth ha nos
    gul oberov a thadder

COMES VENETENSIS

Me a vyn don an neyll pen
4492 bythqueth ny gerys moy den
    me a greys in norvysma
eff a thadder o lenwys
ha benesygter kefrys
4496   genys vvue in termen da

p. 175.

GLOBUS COMES

Me a thek an pen arall
meryasek purguir heb fal
am sawyas pan ena* dal

* leg. eua, enua?

THE EARL OF VANNES.

This is much of loss
4468 In Brittany surely to us all.
    Masters, if ye are ready
We will go to the church
To bury certainly
4472   The body quickly.

THE DEAN.

Everything here is ready.
The quire is arranged
    As behoves to meet a worthy man.
4476 The country folk are coming fast.
Loved was he by young and gray
    In this world above lords.

THE EARL OF VANNES.

He deserved to be loved.
4480 Many weak persons in this world
    Right truly he comforted.
Blind and deaf, maimed men,
Palsied people, and divers lepers,
4484   We cannot say how many.

THE DEAN.

Let us come away in the name of God,
And of Mary, Jesu's Mother:
    Help ye at the bier
4488 That we may go into the church,
May Christ grant unto us day and night
    To do works of goodness!

THE EARL OF VANNES.

I will carry one of the two ends.
4492 Never loved I any man more
    I believe, in this world.
He was filled with goodness
And blessedness likewise:
4496   Born was he at a good time.

EARL GLOBUS.

I will bear the other end.
Meriasek right truly without fail
    Healed me when I was blind.

4500 gorthyans dotho benitha .
kep*a*r del oma sensys
ben*y*tha in ov de*n*sys
   thy enora   [*finit*

DECANUS

4504 Leme*n* canens an clergy
in hanov du a ve*r*cy
   han due*n* usk*is* alema
y tendelas
4508 boys enoras
   sur in povma

Hic cantant

SECUNDUS EPISCOPUS

Lemen p*a*rusugh an beth
in hanov c*r*ist del deleth
4512   may hallen y anclethyas
del yv dufer de*n* worthy
in age*n* meske e*r*edy
dadder the lues huny
4516   eff a ruk ʒ*e* ihe*s*u gras   [*finit*

p. 177.   ### NUDUS

An beth gene*n* ny yv grueys
kep*a*r del enua* sensys
   thy wonys in norvysma
4520 efrethek ha claff pa*n* en
eff an† sawys in certe*n*
   may coth dymo y gara

CONTRACTUS

An beth gene*n* yv glanheys
4524 arlythy del vugh plesijs
   gruegh why leme*n*
du asson ny herethek
ov queles corff me*r*yasek
4528   ov mones in dor certe*n*   [*finit*

EPISCOPUS KERNOV

Both du nynsus offendia
an corff in beth y wora
   gruegh leme*n* in hanov du

* Perhaps *enna*.   † leg. *am* ?

4500 Worship to him always
As I am bound
Always in my manhood
To honour him.

THE DEAN.

4504 Now let the clergy sing
In the name of God of mercy,
And let us come quickly hence :
He deserved
4508 To be honoured
Surely in this country.

Here they sing.

SECOND BISHOP.

Now prepare ye the tomb
In Christ's name as is meet,
4512 That we may bury him,
As is the due of a worthy man.
Amongst us readily
Goodness to many a one
4516 He did, to Jesus thanks.

THE NAKED MAN.

The tomb by us is made.
As I was bound
To serve him in this world,
4520 Maimed and leper when we were
He healed us certainly
So that it behoves me to love him.

THE CRIPPLE.

The tomb by us is cleansed.
4524 Lords, as ye are pleased
Do ye now.
Pardie, we are yearning
Seeing Meriasek's body
4528 Going into the earth.

BISHOP OF KERNOU.

God's will is not to be resisted.
The body in the grave
Now put ye it in God's name,

4532 ha me an benedicconn
a ra oma purdyson
abarth ov arluth ihesu

COMES VENETENSIS

In beth me an gor lemmen
4536 gueres dym ser surle y len
in hanov map maria
atta an corff y wroweth
kyn fo mar fur an roweth
4540 oll ny a thue the helma

p. 178.   EPISCOPUS KERNOV

Arluth neff ren benyga
ov flehys gruegh y gutha
in hanov du
4544 ha duen the dre alema
hereth us orth ov grefya
ha lues heboff oma
purguir hythyv   [*finit*

COMES VENETENSIS

4548 Pes in hanov du avan
mens us oma kuntullys
bevnans meryasek certan
genen revue dysquethys
4552 in keth dethyov ma dywy
trestia inno a rella
ha lel pesy warnotha
ihesu re grontias detha
4556 age desyr eredy

Dywhy banneth meryasek
ha maria cambron wek
banneth an abesteleth
4560 evugh oll gans an guary
ny a vyn agis pesy
kyns moys an plaeth

p. 179.   Pyboryon wethugh in scon
4564 ny a vyn ketep map bron
moys the donsya
eugh bo tregugh
wolcum vethugh
4568 kyn fewy sythen omma

Finitur per dominum HADTON anno domini M^{l}v^{c}iiij.

4532 And I the benediction
Will make here at once
On behalf of my Lord Jesus.

EARL OF VANNES.

Into the tomb I will put him now.
4536 Keep for me, sir Earl, his cloak
In the name of Mary's Son.
Behold the body lying.
Though so great be our sway,
4540 We shall all come to this.

BISHOP OF KERNOU.

May Heaven's Lord bless him!
My children, cover him
In God's name.
4544 And let us come home from hence,
Yearning is grieving me
And many besides me here
Right truly to-day.

EARL OF VANNES.

4548 Peace in the name of God above,
All that are here gathered!
Meriasek's Life certainly
By us hath been set forth.
4552 In these same days to you.
Whoever trust in him
And loyally pray to him
Jesu has granted to them
4556 Their desire readily.

To you the blessing of Meriasek,
And of sweet Mary of Camborne,
The blessing of the apostles!
4560 Drink ye all with the play
We will beseech you
Before going from the place.

Pipers, blow at once.
4564 We will, every son of the breast,
Go to dance.
Go ye or stay,
Welcome ye shall be,
4568 Though ye be a week here.

p. 180.

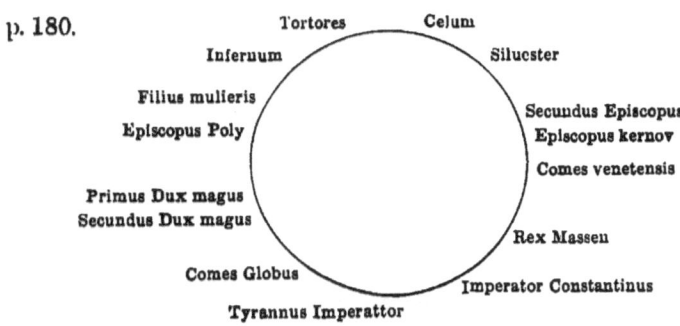

Tortores   Celum
Infernum   Siluester
Filius mulieris
Episcopus Poly   Secundus Episcopus
Episcopus kernov
Comes venetensis
Primus Dux magus
Secundus Dux magus   Rex Masseu
Comes Globus   Imperator Constantinus
Tyrannus Imperattor

NOTES.

[*Notes by the Rev. Robert Williams of Rhydycroesau are marked thus*: (W.)]

7. *gwarthevyas* cognate with W. *gwarchad* 'a guarding' (W.): *th* may here be for *gh* as in *bothosek* 779, *berthuth* (for *berthugh*) 1376, 41 36. *latha* 1629, *arthelath* Cr. But I would rather compare W. *gwarthaf* 'summit,' and perhaps the Latin *vertex* (vertices principiorum).

16. *perhennek* = W. *perchenog* 'possessor,' 'owner,' Br. *perchen.*

20. *angeffa* 3d sg. 2dy pres. of the irregular verb *cafus* 'to have,' 426, 1053, *cawas* 85. 255.

The other forms of this verb which occur in the foregoing drama are these :—

Present sg. 1. *ambus* 301. 494. 1367. *ambus vy* 1385. 2008. *numbus* 356. 566. 2560. 2632. 3192. 4098.
2. *kyn feste* 2046.
3. *angeves* 2834. *nangeves* 1937. 2754.

Secondary present Sg. 1. *ambeua* 1686. *maymbeua* 47. *ambethe* 1055, *numbethe* 3371. *numdarfe* 3727, *numdarfa* 1477. 1808. Sg. 2. *kyn feste* 2046. Sg. 3. *angeffa* 20, *nangeffa* 159. Pl. *astefe* 1935.

Preterite Sg. *ambuevy* 1726. *me rumbue* 1580. *ty re fue* 3570.

Future Sg. 1. *me am beth* 681. 1889. 3494. 4293. *ty a feth* 409. 2442. *a feth* 2818. *y feth* 304. 1218. 1466. *ny feth* 3578. *eff an geveth* 2090, *angeveth* 1001. *nyngeveth* 1124. Pl. *nygynbethen* 4268. *wy agis beth* 2508. *why agys beth* 1305. *y astevyth* 765, *y asteveth* 1199. *nygisbeth* 1770.

Conj. and Opt. *rethvo* 3230 [better *rethfo* O. 2265]. *kyn fy* 2018. *mengeffo* 1248. *kyngeffo* 2270. *rengeffo* 1022. 1277. *nangeffo* 4027. Pl. *maystefons* 4287. 4291. *nystufons* 2785.

22. *helma*, *helme* (ex *hen-lemma* 'this in this place'? Rhys), a masc. and neut. demonstrative of constant occurrence in this play (see 135. 723. 742. 838. 999. 1010. 1054. 1073. 1129. 1269. 1455. 1522. 1641. 1923. 2012. 2023. 2080. 2190. 2251. 2627. 2762. 2835. 3153. 3389. 3564. 3698. 3823. 3959. 4100. 4111. 4467. 4540). The feminine is *holma* 1072, 1090, 4148 (=*hon-lem-ma*?).

25. 2025. 2034. 3879: *megyans* (if the g be soft)=W. *mawsiant*, if hard, (as in *megys* 3872, 3886) cf. W. *magu*, Br. *maga*.

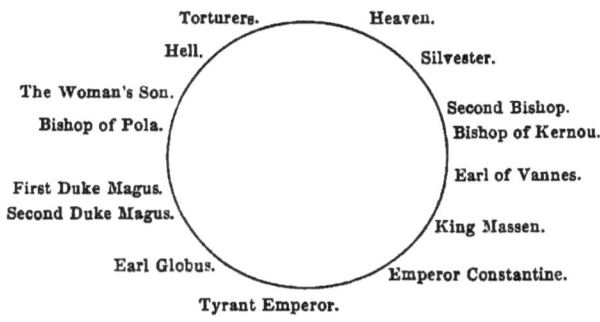

Torturers. Heaven.
Hell. Silvester.
The Woman's Son.
Bishop of Pola. Second Bishop.
Bishop of Kernou.
First Duke Magus. Earl of Vannes.
Second Duke Magus.
King Massen.
Earl Globus. Emperor Constantine.
Tyrant Emperor.

27. *attendie, attendya* 848, 867, 1632, 1913 ' attendere.'
30. *ewnadow* for *yeunadow,* a derivative from *yeuni* 'to desire'. As
   to the forms in *adow* ex *atvo*—see Z^2. 832-3. and add *usadow* 35.
32. *colonnek*=W. *calonog* ' hearty,' 'valiant' 641. 672. 2719. 2944. 3132.
40. 641. 672. *densa* from *den-da* 'a good man' (W.)
61. *martege* (Br. *martese* ' forte' ' forsan,' Z^2. 726) for the usual *martesen*.
64. *mannafi, mannavy* 2123. *clowevy* 1957. *bethevy* 2130. *sensevy*
   2406. *ovy* 3122. 3853 (=*ove* 4375), *nynsen-vy* 3700. cf. W.
   a-garafi Z^2. 506.
65. *leuf* from A.S. *leóf,* Eng. *lief,* Goth. *liubs.*
79. *dyvyn* W. *dyfyn* ' citation.'
80. *tos* borrowed from Eng. *tot* ' a small cup.'
96. *dyth* ' dictum,' Eng. *ditt, dite.*
98. *gobrow* pl. of *gobr* ' reward ' (W.)
103. *yn-newer* W. *yn-hwyr* (W.) But cf. W. *dewaint* ' midnight'.
104. *lyfye, lyvya* 113, *lyfya* 270, Br. *lein.*
117. i.e. I make my livelihood by the profit on the boys' food (W.)
121. *worth un pris* ' for a while ' (W.), or perhaps 'at one time'.
132. *dhe udhyll,* the infinitive of the verb meaning *facere.* Other forms
   are:—Infinitive *guthel* 639, 691, 2345, *gul* 378 (*dyswul* 1169,
   umwul 2366), *ou cuthel* 785, *ou cul* 688. Pres. Sg. *gruaff* 503,
   1830, *y raff* 537, *y raf* 143. *gureth* 69. *mar qureth* 904, 1218.
   a reth 937. *me ath ra* 300, *ny ra* 425, *ny an grua* 964. *me an
   grua-e* 3201. (*om*)*grua* 477. Pl. *ny ren* 1124, *pendra reny* 958, *a
   reny* 3950. *ny regh* 1747 *a regh* 1912 *mar quregh* 3525. *a rons*
   4000, *mar crons* 2085. Conjunctive Sg. *na rylly* 110. 4144. Pl. *a
   rellogh* 2351. Imperative Sg. *gura* 136. 1004. *grua* 637. 901.
   gruens 1202. 3697. Pl. *gruen* 3013. 3845, *gruegh* 372. 497.
   grugh 2838. *grueghwy* 1093. *na reugh* 108. Secondary present
   Sg. *na ren* 1198. *may ren* 1794. *me ren* 2402. *may rellen* 1777.
   3819, *ny rellen* 3756, *pendrellen* 1065. *mar ny reva* 334. *am
   gruelle* 1488. *na relle* 4005. *na rella* 615. *a relle* 1474. First
   Preterite Sg. *ny ruk* 1987, 3484. *del russys, na russys* 1707
   pendrussis 379. *na ruste* 3334. *gruk* 365. 475. 871. *a ruk* 949,
   reruk 1094, 2156. *y ruk* 2229, *mar a cruk* 32 and perhaps *am ros*
   3728, if we have here the Bret. *e grez* Z^2. 594 (but see note on
   472).

Pl. *a russyn* 2097. *ny russugh* 1531. *y russugh* 3804. *del russons* 26.

Secondary preterite : *na russen* 2590. *ny an grussa* 1763. *a russe* 1648, 3339 *a russa* 111. 2424. *ny russe* 2053.

Passive : *y rer* (= *y wrer* O. 1936) 3440. Participle *gwrys* 17, *grueys* 423. 436. 2767. *deswreys* 3962.

137. *sansoleth*=W. *santolaeth*, Br. *santelaez* Z². 847. cf. *skyentoleth* 157.

138. *gon* W. *gwnn*, Ir. *find* :—

Infinitive *gothfos* 1987, *gothvos* 28, *gothvas* 104, *gothfes* 828, 2273, *aswonfos* 1983.

Pres. Sg. *gon*, 138, *ny won* 101, 1483, 1487. *a won vy* 1478. *aswen* 73 *y wothes* 2974, 3649. *a wor* 38, 2843, *a wour* 1931, *a wore* 19, *ny wor* 4440. Pl. *y wothen* 309, *ny wothen* 1036, *del wothen* 2626. *a wothogh* 1439. *mar cothens* 1382. Secondary pres. *ny wothyan* 3088. Form compounded with the verb subst. *a cothfes* (si scires) 867. Imperative Sg. *gothfeth* 935, 2453, 3548. Pl. *gothvethugh* 1913.

139. *dus* (misprinted *due*) 2d sg. imperative of *dôs*.

Other forms of this irregular verb are :—

Infinitive *doys* 796, 824, *y thoys* 3012. *ou tos* 2466, *ou toys* 4476, *dones* 2436, 3045. Pres. sg. *mar tuff* 3365. *a due* 1296, 3991, *a thue* 907, 2024. 2429. *ny dhue* 250, *ny thue* 891, *mar a tue* 1106. *athue-a* 3902. *dua* 3976. Pl. *mar a tuen* 3476, *mara tuny* 3907. Conj. sg. *kyn teffo* 251 ; *na thefo* 415, *may teffo* 1274, 1712. Pl. *may teffons* 1738. 3290. Imperative sg. *dus* 139. 596. 1083, 3002. *duys* 4056. *dens* 2467, 3260. Pl. *duen* 798, 1201, *duen ny* 1027. *dugh* 952, 1171, 1346. *dens* 1538. Secondary Present. *pan deffen* 906. *a teffes* 3837. First Preterite, sg. *y tuth* 3197, 3676, *pan duthe* 4396. *me re deth* 234. *y tuth* 1727, 2148. *mar tuth* 746. 2908. *a thuth* 1787, *a thueth* 2219, 3768. *re duth* 2700, 2899 ; *deve* 944. *dufe* 2095, 2950, 3287, *dufa* 1086 : *re dufe* 1432. 3995. *redufa* 623, 650, *pan duthe* 2666, *y tuthe* 2274. Pl. *duthen* 1981. Passive pres. sg. *deer* 2833. Part. pret. *due* 1869. *devethys* 625, 1091.

149. *cowgegyow* (both *gs* soft) pl. of *cowsss* Br. *coudet, caoudet* (internum) Z². 108, *drok-cowsys* 3859.

151. *clour* 1312, *in clor* 4220, *pur clour* 4332. Br. *clouar, clouer* translated by ' doux.'

156. *drefa*=*drefe* 1450, for *dreheva* 'raise' (W.).

167. *newyth, henys* derivatives from **naw* (=*novus*) and *hen* (=*sen-ex*).

184. *arlud flour* (flos dominorum) : here *arlud* is in the gen. pl. so in *an werhes flour*, 631, *mester flor* 1076, *turant floyr* 3296. *doctour flour* 1391, *epscop flour* 1434, *empour flour* 1600.

186. *par.* cf. Quant deus out fait Adam et Eve sue *per*, *Vie de Seint Auban*, ed. Atkinson.

192. *moy gracyus*, cf. *moy worthy* 4389.

198. *bedneth* (also in 224, 225) for *benneth* 202. *mestrigy* (*g* soft)=magistratio. so *deulugy* 2096.

203. *benegycter*=*benesygter* 4495, so *tecter* 2935, *honester* 3027, *glander* 533. *eselder* 1166. *golouder* 2101=*goleuder* 3669. *creffder* 2406, *uvelder* 2941, *reelder* 2942. *guynder* 3667, *caradeuder* 3668. More in Z². 829.

213. *re-woloways :* cf. W. *goleuo* ' to light,' ' to illuminate.'

230. 4526. *du* an interjection as W. *myn Duw* (W.).

236. *kes-talkye.* Here as in *kes-colon* 1756, we have the W. *cyd.*

247. 2268. 2286. *plass, plas*=W. *plas* ' palatium.' In 4298 *plas* is= ' place.'

251. *kynteffov*=*kyn*+*deffo*+*ou* ' my.'

293. *nywy :* cf. perhaps W. *nyw* ' vivacity.'

296. *omgersyogh* from **omgesuryogh :* cf. W. *ymgysuro* : so *omry* 326, 2122. *omgrua* 477. *omguythe* 533. *omprevy* 1194. *ombrene* 1252. *omguytha* 1339=*omguythe* 1347. *omgolhugh* 1642, *omgemer* 1882. *omsone* 2319. *omdok* 2344. *omleth* 2491. *omheres* 3666. *ommeras* (ex *omwheras*) 2560. *ompredery* 2857. *omconfort* 3071. *omconfortya* 3080. *omgellys* 4120. *omparusen* 3244. *omthegen* 3451. *omdenna* 3474. *omgu*[*e*]*ythe* 1989.

309. *gras y wothen* ' we give (lit. know) thanks :' cf. *gothfeth thym grays* 3548.

311. *greffe* a mutation of *creffe, creffa* 321, the compar. of *creff.*

313. 357. 4539 *roweth* ' sway,' *royauté ?*

327. 334. 341. 371. 396 *domethy, ty a dhommeth* 329. Br. *dimiziff* ' soy marier :' Cath. *dimezabl* ' nubilis,' ib., *dimezer* ' espouseur,' *dimezez* ' a bachelor,' ib. Root *vad* with the compound prefix *dom (dim)* =Ir. *timm (do*+*imm).*

379. *pendrussis* for *pe*+*an*+*tra*+*grassis,* as *pendrellen* 1065. 2355, for *pe*+*an*+*tra*+*grellen.*

387. 1100. 1954. 1984. *nessevyn* formed from the old superlative **nessav* (Ir. *nessam* ' proximus') as *guelhevyn* (optimates) 2724, 2928= *guelheven* 2791, from the old superlative **guelhav* (optimus).

406. 1655. *am govys vy. govys*=O. Ir. *fobith* Z². 659.

433. *degemorys, degemerys* 2573. cf. W. *dygymeryd* ' to accept.'

439. 830 *devethyans* lit. a coming : cogn. with the participle *devethys.*

440. 3919 *in hans* from *in-nans* as in *hoth* 3064 from *in-noth* 1933.

468. *trou* Fr. *trou : nasweth*=W. *nodwydd,* Ir. *snáthat.*

472. 521. *ry :* other forms of this irregular verb are :—
Present Sg. *rof* 150. 217. *reyth* 3620. *ree* 1694. 2836. Pl. *regh.* Conjunctive Sg. *roy* 532. 2540. 2847. Imperative Sg. *roy* 549. 4489. Pl. *regh* 536. 1667. 3041. 3151. Secondary present Sg. *rollen* 2593. First Preterite Sg. *a reys* 1753. *a ros* 3463. *re ros* 1930. *am ros* 2252, and perhaps in 3728 *re roys* 3428. Secondary Pret. Sg. *rosen* 1687. *a rose* 2881. Part. pass. *reys* 3095.

481. *lee*=W. *lleiâu.* The original guttural is kept in *a leghya* 2981.

516. 1345. 4158. *mebyen lyen* pl. of *mablyen* 3163=Ir. *macc légind.*

541. *podrethek* 10.=W. *pydredig.*

542. *in gron.* cf. W. *cron* ' round,' ' circular.' Ir. *cruind.*

543. *schanlour,* better *scant-lor* 3459. *schant* 3929. *ascant* 658.

544. *kynweres*=*kyn* + *gueres* Z². 901.

566. 590 *numbus* ' I have not'=*nymbus* O. 356.

576. 1179. 1749. 3271. *lafurya,*=*lafuria* 1388, 2768. *lafurye* 3286. *lafuryys* 1567, *lafuryans* 480 : cf. the English phrase ' to labour on the way'=to go onward.

579. *sansesou* pl. of *sanses* fem. of *sans.* So *arlothes* 237, *kentrevoges* 1551, *mowes* 1646. *myternes* 3684.

587. 4194 *dorsona, dursona,* compounded with the prep. *dar* and *sona*
W. *swyno* to preserve, to charm, signare, to *sain.*

605. 610. *go-ny* formed like *go-vy* 793, *gogy* 3576, *yo-ef* 1895 : *go=vae*
Ir. *fē,* in the phrase *fē amai.*

607. *yeys* a verb formed from the participle *yesseys* 2162, 2747. 4272.
4279.=AS. *gesed* ' confessed,' p. part. p. of *gesecgan.*

650. *dressen=dres + an.*

659. 1338. 1347. 3655. *polge,* pulsus (venarum) : here as in *falge* 987.
1161. 1721. 2045. 2306. 2448. 3803. *felge* 1273. *calge* 2046, *s*
has become soft *g.*

661. *corff* = W. *cwrw,* Ir. *coirm,* Z.² 821.

662. *effsen* (so *mensen* 1042, 1368. 2067. *rosen* 1657. *carsen* 1990. *god-
haffsen* 2634) 1 sg. 2dy present of *eva* ' bibere.' Note the sharpening of the *v* before *s.*

668. *dovyr=dovr* 673, W. *dwfr,* O. Ir. *dobar. a wur* (leg. *vur*) *speys.* W.
byr brevis, so 1012, 1741.

681. *schorys* re-occurs in line 2633. I think now it must mean ' shivers,'
' shivering-fits ;' Mr. Williams would regard it as the English
word *scores* ' marks,' and compare the Welsh name for the plague
haint y nodau ' the disease of the marks.'

709. *omglowugh* cf. W. *ymglywed* ' to feel oneself.'

719. *adar,* W. *adrawdd* ' say ' (W.) But v. note on 4311.

746. *mar tuth an nur* perhaps ' if the hour (*an n-ur*) has come. ' cf. *ty
an n-oyll* 929.

757. *asogh* 1237. *assus* ' est ' *asson* sumus 1120.

760. *regniis,* like *tregys,* 816, has an active meaning.

759. *me a veth* lit. ' I shall be', future for present as in 681 and elsewhere.

764. *penag=panak* 3104.

778. 953. 3287. 3346. 3745. *dar* seems an interjection or imprecation,
W. *dera* ' fiend.' In 953. 2445. *dar* seems a preposition.

792. *y meth-e* here the *e* is a suffixed pron. of 3d sg. m. See Z³. 606.

806. *dethe cloweys* lit. ' hearing to them ' (W.), *clowes* 3709, *clowas* 2636.

847. *breys* ' womb ' seems borrowed from Eng. *breast.*

850. *genegygva,* like *genesygeth* 4387 a deriv. from *genesek, genesyk* 3211.

864. 1019. 1478 *malbe dam,* an imprecation which I cannot explain.

867. *a cothfes y attendya:* cf. the imperative *gothvethugh y attendya* 1913.

892. *vyketh* = vyth-keth, *bythqueth.*

897. *peb les* perhaps ' of every court ' (Ir. *lis*).

903. 24 39 *campol* p. part. p. *campollys* 2204. sg. pret. *campollys* 2791.
Engl. *cample,* ' to talk, contend or argue.' Halliwell, *camble* ' to
prate saucily,' ib.

908. *ruthy* W. *rhwyddad,* or compare (with Mr. Williams) *ryth* or *wryth*
sorrow ?

929. *ty an noyll* cf. *ty a oyl* 3572.

938. *sevuruth=severitas* ?

957. should have been printed *y bescherev your patis,* which is wholly
English (' I beshrew your pates ') : cf. line 1451.

984. *besyon* from *vision(em),* as *belan* from Pr. *vilan.*

997. *vij ...* to be read *syth.*

1006. *den varijs* cf. W. *bâr* ' fury '. But why the *v* in the Cornish ?

1035. 1749. 2788. 2885. *dour* an adverb (in 4323, an adjective)=O. W.
deurr (gl. acri) now *dewr.*

1047. *drues* for *drus* = W. *drud* : the *e* is inserted to make a rhyme with mes. So *graes* 669, *plaes* 635 so *pur-goeth* 1979. *taem* 2093. *fael* 2249 *ragoen* 2742 *gluaes* 2782, *vyen* 2998, *dremaes* 3074, *scoen* 4066. So *suyr* 1924. *luyr* 2263, *duys* 405 6, *voas* 2943, *beas* 4275. In *turent* 3246 *e* is written for *a. fuir* 905.

1048. 3467. *ke war the gam*: so *a war agys cam* 2022, *eugh wy war gam,* 3974 so *cry war the gam* 3043

1060. *ny warth mas-ran* ' a good part (of the torturers) will not laugh.' The same phrase re-occurs 3342. *mas ran* 4440.

1075. *mach*=mates : for the change of *ts* to *ch* cf. *lych* (for *lits, list*) 2832.

1077. *damach* from *damage* as *ymach* 1805 3789 (*yamach* 3785) from *image, lyche* 240 from *liege, maryach* 332, *charych* 2831 from marriage, charge, with the sharpening of the final characteristic of Cornish : cf. *caff* 3906 from *cave, manhot* 3174, *gront* 3471.

1081. *hevelsa* 3d pl. *havalsens* 1206.

1090. *holmyu*=*holma*+*yu* : so *helmyu* 1522, 2762=*helma*+*yu*.

1100 *mar a s-aff.* note this form of *aff* ' eo ' ' ibo ' with prosthetic *s*. The other forms of this irregular verb found in the present drama are as follows :—

    Infinitive *mos* 665, *mois* 130, *moys* 4364, *mones* 173, 3159, *myns* 1989.

    Pres. & Fut. Sg. *marasaff* 1100. *nynseth* 2409. 2823. 3561. *marseth* 4315. *eseth* 2462. *a* 853, 1029, 3634, *ty a* 2968, *ny a* 801, *yth a* 1192, 1214, 3630, *pyth a* 369, *nynsa* 2347. Pl. *ythen* 3876, *marsegh* 588 *ythegh* 1521. Conjunctive : Sg. *pyth-ylly* 1103, *nuthylly* 4142. Imperative : Sg. *a* 2022, *ke* 139, 3467, 3737, *kea* 1417. *kegy* 35. *kedhegy* 58. *ens* 1541, 2794, 3522. Pl. *eugh* 113, 965, 1354. *ens* 373. Secondary Present, Sg. *ellen* 1257. *maythellen* 985. 3775. *kynthellen vy* 3064 *ethe* 1588. *ythe* 4453. *maythella* 4284. Pl. *pythellen* 3438. *pythellens* 374. First Preterite : Sg. *ytheth* 2236, 3362 *pytheth* 448. *ytheth-a* 1028.

1110. 1124. *dregyn*=*dregen* 4005, *dregan* 4139 pl. of *drok ?*

1115. *levays* 3d sg. pres. of *levasy* (W.)

1127. *guelfos* (*guylfoys* 1132)=*guils-bos* (W.)

1187. *debron*=*debrén* 3432=M. Br. *debruan* ' prurigo', in late Cornish *debarn.*

1253. 1896. 4186 *pur* ' when' (*pa-ur*)=Br. *peûr* ' quand '.

1257. *fors ny raff,*—English ' I do not force ' i.e. I care not : *nynsus forse* 1440—Eng. *no force* ' no matter ', *fors ny reyth* 3620 force thou givest not i.e. (thou carest not) cf. *they give no force* ' they care not ', Halliwell. *ny reys dyn fors* 2355.

1264. 1335. *usons.* This new and obscure form belongs to the verb substantive. The other forms occurring in this play are as follows :—

    1. Root I: Pres. Sg. *off* 577, *ythof* 6, *ythoff* 984, *maythoff* 1311. *nynsoff* 2975, 3482. *assoff* 509, 4184, *ovy* 2308, 3122, 3853. *maythovy* 2158, *oma* 4501. *ythonna* 1359, *maythonna* 1943, *ythama* 794, *ydama* 3393, *asoma* 2522, *assoma* 4181, *marsama* 3288. *os* 137, 203, *oys* 299, 462, *ythoys* 1854, 3012. *nynsos* 1996, 3016, *nynsoys* 2976, *nynsesos* 848. *ote* 2114, *ota* 1841, *nagote* 377. *yw* 1, *yu* 17, *ew* 307. *assyu* 4467,

marsyu 14, 2120 (= Br. *mardeu*), *nynsyu* 98, 360, 1438, *nansyu* 682, *kynthyu* 1145 : with suffixed pron. *marsew-e* 1041. *yw-a* 1415, *yw-e* 3398. Pl. *on* 257, 1091, 2312, *onny* 2671, 2892. *asson* 1120, 4526, *ython* 1174, 1308, 1529. *nynson* 2719. *ough* 233, *ogh* 240, 241. *asogh* 1237, *ythogh* 1769, *maythogh* 288, *kynthogh* 492, *owhy* 2705, 2824. *yns* 3187, *ythyns*, 4169, *marsyns* 1806, *marasyns* 4122, *nynsyns* 2045. Secondary Pres. Sg. *esen* 3771, *nynsen* 3700, *enua* 4518. *maytheua* 3760, *pan eua* 4499, *es* 3786, *kyntheste* 1853. *ythesta* 2412. *o* 447, 450, *nynso* 1801, 2495, *marso* 874. *kynnago* 2400, *ove* 4375. Pl. *esen* 2145, 3350, *ens* 579, 916, 1280, 1791, 1800, *pythens* 2157.

Obscure to me are Sg. *ytheseff* 834, 4023=*ythese* 1387, 1963. *kyntheses* 3888, *fetel esta* 3659. *nynsese* 3586. *nynsusy* 1019, 1403. *pan usy* 3780. Pl. *ythesen* 3333. *esogh*, 4310. *usons* 1264, 1335, *kynthusons* 2366. Secondary present *ese* 872, 2672, *ythese* 862.

2. Root ĀS? Sg. 3. *us* 229, 238, 655. *nynsus* 366, 380, *nynsues*, 291, *kynthus* 1453, 2364, *nansus* 3949, *marsus* 1203, 1373, *marsuys* 3621, *pendrus* 1412, *namsus* 1554, *asus* 635, *assus* 757. *nynses* 180, *kynses* 908.

3. Root MAG. Pres. Sg. *yma* 8, *ima* 900, 2036, *ymae* 1978, *may-me-ve* 2922. Pl. *ymons* 1954, 1985, 1986, 3309, 4476. Secondary present (?) *y myens* 2808.

4. Root BU (Skr. *bhu*). Infinitive *bos* 26, *boys* 522, *boas* 2943, *bones* 352, 401 : with possessive pronouns : *ou bosa*, 3062, *the vote* 3089, *the vota* 571, *y vose* 2052, *y vosa* 4126. Future Sg. *ny vedhaf* 109, *y fethaff* (misprinted *y sethaff*) 1101, *bethe* 3802, *ny vetha* 4095, *bethevy* 2130. *betheth* 531, *y fetheth* 1242, *mar a pethy* 2585, *vyth* 1073, 4263, *a vyth* 37, 89, *a veth* 331, 368, *ny veth*, 774, 811, *nynse feth* 3890, *mar peth* 422, 1607, *mara peth* 2315, *y feth* 725, 1298 : with suffixed pron. *ny veth-e* 769, 810, *na vethe* 771, *a vetha* 1636, *a vethe* 1925, *mar pethe* 4301. Pl. *bethen* 1341, 3945, *ny vethen* 3354, *mar pethen* 420. *y fethenny* 3443. *bethugh* 1460, *vethugh* 4567, *ny vethugh* 1492, 2729, *y fethugh*, 1513, *fethogh* 2352.

Conjunctive Sg. *pan vy* 139 *reby*, 672, 2670, *may fy* 1823. *bo* (used as a disjunctive conjunction) 373, *may fo* 16, 761, 895, *na vo* 91, 1277, *a vo* 127, 1122. *kyn fo* 439, 1255, *kyn fo ve* 976, *na vova* 2064, *rebo* 556, 624, *pan vo* 1215, *py fo* 1880. Pl. *may fegh* 2162, *pan vegh* 1520, *pan vowhy* 3524, *kyn fewy* 4568, *may fons* 3344. Imperative Sg. *beth* 905, 3866. *bethens* 972, 1517, etc. *bethyns* 818. Pl. *na vethen* 3245. *bethugh* 292, 611. *na vethugh* 3238, *bethens* 274, 1614, 1637, 3299. Secondary Present Sg. *hedre ven* 55, 354, *na ven* 1135, 2999, 3838, *pan ven* 525, *kyn fen* 3895, *may fena* 4285, *y fethen* 1731, *mar pethen* 2159, *ny vethe* 2958, *kyn fes* 861, *may festa* 1710, 1717, *pan vesta* 1719, *pan veste* 2819, *pan ve* 80, *na ve* 1863, *ny ve* 204, *a pe* 1762, *mar pe* 614, *a vethe* 2151, 2382, *a vetha* 4462, *ny vethe* 4448 : with suffixed pron. *pan veua* 3210, *na veva* 152, 2116, *appeua* 686. Pl. *pan venny* 68, *kyn feny* 892, *del vugh* 4524, *pan vegh* 1520, and perhaps *a pegh* 1496, *mara pewy* 194, *na vewy* 119, 322, *a vewhy* 1494 (these may be conjunctives). *kyn fens* 1540 : with suffixed pron. *kyn fens-i* 3655. First preterite Sg. *na vuff* 795, *re vuff* 3798, *y fueff* 4393, *y fuff* 2154, *na vu ma* 4099, *na vef* 102, *pan vus* 3576, *aban vys* 3969. *y fus* 338, *nyn fus* 1855, *fetel vusta* 3764. *bue* 792, *rebue* 1304, 1490. *vue* 2249, *vvue* 4496. *ny vue* 2234, *del fue* 397, *a fue* 564, 887, *a fua* 1775, *y fue* 859, *may fue* 3416, Pl. *pan vuen* 605. Secondary Preterite Sg. *me a vyen* 2998, *y fyen* 3704. *bya* 3600, *vye* 1656, *ny vye* 663 *ny vya* 2883, *y fye* 1654, 3169, *a fya* 1497, *a vya* 1504, 1665: with suffixed pron. *y vyea* 21, *mara peya* 186. Pl. *y fyen* 311, 317. *y fyen ny* 2170.

1268. *respela* : cf. *pelys* 3418, *pyle* 3430. *pylse* 3828, W. *pilio.*

1288. *grueys* is=*gurys* D. 1790 (W.)

1307. *hensy*, this is very obscure : cf. W. *hynhad*? Eng. *hent* furrow?

1311. *amuwys* Fr. *ému.*

1312. *gefugh* may be 2d pl. imper. of *cafus*, the infection of *c* being caused by a particle understood. If we read *gesugh* 'beseech ye,' cf. Ir. *guidid*?

1356. *lovrygyon* a deriv. from *lovr*, Ir. *lobar.*

1368. *stak*=Br. *stâg* 'attache', 'lien.'

1390. *strechya* Eng. *stretch* 'to walk in a dignified manner,' Halliwell.

1393, 2030 *trettya* from Eng. *tread* ?

1408. 1469. *mayl* (i.e. *mâl*) is apparently an imprecation: cf. *malbe dam.*

1410. 1417. *preytha*=*preys* + *da.*

1412. *pendrus*=*pe* + *an* + *tra* + *us* : so *pendryu* 2015.

1413. *claff deberthys.* pl. *clevyon* d. 3130 : cf. *ij then debertheys* 3108. A leper in Welsh is *claf gwahanol* (*gwahan* 'separate') : *gwahan-glaf* 'leprous' (W.).

1419. *gasel* a mutation of *casel*=W. *cesail*, Br. *kazel* (W.).

1420. 2241 *gormel* W. *gorfoli* 'to flatter.' But why is the *m* uninfected ?

1421. 1427. *connek* a deriv. from **conn*=Ir. *conn* sense, reason, Glück 69.

1423. *tarthennou* : W. *dyrthon* (W.): cf. *les-derth* (gl. febrifugia) Vocab.

1433. *an gannas*=W. *y gennad* (W.).

1463. *stoff* here and in 1869 (cf. 1873) seems to means *cash*. In 3167 it means 'wealth' or 'store.'

1487. *methegyeth* a deriv. from *methek*=medicus.

1516. 1546. 4374 *ea* (a dissyllable), Lat. *eja* ?

1518. *ysawys*=Eng. *y-saved*, as *yeseys*=ge-sed.

1526. *dufunugh, dyvune* 1785, *dufen* 3770, from the prefix *de* and the root *svap.*

1528. *gal*=W. *gwael* 'vile' (W.).

1530, 1800 *crese*, a corruption of *cresa*(*f*).

1537. *blythy* pl. of *blyth*=W. *blwydd* 'year.'

1552, 1555. *trussogh*, Eng. *truss* · to pack up,' 'to make ready.'

1554. *namsus* probably a scribe's mistake for *nansus* : but Lhuyd has *nam* 'now.'

1556. *dewogys* (the *g* soft) p. part. pass. of *dewosa* 1575, *dewose* 1584, 1619. 3d sg. *dewoys* 1652. Br. *diwada* 'saigner.' From *de*- and *goys, gos*, O. Corn. *guit* (gl. sanguis), W. *gwaed.*

1565. *wegennou* for *whegennou*, a deriv. from *whek.*

1581. *malbew, malbe* 3303 seems an imprecation like *malbe dam.*

1589. *ievuje*=*ievody* of the Oxford plays 'je vous dis.'

T

1590. in the MS. rag astevery ancoel.

1604. *sul, sul voy* 2351. W. *sawl.*

1609. *ou thola = outh ola.* So *ou thumwul* 2366 *=outh umwul.*

1644, 1652 *knak=*W. *cnec.*

1692. 1705 *gruegh, greegh* (?) 1776 connected with W. *gwrachell* 'a puny dwarf,' *gwrachen* 'a crabbed dwarf' *gwrachan* 'a little creature.'

1760. *a wetsa* cf. W. *gweddu* (W.).

1768. *drokcoleth* from *drok-goleth.* So *drok-cousys* 3859.

1811. *alwethou* pl. of *alweth,* Br. *alchouez.*

1824. *luyst* from *lust* with *y* inserted for sake of rhyme with *crist.*

1827. *omdhevas=*W. *amddifad,* Br. *emzivad.*

1853. 2630. 3072. 4184 *anhethek.* It is not easy to fix the meaning of this adjective. W. *annhuddawg* 'uncovered' and *anheddog* (unpacific) would suit phonetically, but the meanings are inappropriate. Br. *hêtuz* 'souhaitable' is perhaps cognate.

1878. 2747. *in sol* a corruption of *in sevel* (W.).

1926. 4367. *trogel* 'body' O. Ir. *troicit.*

1968. *hevys ruen=*W. *hefys rhawn.*

1971. *goverou* pl. of *gover* O. Corn. *guuer* (gl. rivus).

1989. *myns* ex *mynd,* W. *myned* 'to go.' *omguythe* better *omguethe* 'to make oneself worse' (*gueyth* 3378) : cf. W. *gwaethu* 'to grow worse.'

2015. 2099 *pendryu=pe + an + tra+yu.*

2054. *annye, annya* 3637, *ynnio* to urge (W.). Is it not rather from the English *annoy?*

2069. 2194 *gortheren=*Br. *gourêlin.*

2073. 2197. *est=*Br. *éost, est,* W. *awst,* all from (mensis) *Augusti* with loss of vowel-flanked *g.*

2076. 2200 *gwyn-gala=*Br. *gwengôlô.*

2078. *neffrea* : here *a* is added for sake of rhyme.

2099. *fesky,* W. *ffysgio* 'to hasten.'

2100. *terlemel=lemmel* 'to leap,' with the prefix *ter* (=Ir. *tair* ex *do-air*) Z². 906.

2106. *tanges* (*g* soft)=W. *tandod.*

2145. *dethwyth=*W. *dyddwaith.*

2243. *dyrhays* a mutation of *tyrâs,* cf. W. *tirio* 'to land.' (W.)

2270. *myllyou cans=m*[*y*]*llyou cans* 2471.

2287. *genesek=*Br. *ginidik* 'natif,' *genesyk* 3211.

2313. *schakyage=schakya+age.*

2328. 3427. *tassens,* the translation is a guess.

2368. 4134. *grueff* (*e* inserted for rhyme) from Eng. *groffe* 'face.'

2379. 2655. *myngou* seems a nickname for Christ.

2390. *devenys=dufunys* 3224 p. part. p. of a verb=W. *difynio.*

2396. *darvyngya* perhaps 'through (*dar*) taking of vengeance.'

2399. *treythy* perhaps connected with W. *traeth* 'sand.'

2409. *nuk* Fr. *nuque?* *war nuk* 'backwards'? see Z². 693, 697 as to using names of parts of the body to form prepositions.

2418. *crehy,* W. *crech* 'a crash' (W.).

2419. *brehy* is obscure, Nhg. *brühe* broth?

2423. *gargasen, gargesen* 3322=Br. *gargaden.*

2450. *pastel, pastell* Br. Cath. *pastel* 'morceau,' 'panneau,' *pastellaff* 'frusta facere.' With *genys the pastel dyr* ('born to a morsel of land') cf. *genys then eretons* 3469.

2453. *routyyth* for *reoutyyth* (cf. *reoute* 2985) ?   or cf. M. Eng. *rout* ' to assemble' Stratmann.

2477. *atlyan* pl. of *atal* offcast.

2489. *darne*, 2496 *darnn*, W. *darn* a piece, Br. *darn* partie, portion.

2555. *reff*=W. *rhyf* ' presumption' i.e. ' before I presume to speak to thee' (W.).

2590. *nes*, Br. *nesaat* ' faire alliance.'

2613. *opery* seems=*obery* (as *capel* 467=*cabel*), but the meaning of the line is not clear.

2616. *nebes an fa*=*nebesa* (Br. *nebeutoch* ' moins')+*un fa*.

2644. *teythy*=W. *teithi* (W.) : in *antythy* 3052 we have a cognate adjective with the negative *an-*.

2652. *oudomhel :* either this is for *outh om(w)hel* (cf. *umhelaf*, Cr. *ommelys* p. 203, *umhelys* p. 244, W. *ymchelwyd*), or *domw(h)el* is compounded, like *domethy* (see note on 327) with *dom-*=*do+om*.

2655. *atty* for *otty* Z². 606.

2681. *adar* seems=*ater* infra 3631.

2730. *y troff* ex *yth+droff* ' affero.'
   Infinitive *dry* 3819, *ou try* 673, *thy threy* 1008.   Pres. Sg. *y troff* 2730, *a doro* 3981.   Imperative Sg. *dore* 508, 3685., *dro-fa* 3835. *drens* 3696.   Pl. *dregh* 2487, *drewhy* 1290. First Pret. Sg. *dros* 873, *redros* 3848, *droys* 3415.   Part. pass. *dreys* 2673, 4114, 4130.

2738. *mo ha meten :* the *mo* seems opposed to *meten*, and is perhaps akin to W. *much* ' gloom.'

2832. *har* (compar. *harhe* 2842) for *her* (compar. *herre* 2920).   W. *hir*. Ir. *sir*.

2833. *deer* lit. venitur.

2852. *tasek*=Br. *tadek* ' paternel.'

2833. *dynnya :* W. *denu* ' to entice' (W.).

2900. *govenek* cf. O. Ir. *fomenaid*, *fomentar* Z². 998, root MEN.

2969. *cumyys* Br. *kombout*, *kombot* ' étago'?   Or is it W. *cymes* ' sufficiency' (W.)?

2985. *revvte* for *reoute*.

3018. *gore* W. *goreu* ' best.'

3052. *antythy* see 2644.

3066. *poth* is perhaps the W. *pwd* ' rot in sheep.'

3086. *dealer*=*de + galer* 4225=Ir. *galar*.

3104. *panak*=*penak*.

3113. *ues* i.e. *ves* for *aves* ?

3133. *heweres*=*he + gueres :* *he*- or *hy*- (*hebasca*, 3753, *hyblyth* ' flexibilis ') W. *he*-, *hy*-, Br. *ho*- *he*-, Z². 93, is Ir. *su*, Gr. *ɛὑ*, Skr. *su*-.

3144. *knesen*, *kneys* 4054=Ir. *cnes*.

3171. 3899. *dufer* from *devoir*.   In 4513 it means ' due.'

3201. *arveth*=*arfeth* D. 2262.

3224. *bowyn*=(caro) bovina.

3231. 3632. *dulle* ' let go '=*dul* (Ir. *dul* to go ?)+*le* (Goth. *letan* ?)

3232. *busch* Eng. *bush* ' a flock of sheep.'

3235. *hethou* W. *heddwch :* the final guttural lost.

3253. *kerethys* Ir. *cairigthe*.

3259. *indan onen* i.e. with an ashen stick (W.)

3291. *keher* W. *cur* ' ache' (W.)

3300. *tountya* Eng. *taunt* ' to tease,' Halliwell.

3312. *du-klyn*=*duo-clunes.*

3313. *lemyk*, W. *llymaid* (W.), a diminutive of some word=Ir. *loimm* 'a sup.'

3314. *plemyk* a dimin. of some word=W. *plwm* 'plumbum.'

3331. *raghyl* I conjecture to be the Eng. *rascal*. Mr. Williams would read *rag hyl* and regard *hyl* as a mutation of *cyl*=W. *cul* ' narrow.'

3338. *calame*=Br. *kala-mae* 'le premier jour de Mai.'

3341. *hot* AS. *hôd*, or is it 'head,' AS. *heáfud?*

3344. *teharas* a mutation of *deharas*, W. *diheurau* (W.).

3360. *thyek* for *dhyek*, *dioc* (gl. piger). *di + oc*=ὠκυς.

3368. *snel*, *snell* 4342 Nhg. *schnell*.

3375. *lok* 'lock' was any close place of confinement,' Halliwell.

3391. *schylwyn* W. *ysgilwyn* 'whitenaped' (W.)

3396. *gorourys* p. part. p. of a verb=W. *goreuro*.

3397. *gernygou* a mutation of *kernygow* pl. of *kernyk* 'corniculum.'

3403. *skyrennou* pl. of *skyrenn*=O. W. *scirenu* (gl. stella 'splint' Ducange) now *ysgyren*.

3413. *lawen-cath* cf. W. *cath llawn-duf*.

3414. *legessa*=W. *llygota*, a denominative from *llygoden* Ir. *luch* f. gen. sg. *luchod*, acc. pl. *luchtha* a t-stem.

3427. *an barth north*, cf. 'make their last head like Satan in the North,' Tennyson.

3453. *ewyas*, cf. W. *euain* 'to move' (W.).

3470. *tont* Eng. *taunt* 'lofty,' 'loftily-masted,' Halliwell. *re-dount* 3570.

3482. *omager* Eng. *homager* 'vassal.'

3483. *danger* Eng. *dangere*, the power which the feudal lord possessed over his vassals. Halliwell.

3490. *lendury* a deriv. from a word=Eng. *lent* 'a loan;' cf. *falsury* from *fals*.

3492. *avond*, like W. *afwyn*, borrowed from *habéna* (W.) *tellek* 'perforatus' i.e. formed into a noose (W.) (from *tol*).

3517. *nag yedhou:* observe the *g* of *nag* kept before the semivowel.

3523. *acectour* 'assectator.'

3524. *remyu*=*re-ma-yu.*

3564. *in bagh* 'in a little.'

3570. *re fue* (if not a mistake for *re vue*) means *habuisti;* see R. 2628. *napyth* for *nep-pyth:* redount from *re + tount*.

3631. *ater* (*adar* 2681) is perhaps W. *eithyr*, Ir. *echtar*, Lat. *extra*.

3645. *me yu lowenheys*, as to this mode of expressing the passive see Z². 540, and cf. 4258, 3640, 3654, 3673, 4232, 4251, 4518.

3667. *dyegrys* as if *deoculatus: egr*=oculus?

3674. *dyglon*=*dy-calon.*

3677. *grous* a mutation of *crous*, the interjection *a* being understood.

3681. *golvygyen* W. *goleuad* illumination (W.)

3721. *a molleth du in gegyn*=*a m. d. in gegen* 3928.

3727. *num-dar-fe* (=*num-darfa* 1477, 1808), note this instance of the prep. *dar* compounded with the verb subst. and cf. W. *dar-oed* Z². 573.

3751. *lest*=W. *llest* to hinder (W.).

3753. *hebasca*, cf. M. Br. *habasq* 'facilis,' 'suavis,' Cath.

3805. *myllusyon* pl. of *myllus* an adj. formed from *myl* 'beast.' Ir. *míl* (*étaig*) 'louse.'

3817. *mes ay reule*, cf. Lat. *delirus* 'deviating from the straight line.'

g him ': *dro* 2d sg. imper. of *drey* and *fa* the suffixed
the 3d sg. masc. So the suffixed pron. of 2d sg.
gy=(*reth-sawya-gy*) 3844, 3d pl. *kemer-y* 4034.
the final *a* is added for rhyme's sake.
W. *cest* paunch ?
erhaps *teruans* ?) lit. land of (the) valley.
om *bishop* with progressive assimilation.
ng. *scumber* ' to dung.' Halliwell.
tion of *gwy* ' water.'
ryens 3963) a mutation of *bryans*=W. *braint*, O. W.
privilegium ' Z². 845.
welen *indan droys*, a proverbial expression, I suppose,
grass grows under his feet.'
for *dag*+*guereys*. Or is it for *dhe guereys* ' to help

anal, anadl, Ir. a*nál*.
W. *annwyd*.
from *caffsen-va* : cf. *may fe-ua* 4285.
cf. *sclaldya*, *sclandra*.
cf. *pedrevan* ' lizard, elf, newt.'
=*reth*+*drehava*.
. or *diwedd*)=*wotyweth*.
W. *mehefin*.
this *a dar* (778) or=*ater* 3631, and used here (and in
n intensive ? (' very greatly weakened you are ').
hek, W. *hiraethog*, derived from *hereth* 4545.
utation of *basken*, Br. *bazkañv*, *bazkaoñ*.
had, Ir. *rath* ' grace, favour.' This is not here, at all
mutation of *gras*=gratia.
ms to mean ' coverings ' ' housings ' (W. *hws*), with *th*
ten in auslaut (*plath*, *fath*, *rychyth* 429).
=W. *hunedd* ' somnolence ' (W.).
. *chwyddo*.
for *trevythyou* pl. of *treveth* O. 799, or should we read
ou ' between times ' ? (W.)
re+ou.
eglos.
. *traul* 'cost,' 'charge' (W.), or a mistake for *tra*? cf. 268.
r. Other forms of this verb are as follow :—
ve *don* 4491. *ou ton* 2638. Present. Sg. *a thek* 1812,
. 4997. Pl. *degen* 3880. (*om*)*thegen* 3451. Conjunctive
oga 3746. Imperative Sg. *dok-hy* 1419, (*om*)*dok* 2344.
s 3417. 4070. Pl. *degogh* 2796. *degeugh* 4067. First
rite Sg. *a thuk* 451. 790. 1239. 2380.
wroweth lit. ' the body, its lying ' (*groweth*).
out me,' *hebogh* ' without you ' 2693.

CORRIGENDA.

B. in the translation.

Line 7. *after* warden *insert* [?] 119. *for* be not *read* you should not
be 223. *after* Conan *insert* surely 247. 2286. 2286. *for* place *read*
palace 292. *for* lord *read* king 304. *for* will be *read* thou shalt have
309. *for* I *read* we 322. *for* be not you *read* you should not be 420,
422. *before* be *insert* shall 426. *for* find *read* have 565. *after* world
insert a full stop. 566. *for* had *read* have not 579. *for* are *read* were
641, 672 *for* Kind (sir) *read* Good man 681. *for* marks *read* shivering
fits 746 *mar tuth an nur* is perhaps ' if the hour (*an n-ur*) has come '
790. *for* died *read* bore death 856. *for* Went *read* Came 867. *for* Thou
oughtest to *read* If thou couldst 916 *for* are *read* were 929 *for* catch
read bewail 953. *for* regard *read* give heed 957. 958, 959 *read*

> I beshrew your pates !
> What thing shall we do through napping ?
> Ah, you hear me not calling ?

966 *for* Cambrea *read* Carnbrea 1001. *after* Christian *insert* have 1020.
for have *read* get 1025. *for* sitting *read* has gone 1027 *for* go *read* come
1035 *for* country quite *read* country's land [?] 1044. *read* I would not
again 1060. *for* not a laugh but a cry *read* a good part will not laugh
1061. *omit* to 1072. *for* rock *read* Rock. 1115. *for* has ventured *read*
ventures 1253. *for* Hast thou really *read* When hast thou 1280. *for* are
read were, 1312 *for* clear *read* gentle 1477. *for* has not happened to me
read I had not 1530. *omit* should 1531. *for* would not have *read* have
not 1589 *for* for thee *read* children 1590 *read* For the omen (?) has les-
sened them 1594. *for* This *read* There 1607. *for* needs *read* need shall
be 1636 *for* Whether *read* If 1694. *for* shall *read* He shall 1698 *after*
For *insert* that 1719. *for* shalt *read* mayst 1800 *for* believed *read*
believe 1812 *for* bore *read* who bears 1813 *for* were *read* have been
1855 *for* There has *read* Thou hast 1858 *add* for it 1896. *for* . . .
read When 1898 *for* sin, *read* evil ? 1963 *for* have been *read* am
2044 *for* have I loved *read* used I to love 2051. *for* If he were not
read Were it not that he was 2053. *for* work *read* have wrought 2076.
2200. *before* month *insert* in the 2217 *for* opposite to *read* hundred

(Br. *kevren*). 2335 *for* go *read* come 2351. *dele the point.* 2386 *for* you *read* them 2449. *after* born *dele the point* 2450 *for* to break up deer *read* a morsel of land 2462 *for* be *read* go 2489. *for* Ruin ! *read* Part of 2495. *for* is now *read* was 2496. *for* Through me *read* Part of 2585 if *bethy* be, as I now think, for *bethyth*, translate 'if thou wilt be wise' 2654. *for* go, *read* cause more 2655. *for* To sow for thee, thou, *read* For lo (there is) to thee a 2681. *for* Through *read* Without 2763. *before* sweet *insert* my 2785. *for* will *read* would 2836. *for* cause to reckon *read* give an account 2837. *for* The *read* Of the 2839. *after* there *insert* shall 3117 *before* certainly *insert* very 3245. *for* we should *read* let us 3287. *for* will *read* has 3415 *read* Morvelys 3632. *for* come *read* go 3721. *omit the asterisk and the note* 3770 *add* quietly 3992 *after* ever *add a point.*